She was a damned
fine-looking female . . .

But no decent woman he knew would be with him at this hour of the night, unless she was interested in getting him in her bed.

That thought didn't appall him, exactly.

She gazed up at him, studying his face, as though seeing things in it that he had never seen, looking as fascinated by him as she was by the portraits of his ancestors.

He took a quick step back from her, feeling as though he'd stood too close to the edge of a precipice. Of course she was tempting. He was a man, and she was a lovely young woman, and more, she seemed free of all the constraints and restraints of polite society.

She was an interesting woman, he had to grant her that. And a promising-looking one. But he had no time or reason to contemplate her.

He had a mission . .

EDITH LAYTON

FOR THE LOVE OF A PIRATE

AVON BOOKS
An Imprint of HarperCollinsPublishers

This is a work of fiction. Names, characters, places, and incidents are products of the author's imagination or are used fictitiously and are not to be construed as real. Any resemblance to actual events, locales, organizations, or persons, living or dead, is entirely coincidental.

AVON BOOKS
An Imprint of HarperCollins*Publishers*
10 East 53rd Street
New York, New York 10022-5299

Copyright © 2006 by Edith Felber
ISBN-13: 978-0-06-075786-1
ISBN-10: 0-06-075786-8
www.avonromance.com

First Avon Books paperback printing: December 2006

Avon Trademark Reg. U.S. Pat. Off. and in Other Countries, Marca Registrada, Hecho en U.S.A.
HarperCollins® is a registered trademark of HarperCollins Publishers Inc.

Printed in the U.S.A.

10 9 8 7 6 5 4 3 2 1

For Miss Daisy:
dear companion, inspired jester,
and master thief who pirated my heart,
but still has some pretty big pawprints to fill.

Chapter 1

⁓⁓

"They say I have everything, but they're wrong," the gentleman said. "There's one thing I lack. Your hand, in marriage. Will you marry me, Miss Winchester?"

The lady nodded. "I will, Lord Wylde."

"You have made me the happiest of men," he said.

They were in the lady's salon, alone for the first time since they'd met, because they'd been allowed this private moment together.

He bent to her and placed a light kiss on her

1

lips. Then he straightened and smiled. "Well, then. Shall we place the notice in the papers?"

"I believe my papa has already prepared one," she said. "In fact, I believe he has already sent it to the papers. It should appear this very day. I hope you don't mind."

"Why should I?" he asked. "I asked him for your hand, and he agreed. I assumed that you would as well."

She smiled. She was a passably attractive young woman, too angular for beauty, but thin enough for fashion, and sufficiently pale and blond for current tastes. "Father told me about your offer, of course, and after he had you investigated, he broached the matter to me."

"*Investigated?*" Constantine asked, raising one eyebrow.

She shrugged. "There is talk about everyone in the *ton*, and he's a thorough man. When he was satisfied, he told me of your proposal. When I said I'd accept, he and Mama said they would take care of the business of being wed. October, you said?"

"So I did. But perhaps you think that's too soon? It is April now, after all."

"My thoughts exactly," she said. "Marrying in such haste might give rise to gossip. Shall we say January, instead?"

"If it pleases you. I think we will be quite happy together," he added, raising her hand to his lips. "Shall I see you at the Blaynes' ball tomorrow night? I should have asked you as my guest, but had you not accepted my offer it would have been, you'll grant, uncomfortable."

"Did you really think I would not accept?" she asked.

They both laughed.

There was little chance she, or any woman, would have refused him, and he knew it. Constantine Wylde, Lord Wylde, was an attractive man, long limbed and fit. He had dark brown hair, dark brown eyes, and winged eyebrows that gave his handsome face a slightly wicked cast. But that was an illusion; he was a gentleman in name and behavior. He also had a title, and a considerable fortune. His reputation, if not spotless, was at least less spotty than many other young gentlemen of similar breeding. He was intelligent, and knew how to be charming. If he'd any fault, his friends agreed, it was that he was too moderate, sobersided. But even they agreed that was because of his excellent upbringing by his uncle, a vicar and justice of the peace, and his very correct wife.

Still, he did everything a young gentleman about London was supposed to do: he fenced; he rode handsome Thoroughbred horses and, as a member of the four-in-hand club, drove a fine light high curricle. He belonged to the right clubs and knew the right people, and had political ambitions with the right party.

He also knew the best wrong things to do, and did them well. He occasionally gambled, but never too high. If he kept any light ladies, he kept their names as secret as his doings with them. In short, he was a prize, a *catch* he knew his new fiancée could be proud of landing.

Catching had been no part of his proposal though. He'd studied the available crop of unwed ladies, and after much thought decided upon Miss Charlotte Winchester, daughter of a baron, wealthy in her own right, educated and nicely behaved.

"Until tomorrow night, then," she said comfortably.

He bowed, left her, and went to celebrate.

The sun was sinking low in the west, so he went to his favorite club, and gave the news to some of his friends.

"Well done," one of them said.

"Going to be shackled soon, are you? How many of us does that leave single?" another asked.

They talked about that a while, and then repaired to a nearby inn to toast him in louder fashion. They soon found the place too dull, and took their newly engaged friend to a gambling den. That palled, and they dragged him to a bawdy house, where all they did was sing bawdy songs.

"We'd do more," one of his friends told a disappointed young woman who was sitting on his knee. "But that wouldn't be polite. That is, knowing the guest of honor wouldn't takes some of the fun from it. Connie . . . Con here is very laced straight, y'see." He frowned. "Straitlaced, I mean."

"Lord Wyatt?" she asked with a laugh. "No, he's just a very sober fellow, and so say all."

Constantine raised an eyebrow, and then his glass to her. When the clock struck ten, he left with a few friends who took him to another festivity, because the nightlife of London was just starting, and he'd a sudden longing to be less sober.

He celebrated the next night, and on the next, he began to believe that the celebrations were becoming a bit forced. He had many friends, and even more acquaintances, so it was hard to refuse anyone willing to propose a toast to his future. Being polite, he drank with them; being politic, he decided to stay away from his friends for a few days until the novelty of his engagement wore off. Still, he had obligations.

It was almost dawn on the third night after his announcement when Constantine began to weave his way home again. He was a little unsteady on his feet. But no one accosted him. The villains in the shadows knew that sometimes a young blade like him, dressed to the nines and looking like easy prey, was just looking for a chance to fight with people they, and the law, didn't care about killing. And such young gents often carried pistols in their pockets, or sword-sticks, or iron fists hardened by bouts at fashionable boxing salons. Constantine had nothing in his pockets but coins, his walking stick was only that, and he disliked sparring because he'd been taught, and believed, that hitting his fellow man was no way to prove he was a superior man. But the lurkers didn't know that, and so he wasn't bothered by any of London's many thieves.

He never got very drunk either, and so he was walking straighter and humming a little tune to himself when he made his way into a better district. Like everything else about him, the tune was perfectly on key. It was a wedding march. He finally stopped in front of his town house, and went up the stair to the front door.

The door swung open.

"Good evening, sir," the butler said.

6

"Still up, Clarke?" Constantine asked in a clear, sober voice. "I told you not to wait for me."

"Indeed, my lord, I had not thought to. But you've a visitor."

Constantine frowned. "At this hour?" His eyes grew wide.

"It is no one I know, my lord. I doubt, in fact, that you know him either. But he was most insistent, as well as persuasive. He's waiting in the library."

"That I am not!" a loud voice announced.

Constantine looked up at the man standing behind his butler. He shook his head to clear it. He wasn't that drunk, but damned if the fellow didn't look like a villain. He was a big, wide older man with a seamed face and a scruffy gray beard—and two heavy old horse pistols in each huge hand. Constantine squinted, wondering if it was the liquor or his eyes playing tricks on him. Such a fellow didn't belong in his house, or indeed, in his world. Then he smiled. Of course. It had to be one of his friends playing a joke on him after their night of revelry.

"That you, Richard, behind that gray bush?" he asked, smiling. "I don't mind, but you've no right to frighten the breeches off my butler."

"Aye, well, I didn't," the man said in a voice

more like a roar. "Because he had none on when he came to the door. I don't hold with nightshirts, myself. A fellow has no place to stow his pistols and knives. Be that as it may. I've got to have a word with you, my lord, and now."

"Very well," Constantine said, "but let us go into my library, shall we? That way Clarke can go back to bed."

"Indeed I will not, my lord," his butler protested, making little movements of his head to indicate the man behind him.

"I think you should, it lacks some hours till dawn," Constantine said. "Don't worry about my guest, Mr. . . . ? Sorry," he told the big man with the pistols, "I didn't catch the name."

"Didn't throw it," the fellow growled. "But it's Captain Bigod."

"Indeed?" Constantine said, still just enough under the influence to not be taking any of this seriously. "I don't believe we ever met."

"Nor did we, but I'll wager you heard of me."

"How much?" Constantine said with interest. "Because you'd lose. At any rate, Clarke, be at ease. If the captain here wanted to shoot me, he'd have done it by now."

"Right you are, lad!" the big man said, shoving

one of his pistols into his belt. "Well, then, come on," he said, gesturing with the other pistol. "We've got to talk, and now!"

Constantine led his strange visitor down the hall and into his library, and shut the door behind him. He knew his butler would have the watch and all the footmen in the house at the door within minutes. He turned up the lamp on his desk, and studied his visitor.

"Well, sir, and what is it that couldn't wait until morning?"

"Wait?" the man roared. "Not another hour, lad. It's this," he said, extracting a rumpled newssheet from a pocket of his coat. He put it down on the top of a highly polished mahogany desk and pounded his fist on it so hard that the desk trembled.

"It is difficult for me to read it from here," Constantine said. He took the top off a decanter on his sideboard. "Can I interest you?" he asked. "I find a jot in the morning after a hard night often clears the head."

"No!" the captain shouted. "Not until you tell me what's the meaning of this."

Constantine poured brandy into a goblet that stood on the sideboard. He picked it up, swirled it in his hand, and cocked his head to the side. "If my eyes do not mistake me," he said, "that is a copy of the *Times*. What does it have to do with your visit?"

"Everything," the fellow said darkly. "It's a notice of your engagement to Miss Charlotte Winchester, daughter to Baron Pierce of Sussex."

"So it is," Constantine said. "Here to congratulate me, are you?"

"Aye, with a letter from my man-at-law! And my pistol, if need be."

"Why?" Constantine asked with fascination.

"Because, you dog, you're already engaged—to my granddaughter!" the fellow shouted.

The goblet of brandy hit the floor after falling from Constantine's suddenly numb fingers. "Oh, dear," he said a second later. "And it was the last of the '49 too. Want to tell me that again?"

Constantine pressed his fingers to his forehead. The ache he felt had nothing to do with how much he had drunk this night. He simply couldn't believe his own eyes or ears. He sat still and waited. His strange visitor said nothing. This gave him a feeble random hope that what he had seen had been some sort of visitation, rather than a human visitor. A visitation brought on by too much liquor and the lateness of the hour. He hoped and half believed that when he opened his eyes again, his weird visitor would be gone, vanished with the growing light. It was, after all, by his reckonings, not far to dawn.

The room had been quiet since his bizarre guest had stopped telling his bizarre story. Constantine didn't accept it. It was easier to believe the captain was something brought on by mixing ale, wine, and good whisky.

He opened his eyes. And didn't see anything in his study that shouldn't have been there. He sighed. It had only been a terrifying dream, after all. But he *had* been drinking too much, and decided to remain more sober now.

"You keep a good cellar," a deep voice boomed from behind him. "That much I give you, lad."

Constantine closed his eyes again. "Thank you," he said carefully. "Now, as I understand it, to recapitulate, you're saying that my father and your son were bosom friends?"

"Don't know about that," Captain Bigod said. "Know they were close as thieves, which is what they were then. Not an ounce of harm in either of them, mind. Just young rapscallions, looking for adventures in all the right places."

"If they were shot in commission of their crime, I should not call that the right place," Constantine said.

"Nay, what they were after, they got," the captain said, his voice thick and deep, sounding like a bass organ playing a dirge. "What could be righter than that? I was fair demolished, I can tell you. My Jeremy was a fine lad; handsome as he could stare, full of old Nick, and good to his father and every female he ever met." He sighed. "I liked your father too. And wasn't your ma a fine piece of mischief? My boy swore he'd have married her had your father not clapped eyes on her first. Always one to play fair, was my Jeremy. But she died soon after they did. Pined away, I think, aye, that's what I think it was. For she loved them both, although in different ways, mind. Nothing shady about your mam, and that's a fact."

Constantine nodded absently, until he realized how much that hurt his head. He had never met his mother or his father. "I see. Now, to be sure I have it all," he said slowly. "You say that my father, Constantine Roger Wylde, Lord Wylde, was a good friend to your son, Jack Bigod. And that they both met my mother at the same time, at a soiree, but it was my father who won her hand?"

"Aye, but I think that . . ." the captain said, wagging a sausage-sized finger. "Not meaning no harm to your father's memory, but I think that was only because my Jeremy bowed out when he saw where your father's heart was. Now your father was a handsome lad; you're the spit and image of him, by the way. But my Jeremy was a taking fellow too, glib as he was bonny, and a treat for the ladies. Still, he had morals, and wouldn't graze in someone else's pastures, especially not when he saw how the wind blew. Your father was daft about her."

"Yes," Constantine said wearily. "And then, you say, the two of them took to the road together." He cleared his throat. "As highwaymen."

"Straight truth," the captain said. "My Jeremy was up to every rig. Gave him an education, which is where he met your father, at school. But his learning didn't slow him down; it just gave him better ideas. He loved to run rigs. He loved laughter more than money. He rode a horse up a staircase in a noble house, for starters. Why, I could write a book about what he did with horses. He once painted one, to addle its owner. He rode to the hounds, after he trailed three foxes in different directions. That was a scene. He once moved a cow into a stable, after moving a fine-blooded horse out, and bragged about the look on the face of the toplofty fellow who owned it when he saw a cow instead of his prime blood there."

The captain wiped his eyes with a handkerchief.

"Ah, he carried on one way or another, all the time," he said in happy remembrance. "That was what attracted your father. See, your grandfather had the raising of your father, and as I heared it, he was a prosy old fellow. Not an ounce of life in him. And stupid, to boot, because if you give a young lad his head, he'll find his feet soon enough. But no, he couldn't back off. He sermonized and moralized, and then when he heard about how your father was living, cut him off without a penny. It only made your father more eager to get rich and rub his father's nose in it. It was the tight purse strings that set him on the high Toby in the first place."

"I see. That was what set your son on that road as well?" Constantine asked.

"Nay," the captain said sadly. "I gave him money enough. Pure deviltry was what sent my Jeremy out with his pistols at midnight. He loved the risk, and knew his friend needed the gold, so he was glad to ride out with him to demand that travelers stand and deliver. I didn't know about it, or I'd have knocked his head off for him. But he got it shot off before I could," he added sadly.

"So my grandfather was no more wrong in his treatment of his son than you were," Constantine said.

"Well, if you want to look at it that way," the captain conceded. "But my Jeremy loved me, and your father couldn't stand in the same room as your grandfather."

Constantine was silent. He remembered his grandfather too well. The old gentleman had been a model of rectitude and a pillar of Society. And he had terrified his servants, his community, and his only grandson. But then, Constantine had only been five when the old man died. He had never discussed his dead son. But Constantine's uncle had.

"My uncle," Constantine said carefully, "always told me that my father died a hero, while he was in the service of His Majesty, on the Continent."

"Hard to do when he was cashiered out of the army, lad. For gambling. Well, not so much for gambling as for cheating. Well, not so much cheating as shaving the cards, because he thought it fun to run a rig. But you can't, not with gents, not when you're gambling, y'see."

Constantine closed his eyes again. "You can prove that?"

"Aye," the captain said. "He'd been quit of His Majesty's service for two years when he was felled."

"By the pistol of a disgruntled traveler who

refused to give up his purse," Constantine said woodenly.

"Aye. The lads didn't know that the guards on that coach had been warned about them. A sad day. My Jeremy wept for a month, and he wasn't a soft man."

Constantine's head came up. "Your son didn't die when my father did?"

"Oh, nay," the captain said in surprise. "He got winged, but got away, though he had to wear a sling for weeks. But he lived to go to your poor father's funeral. Nay, my Jeremy died later, at the hands of a jealous husband. Well, but if that bastard hadn't of killed him, his wife would of done it when she found out he had a few other women on the side. So he was dished either way. Your father was betwixt a rock and hard place where money was concerned. Too proud to take a loan from my boy, and my lad too full of devilment not to join him on the high Toby out of friendship."

"And you say I'm betrothed to your orphaned granddaughter because my father and your son signed a pact saying that if your son ever had a daughter, I'd marry her?"

"Signed in blood," the captain said proudly.

"May I see it?"

"Aha!" the captain said craftily, wagging a finger

"And wouldn't I be the fool for carrying it here, to you, where you could read it and then throw it in the fire—over my dead body, of course," he added.

"And the fact that my father was a nobleman, and your granddaughter obviously is not of noble blood, didn't matter to my father?"

"Ha," the captain said without humor. "We ain't so highly placed as you, but if you rattle our family tree, it would rain barons and lords down on your head. Some of us are wanderers, some are gents, but the name is a good one and the fortune's solid. My son went to the same school as your father, with all the nobs. That's when they partnered up."

Constantine slowly rose from his chair. "I'm sorry," he said. "It might have been amusing to see the document, at least. But I thank you for a most entertaining evening anyway. A stranger tale I have never heard, quite gothic. I don't believe a word of it. Even if I did, that pact, signed in blood, or spit, or ink, wouldn't stand up in any court of law."

"Maybe not," the captain said, scratching his beard. "But it would certainly get the world's attention."

Constantine sat down again.

"Why didn't you come to see me before this?" he asked slowly.

"Well, first my girl was too young. Then, I figured you were biding your time. Then I saw that announcement and knew you'd left her in the lurch."

"There was no lurch to leave her in," Constantine said. "Again, I didn't know any of this. I still don't. I don't believe it."

The captain shrugged. "Don't blame you. Tell you what. You go see your uncle and ask him. He knows."

Constantine's eyes widened. "My uncle Horatio knows?"

"Aye. Of course he does. He had the raising of you, didn't he? Your grandfather knew too. Everybody did, seems to me, but you."

"I'll go to my uncle and speak with him," Constantine said.

"Aye, that's the ticket, lad. He knows all. Then, come to us."

Constantine frowned as another unbelievable and horrible thought occurred to him. "Why would your granddaughter want to marry a stranger?" he asked.

"Because she's a good girl, and does as I tell her. I had the raising of her, y'see."

Constantine felt a chill just imagining this man's granddaughter, a woman willing to marry an utter stranger. No, she had to be a woman who was of age, who hadn't married yet and was desperate enough to marry an utter stranger.

"I'll discover what I can," Constantine said stiffly. "And act accordingly."

"That's all I ask," the captain said piously.

Constantine meant it, he would discover all. Tonight, he was tired, shocked, and incredulous. But one thing he knew. There was no way on earth he'd agree to the mad captain's bizarre scheme, or honor his long-dead father's idiotic pact, if indeed he'd ever made one.

Still, there was a lot of smoke, and even if there were only a little fire causing it, it would be best to put it out before any hint of it came to his fiancée's nose. Or the *ton*'s ears. Or to his own, ever again.

Chapter 2

It was growing dark, it was getting late, and a thick dank fog was rolling in from the nearby sea, covering the setting sun. Constantine was annoyed, damp, cold, and angry. He couldn't blame anyone for the filthy weather, he couldn't blame his lead horse for casting a shoe a few miles back, he couldn't really hold anyone responsible for the fact that there wasn't a decent inn, or an indecent one, for that matter, for miles along this lonely road.

So he blamed Captain Bigod for the mission that had sent him careering out of London as if his tail were on fire. He also blamed his uncle for being unable to refute the bizarre story, having kept it a secret in order to hide the disgrace. And he definitely blamed the unknown woman who was trying to hold him to his dead father's idiotic scheme. He'd always worshiped the idea of his father, because he couldn't remember the man. Now, he positively disliked him, and his feelings of disloyalty matched his disappointment. Constantine, Lord Wylde, was not a happy man.

The one good thing he'd done, Constantine thought as he rode through the growing dusk, was to take this heavy coach with a team of four. He'd been in a hurry but never traveled without his valet. A gentleman had to present himself correctly, wherever he went. Still, now he almost regretted it. With only three horses pulling, and the fourth going slowly behind, ridden by his tiger, the boy who usually rode with him in his lighter curricle, the going was slow. The coach held his valet and his luggage, and a footman rode on the back of it. He'd turned down the company of his best friends, but only an utter fool would venture into the countryside without a few other men beside him. Especially here, on England's southwestern coast, where smugglers and wreckers, highwaymen, and such villains, were still said to be as common as pickpockets were in London.

But all he'd met up with thus far was misfortune and bad weather.

"Wait! What's that? A light?" he shouted to his coachman as he peered into the murk. He was sitting up on the driver's seat of his coach, because he'd gotten too impatient to sit inside.

"Aye," the coachman said uneasily. "But I doubt we should make for it, milord. This is a wild coast. Y'know the wreckers hereabouts lure the unwary to their doom with false lights."

"That's ships," Constantine said.

"Mebbe," the coachman said darkly. "But if men hereabouts lure ships into ports that ain't there, so they can shatter on the rocks, so's to loot the dead washed ashore, I don't doubt it would be easier for them to lure innocent travelers on land. I've my musket right here by my side. And I thinks if you got a pistol, you should do the same, sir."

Which is how it came to be that when the door at Sea Mews was flung open to see who was pounding on it in the gathering dusk, Captain Bigod saw Constantine standing there, with a pistol in his hand.

Captain Bigod took a step back. Then he drew himself up, planted his legs apart, and seemed to swell to fill the doorway. "So, you've come to end the bargain by killing me?" he demanded. "Well, can't say as to how I'm not shocked, because I am. That's a paltry thing to try to do and I didn't expect it from you. Your father would be ashamed of you, lad."

"What? Oh," Constantine said. "This." He looked at the pistol in his hand as though seeing it for the first time. "This wasn't for you. We've been lost for hours, and my coachman told me to go armed if I went to ask directions. Sorry." He slipped the pistol into his jacket.

"Not saying as to how that ain't a bad idea," the captain said magnanimously. "But didn't you see the marker, down the road? Says 'Sea Mews' clear as anything."

"I couldn't see my hand in front of my face."

"Aye, it is getting dark. C'mon in."

"I will and gladly," Constantine said. "But I've a coach; a coachman; a team of four, one of which cast a shoe; a boy riding him; a footman; and a valet. Have you accommodations for them as well?"

"For them, and all their uncles and cousins," Bigod said happily. "I'll send my servants to help them out, and stow them accordingly. If there's one thing we have here at Sea Mews, it's room, good fires on a chilly night, and good food. Welcome, welcome. Taunton, go see to the gentleman's horses and servants," he told an elderly butler who was standing nearby. "And send someone up to get the sea view room ready for him. We'll have dinner together once we get you warm and dry. C'mon," he said to Constantine. "A swallow of brandy will take the chill off. It's going to rain, y'know."

"I do," Constantine said, and repressed a shudder, because the dampness seemed to have gotten under his skin.

He stepped into the house and looked around. If he hadn't known the crusty old captain lived there, he'd not have believed it. It was a manor house equal to any he'd ever seen. The hall was high and wide, and the tiles on the floor were marble, and gleamed. There was a staircase beyond; it twinned in the middle and went up both left and right from there, leading to a gallery on the second floor. The furniture he saw was of old carved wood, heavy and luxurious. He could smell fresh burning firewood and a delicious dinner on the air. And that air was wonderfully warm. There were no painted ceilings or frescoes on the walls, but otherwise it was a house that spoke of comfort and riches.

He followed his host, both relieved and cautious.

The room the captain led him to surprised Constantine. Not the array of oddments that the captain obviously had collected in his travels, but the fine leather-bound books. Constantine walked in behind his host, who headed straight for the bookcase on the far wall. This gave his visitor a chance to inspect the room. He smiled with pleasure when he noticed a lively fire roaring in the hearth, and lamps everywhere lit and glowing. The curtains were drawn against the night. The room was both sumptuous and cozy, far more pleasant a place than he'd have expected from the brash old sea captain's appearance. And then, as he strolled over to the fire to warm his hands, he noticed that a little old woman was sleeping in a deep leather chair at the fireside.

"Perhaps we ought to go somewhere else," Constantine whispered.

The captain turned his head. "Oh, it's Lovey, is it? Never mind. If she's had her tot, a cannon won't wake her; if she hasn't, she'll be lively company. My daughter's governess," he added. "Or used to be. Now she just lives here. Everyone does," he mumbled absently. "Better if she does wake up. Be blamed if I can remember the book I'm looking for. Wouldn't be here a'tall if I hadn't sent old Taunton scrambling to see to your arrival, and if I wasn't looking for something good and old, better than I usually partake of. Well, special company and all.

Ho, Lovey!" he bellowed so suddenly that Constantine's shoulders jerked. "Give us a hand here, will you?"

The old woman's eyes fluttered open. She glanced up, looking unfocused, Constantine thought.

"Where's the good book, eh?" the captain demanded.

The old woman sat up, blinked, and then frankly goggled at Constantine. "But where are your manners, Captain?" she asked in a strangely youthful, teasing voice. "Who's the handsome lad?"

"He's here for Lisabeth," the captain said. "Lord Wylde. You remember, and if you don't, no matter. Where's the damned good book?"

"Aren't you going to introduce me?" the old lady asked, looking very much offended.

"Aye, here's Lovey, Miss Esther Lovelace, my lord," the captain said. "Lovey, here's Lisabeth's intended."

Constantine frowned.

"Now, must I ask you again, woman?" the captain bellowed. "What's the book?"

"It is the volume of Plutarch's Lives," Lovey said with enormous dignity. "The very rock upon which William Shakespeare built his immortal plays. Do you attend plays, Lord Wylde?"

"What? Who? I?" Constantine said, confused by her sudden change of demeanor, from icily formal to downright kittenish when she addressed him. "Why, yes. I do enjoy the theater."

"And so will dear Lis-Lisabeth," she said, putting her hand over her mouth as she hiccupped "She's never been, you know. To the theater, that is. She's been to local plays, church pageants and the like, of course. But *how* lovely that you will be taking her to the London theater. 'The world's a s-stage,' " she said, her chest leaping with another hiccup. "As the bard said. It's too bad that she has not yet seen famous thespians tread upon it, isn't it? Name a number from one to twenty," she commanded, so suddenly Constantine wasn't sure whom she was talking to. But she was staring at him.

"Ah, eighteen," he said.

She smiled, closed her eyes, sucked in a long breath, and held it. Her pale face was growing pink when she let it out in a sigh. "That's done it," she said with satisfaction. "No more hiccupping. So inelegant, you know. But now you're here, and all will be well. And end well. As the bard— No!" She frowned at the captain, who was about to touch a book on the shelf he was squinting at. "That's never the book. Higher, the next shelf. Yes, there."

Governess indeed! Constantine thought. If she had been, he shuddered to think what she'd taught her young charge. The old woman was either addled or drunk.

When the captain pushed the volume she'd pointed to, the bookcase swung back to reveal another room, complete with what looked like a fine array of bottles and a serviceable counter to put them on. Constantine had difficulty keeping his expression serene. This house was elegant. It was the only thing he'd seen so far tonight that was. A raven might move into a dove's nest. It couldn't change its feathers to suit its new nest. The captain was beneath him; his people were too. All that there was left to do was to meet the captain's daughter, tell her that he was already spoken for, make sure no one was angry enough about it to make a public fuss, and then he could leave this place forever, and good riddance.

He might have to pay the captain a goodly sum for his silence. But Constantine had enough money, and he knew no price was too high to pay for his continued respectability.

"Ah, here we are. Good brandy, old enough to vote!" The captain chortled. "Care to join me?"

"I'll have the Jamaican rum," Lovey said quickly. "I was drinking it and reliving old memories. The islands were where we met, Captain, remember?"

"Can't hardly forget. Took you aboard there and hauled you home again after your man passed on. When I heard you were a governess before you met him, ran away, and sailed with him to nowhere, the thing was simple. My Lisabeth needed a woman of learning and spirit. You'll have your rum. But I was talking to young Wylde here. So, my lord. Care for a tot? This one," he said, squinting at the bottle, "was your father's favorite of a damp night."

"Thank you," Constantine said. "I will."

He accepted the glass the captain handed him, and sipped some of the dark liquid. It was a potent brandy, and drinking it was a strange feeling, because it was the first time he'd actually had a living link to his father, his preferences and personality. Hs uncle never told him anything personal about the man, and as it turned out, what little he had told him was false.

"Ah!" the captain said, turning around eagerly. "Here's our Lisabeth! Lizzie, come meet your . . ." He saw Constantine's expression, and changed what he was about to say. "Won't make your mind up for you, Lizzie, my love. But come on in and meet Lord Wylde."

Constantine turned to see the woman his father

had selected for him as his bride. He breathed a great sigh of relief.

If she'd been a beauty, he would have had a more difficult time rejecting her. He'd always had a soft spot for a beautiful woman. If she'd been a taking young miss, all airs and graces, he might have felt like a monster in denying her. But this! She was a plain little thing in a plain day gown, the hem liberally spattered with mud. Her hair was wet and pressed down flat, her nose pink from the weather, and she had no graces at all because she stood stock-still, gaping at him. Her eyes, he thought absently, were fine, the color of topazes, and very bright. At least the poor creature had something of feminine merit. He decided to be kind to her, because he doubted she'd had a hand in this, any more than he had. And it was easy to be kind to such a female. He'd always been taught to be considerate of those less fortunate.

He gave her a melting smile.

Those great topaz eyes blinked.

"How do you do?" he said, and bowed, feeling as foolish as if he were bowing to a barnyard creature.

She ducked an answering bow. "How do you do?" she echoed. "I was out walking. Then the rain began. I look a fright, excuse me."

"Aye, you do," her grandfather said. "Look like you got dragged through a hedge backward. Go up and change. I'll have Cook hold dinner."

She flashed a sudden smile at Constantine. "I won't make you wait long," she said, and fled the room.

"She'll clean up better, you'll see," the captain said. "Have a seat. Or do you want a wash before we eat? Lovey, go upstairs and have a lie-down until dinner."

"I'll do, right here," Lovey said, her eyes crossing and closing as she tried to stare at their guest.

Constantine bowed. "I think I would like to freshen up, thank you," he said. He had many things to say to his host, but this was neither the time nor place. But he'd say them this very night, so there'd be no mistaking his intentions. And the foremost of those right now was to leave this madhouse as soon as he could.

Chapter 3

Constantine changed into correct evening clothes and then came down the stairs. An ancient footman told him that the captain was waiting for him in his study. Constantine joined him, feeling horribly overdressed, since the captain was still in the casual attire he'd worn when his guest arrived. Although he felt vaguely foolish in his knee-high breeches, tight fitted jacket, shining linen, and correctly tied neckcloth, Constantine reminded himself that a well-dressed gentleman was always dressed correctly.

He was offered another glass, this one of aged Spanish sherry, and was sipping it, appreciating its age and fire, when his eye was caught by a movement at the doorway. A lovely woman appeared there, and was staring at him. Constantine stopped sipping. Captain Bigod was grinning. Miss Lovelace smiled. But no one bothered making an introduction. The young woman was still looking at Constantine, so he recovered enough poise to bow.

"Good lord, Captain," he drawled. "You didn't tell me you had two granddaughters. And this is . . . ?"

She giggled.

The captain guffawed.

Miss Lovelace, in her chair by the fire, tittered.

Lord Wylde's smile vanished. His face became expressionless. He suddenly realized who she was, but didn't see the jest, didn't mean it as a joke, and didn't like being laughed at.

The young woman stopped smiling. She curtsied. "I am the captain's only granddaughter," she said. "So far as I know."

The captain laughed. Constantine winced.

"Now, Lisabeth," Miss Lovelace said. She wagged a finger. "Too ripe a jest, my dear."

"It was my mistake," Constantine said in a

33

deadly calm voice. "I apologize. Your appearance must have so dazzled me that I couldn't see clearly at first."

The young woman's lips curled. It was not a friendly smile.

"Told you she'd clean up good," the captain said, grinning.

Constantine suppressed a groan. This was going to be a long night.

It was the strangest dinner Constantine had ever sat through. He was appalled, amused, and fascinated. The captain's household was eccentric, his servants either so old Constantine wondered if they could successfully teeter around the table with the soup or wind up falling facedown with it, or so young that they didn't seem to know their left side from their right. Miss Lovelace was entirely sober when she sat down, and as the dinner went on, she slowly drank herself almost under the table, or at least down to her elbows, tittering all the way. The captain and his granddaughter didn't seem to notice. Strangely, the food was some of the best he'd ever dined on. It was simple, fresh, and well prepared, and wonderfully good.

Yet, stranger still, the woman he'd come to tell he couldn't marry her obviously didn't like him. She was remote, even a bit disdainful, and largely ignored him, when she wasn't sneering at him. Constantine felt relieved, of course, but also a bit confused, a little annoyed, and entirely fascinated.

Because she was also beautiful. He didn't know why he hadn't seen it at first. Perhaps because she wasn't what he'd ever considered beautiful before? She was small, and although she had a neat little hourglass of a figure, it was definitely on the rounded side. But her low neckline and the thin material of her gown showed she had enchanting upright little pert breasts that bounced when she laughed, which she often did. Except not at any jest he made.

There was nothing classic about her face; her plump lips weren't at all the thing, although they were tempting, no matter what she said, because she said nothing teasing or tempting to him. She was nicely rounded too, not a thready female like those in fashion plates. Not that she was stout, but she was certainly what most men liked, although Constantine had never until this moment realized that he did. She had masses of honey-colored hair, and her long-lashed eyes matched that glorious hair. Her nose was of no consequence, but it was straight.

She did, however, suffer that most dreaded

calamity of all: her flawless complexion had a smattering of freckles. But Constantine was astonished to find them no flaw. They were adorable, as was she. That was the word: "adorable." He'd never met an adorable female before. Or maybe, he thought, peering suspiciously into his glass, he'd had too much of the captain's excellent wine.

And she was clever. Her conversation, with her grandfather, at least, was witty and well informed. She had nothing to say to her grandfather's visitor, so, Constantine thought, she might be trying to interest him by not being interested in him. He couldn't understand why she wasn't. In his experience, most unmarried females, and not a few married ones, were.

"You're mighty quiet tonight, my lord," the captain said. "Tired from your journey? Or is something eating at you?"

"Rather the reverse," Constantine said. "I'm eating too much, and enjoying it far too much to have time to talk. I do beg your pardon."

"Well, thanks for the compliment. Cook did herself proud tonight. But it's simple country fare, not the Frenchified things they serve in London."

"So it is, but simple, countrified things are very appealing," Constantine said, smiling at the captain's granddaughter. He realized his mistake a second later, before he had time to lose the smile.

"Like me, my lord?" she said too sweetly.

But Constantine wasn't a popular fellow for no reason. "Yes, and no," he said smoothly. "You come from the countryside, but you're about as simple as the changing of the seasons. That is to say, there's nothing more simple, and nothing more wondrous to see."

"Lovely!" Miss Lovelace crowed, picking up her head. "What a tongue on the man!"

Constantine heard one of the old footmen, standing behind him, snicker. He was very glad he was schooled in keeping his composure.

"Exactly," Lisabeth Bigod said, shooting a knowing glance at her grandfather, who sighed when he saw it. "Our guest is well schooled in the niceties. Tell me, my lord," she went on, turning her topaz gaze on Constantine. "Do you ever say exactly what you mean? Please don't take offense," she said when she saw him stiffen. "I'm just a simple country girl with no experience of the *ton*. But I've read that you gentlemen seldom say anything to give offense in company, and for the life of me I can't see how anyone can be so amiable all the time. Doesn't that get a bit trying?"

The trembling platter of beef being presented to Constantine by an ancient palsied footman gave him a moment to gain his composure. He drew back, pretending to be more worried about being bathed in gravy than answering the question he'd been asked. He'd rather be thought a fop than a coward, or a fool. But he couldn't afford to insult the woman—or her grandfather, at least. Not until he got the whole story of his father—and who might know about it—from them.

He took a slice of beef, releasing the elderly footman, who then proceeded to stagger around the table toward Miss Lovelace. "You're right, Miss Lisabeth," he said, with a slight smile. "A gentleman in the *ton* tries never to give offense to anyone. But since that includes himself, when he has something uncharitable to say, he simply doesn't say it." There! he thought. What can you say about that?

She nodded, seeming pleased with him for the first time that night. "I see," she said. "So that explains why you're so quiet this evening?"

He tried not to wince. He spread out his hands in a gesture of surrender. "Miss Lisabeth," he said. "I have somehow offended you. Then let me try the candor you want from me. Is it because I didn't recognize you when you changed your gown? Forgive me. I was cold and harried and in a filthy temper when I got here, in no mood to observe anyone or see to anything but my own comfort.

My mistake *was* insulting. I didn't mean it that way. I wasn't trying to be rude. Can we cry quits? I tell you what! Why don't you pretend not to know me tomorrow morning?"

He smiled.

And grudgingly, so did she.

He relaxed. The captain grinned.

Miss Lovelace held up her glass of wine in a salute to him.

The captain then regaled the company with stories about his days at sea, telling tales about the pirates off the China Sea, savage islanders he had met, and fantastical sea creatures he swore he had actually seen. He was a good storyteller, and his granddaughter knew how to prompt him to his best stories. The dinner progressed smoothly, except for the quavering service. It ended in a delicious dessert that left Constantine feeling satisfied, and only a little wary about the rest of the evening.

"We don't stand on ceremony here in the countryside," the captain finally said, as he rose from his chair. "Why don't we go into the salon? Lisabeth can play us some music, if you like, she's a treat on the piano and the harp. But you get enough music in London. We can sit around the fire and talk until you feel like going to bed, my lord. How does that sound?"

Like an order, Constantine thought, tensing. But we might as well get it over with. "Fine," he said. And wondered if when they were done, he'd find himself on the road, in the night, on his way back to London. In one piece, he hoped.

He helped Miss Lovelace stand up straight, put her hand on his arm, and followed his host and his supposedly promised wife into the salon.

They settled in comfortable chairs in front of the hearth, sipped an excellent port wine, and talked about the weather, the roads, and the weather again.

Then the captain yawned hugely, rose, stretched, and said too casually, "It's early for you London gents, m'lord, but I'm an old tub, and better off in my bed now than sitting here prying my eyes open and trying to talk sense. You young people don't have to stir stump. Why don't you sit here a while and get acquainted?"

Constantine rose to his feet. He had been willing to thrash the thing out with the captain, but there was no way he was going to stay alone with the captain's granddaughter and be compromised. "I would, but how can I?" he asked. "A gentleman may not stay alone with an unmarried female, especially such a lovely one as your granddaughter."

The captain waved his hand. "We don't hold

with such finicky ways here. Anyway, you've got Miss Lovelace as chaperone. Don't worry about it."

Constantine glanced over to where Miss Lovelace was sitting, or rather, slumping, in a chair by the fire. Her snoring was just steady enough to insure that she was still breathing.

Constantine sighed, and sat again. He'd talk the matter out with the captain's granddaughter then. She seemed sensible, and hadn't been hostile to him for hours. Best to get it over and done. It was better to drive back to London by day anyway.

After the captain left them, they sat quietly, listening to the logs tick and spit in the fireplace. Then Lisabeth turned to Constantine, and smiled.

"Relax," she said. "I'm not after you."

He was taken aback. The women he knew never spoke so directly. Except for bawds, wenches, and utter romps, of course.

"It's my grandfather's idea," she went on. "And of course, my father's and your father's. But I don't remember my father, and he didn't know me. The idea of my marrying you is not mine, and I won't hold you to it. Still, I must confess," she said wistfully, "I indulged in a few daydreams." She sat up sharply. "But then I met you, and you are nothing like anything I imagined. So, you're free. And so am I."

Constantine relaxed. But then he frowned. He had been rejected. Glad as he was, he wondered why. "What had you imagined?" he asked carefully.

She smiled again. "I thought you'd be like your father and your great-grandfather. Because you look so much like them. But you're nothing like. I know that's ridiculous, and actually I'm awfully glad you're not, because it would be stupid to hanker for a fellow on account of his looks. So, be easy, my lord. I'll explain it to my grandfather. He'll understand. He's gruff and tough but indulgent with me, and always has been."

"I expect that's because of his background," Constantine said absently, trying to decide why he should feel insulted instead of liberated.

She stiffened. "Meaning?" she asked.

"Well, he was a pirate," Constantine began to say.

She shot to her feet. "He was not!" she said, so loudly that Miss Lovelace snorted, woke for a moment, and looked around blearily.

Lisabeth sat again, and said more quietly, "That was his father. He was the man to take risks and defy the law. He was lucky he ended up dying in his own bed, aboard ship. But it was a close thing. Grandy decided that running from the law or dangling from the noose would make it hard for him to raise a family. All he did was to use the knowledge and good will of his father's old acquaintances. He built himself a shipping empire, an entirely legal one. He dealt in goods from the South Seas and the Far East; he never even resorted to smuggling, though half the men living on this coast did. Or so they say," she added quickly.

"Pardon me," Constantine said. "But in truth, he looked the part, and since his son and my father were engaged in criminal activity, I presumed he had been as well. I beg your pardon."

She shrugged. "A natural conclusion, I suppose. He's usually smooth shaven. Why he grew the damned rubbish on his face, I do not know."

As Constantine was trying to absorb the shock of her saying "damned," she laughed. "No, wait! Now I do. Of course! He knew what you'd think and was trying to intimidate you. He did, didn't he? He's a crafty fellow."

"I was not intimidated," Constantine said stiffly. "I was interested. Because I didn't know about my father until your grandfather told me. I came here to find out more. I wanted to meet you too. If I was going to fight this strange pact our fathers made, at the very least I should do it in person."

"You weren't curious about me?" she asked.

"Yes. No. I suppose. But you can understand that finding out my father was a highwayman, when all my life I thought he was a brave soldier killed in His Majesty's service, was a jolt."

"Your father a heroic soldier?" She shook her head. "And your uncle clung to that? From what Grandy told me about him, I suppose he would. But your father wasn't a criminal. Not a dyed-in-the-wool one, at least. He was just trying to get enough money so he could make a home for your mother and you. My father wasn't a true reprobate either, I'm told. He gave up crime, but then was foolish enough to stray with another man's wife. His own, my mama, had passed away, you see. Our fathers were, I think, a pair of boys who hadn't grown up, and never had the chance to do so."

She sat still and stared into the fire. Then she turned to him with a grin. "You've never seen them, have you?"

"My father? Or yours?"

"Both," she said.

"No, how could I?" Constantine said. "My father was gone by the time I was a babe in arms. I do have a miniature of him in his uniform, but now I realize he didn't wear it very long. I never even knew about your father until I met your grandfather."

"Would you like to see them?"

He started. "The house is haunted?"

Her laughter was light and truly amused. "No, good heavens! Did you think I'd ask you to sit up all night by the full of the moon? No, but we have a fine portrait of your father, and one of mine."

"How came you by my father's portrait?" Constantine asked, confused.

She shrugged. "Your grandfather threw it out, along with your father. Your father hired a wagon, took all his things, and brought them to my father and this house—until he made his fortune, he said. He knew they'd be safe here."

Constantine sat up straight. "I'd very much like to meet my father at long last," he said eagerly. "May we see him now? Or would you rather wait until morning?"

She stood. "Now is as good a time as any. The portraits are all in Grandy's study. Come this way."

He hesitated, and cast a glance at Miss Lovelace, who was gently snoring in her chair. "I hate to wake her," he said softly. "She seems so peaceful."

Lisabeth frowned. "Wake her? Oh, Lord! I forgot. You're a London gent, full of airs and graces, and you don't trust me as far as you could throw me, do you?" Her eyes narrowed as she stared at him. "Ah! I see." She put her hands on her hips.

"Well, fine. We'll go by dawn's early light, accompanied by half the staff in the house, or all of them, if you want. Although why you should think I'm longing to catch you or trying to trap you, I do *not* know. You're a handsome fellow, my lord, and rich too, I hear. But I have a fine dowry, a good home, a life of my own, and I wouldn't wed you for a bucket of gold. I told you I was interested because of your father. But you're nothing like him! Your face is similar but you've a different heart. Good night. I'll see you in the morning."

She turned to go.

"Wait!" Constantine said. "Excuse me. I'm sorry." He spread out his hands. "But you see . . . the thing of it is . . ."

She noticed his face looked ruddier.

"Women *have* tried to catch me. And trap me," he added, looking embarrassed. "Not that I'm such a prize, although I suppose I'm considered such. I have my own hair and teeth, a title and a handsome fortune," he said on a weak laugh. "No one speaks ill of me either." He ran a hand through his hair. "That sounds conceited. As if I'm in love with myself. But please understand, the competition is fierce in London. Girls and women come from all over England to find husbands there. So any man declared eligible is considered fair game. Some women actually try to compromise a fellow if they can, by various lures. Getting him alone on some pretext, and then being discovered, is frequently how it's done."

She stared at him. "They do that? How dreadful for you. You must always have to go everywhere with a footman in tow, like a little girl, poor fellow."

"Not exactly," he said, through gritted teeth. He bit his tongue. What he had to say to her would banish him from the house, and he didn't want to leave yet. But when he did, he promised himself, she'd hear all he couldn't say now. And a bit more, for good measure.

"Well, it's a crime and a shame that you don't trust females," she said, her nose going up in the air as though she smelled something foul. "You can come with me now. No one will say a thing. This isn't London. I don't want you and wouldn't have you on a silver platter. But if it would make you feel more comfortable, we can wait until morning, and have grandfather come with us so there's no danger of my ensnaring you. And then," she said forcefully, "you can go. Home."

"Please forgive me," he said stiffly.

"Forgiven," she snapped. "What do you want to do?"

"I've traveled all the way from London, in the fog and the damp. I didn't know you had a portrait of my father. And so I'd like very much to meet him, if you please."

She relented. "Come along, then. The lamps are still lit in Grandy's study. He knew you'd want to see your father tonight."

Constantine walked behind Lisabeth, a bit warily, even though she had said there was no trap waiting. When she didn't speak and infuriate him, he realized again that she was a round little armful, and he was a long way from home. He wondered what she wanted of him, and suddenly found himself hoping for the best. For himself, at least.

She went into the hall, crooked a finger at a young footman who looked as though he were dozing with his eyes open, and said, "Come along with us, Rodney. And stay awake so you can protect Lord Wylde, if he needs you." She shot a murderously amused glance at Constantine, and went on down the hall to her grandfather's study.

Constantine winced, but followed.

The study was dimly lit, so Lisabeth had the footman turn up all the lamps. Her grandfather had a virtual museum in this room, of oddments and whatnots and things picked up on his travels. The walls were filled with portraits, revered because they were his history or the history of those he had admired. These paintings were just as much a personal jumbled treasure trove as his collections of shells and sextants, spyglasses, coins, dried fishes, and exotic carvings on wood or jade, from the South Seas, India, Africa, and the far east, or on ivory, from whales of every sea.

She held the lantern high as she paced along the perimeters of the wall. Constantine saw a handsome blond youth standing by the sea, in a picture of fairly recent vintage.

"My father," she said with simple pride.

"A handsome fellow," Constantine commented.

"And here is my mama," she said, pausing before a miniature portrait of a charming young woman. "It was her engagement portrait, sent to my father. She was to sit for a better picture after I was born." Her shrug was sad. "But she didn't live long enough."

Lisabeth walked on and stopped by a portrait that hung by a window.

Constantine looked up, and halted. The man he saw in the portrait was young, and smiling. The flickering lamplight gave it the semblance of life, and animation. And the face was one Constantine saw in the mirror every day. Only happier. The young man had the same dark hair and tilted arched brows, the same eyes, but with more light and humor in them. The portrait showed a young blade from the last generation, an athletic fellow who looked as though he could laugh as well as wink, as the inconstant light seemed to be making him do. "Mischievous," was the word that came to Constantine's mind. He felt suddenly sad and deprived. This was a man he'd like to have known.

"He is . . . he looks like—he's the image of me," he said.

"He *was* your father," she said. She gazed at him and then at the portrait, and her expression grew grave. "But though the features are similar, look closer and you'll see he's really not so very like." She fell still and waited, letting Constantine look his fill. All the while, she watched his face as intently as he studied the portrait before him.

Constantine was strangely touched and excited; it felt as though a part of his life had been restored to him. Here was a man he'd never known, but one, for all his faults, that he thought he'd have loved, even so. There was such warmth and humanity in that young face. His father must have been his own age when the portrait had been painted. After he'd stared a long while, he slowly became aware of the hour and his surroundings. But he didn't want to leave the portrait. He opened his lips to ask for it, to take it home with him, so this happy young man could make up for all their lost years, and spend the rest of his life near him.

But then he remembered who his father had been, what he'd done, and what people would think if they knew. He understood that though the years had passed, if knowledge of the man's crimes and ignominious end became known, his own reputation would be forever tarnished. Charming, his father may well have been. But he'd also been a criminal.

He closed his lips. "Thank you," he said softly after a moment. "I'm glad I could see him. Perhaps, before I leave tomorrow, I'll come back and see him by daylight."

Lisabeth nodded. "We've grown used to him, and I know I'd miss him. But I'm sure Grandy will let you take him with you. He is your heritage. We would understand."

Constantine turned from the portrait. She was standing closer to him than he'd known; he could actually feel the warmth emanating from her as the room grew chillier with the hour. He backed away a step. "Thank you," he said. "But no. This is his place now. I can rest assured that he'll be safe here."

She tilted her head to the side. "You mean to leave him?" Her eyes widened. "You're *ashamed* of him?"

"Well, but my dear," he said. "He was a criminal. That's why my uncle kept his life, or rather, his death, a secret."

She stiffened. "Indeed," she said. "I suppose he was. And I suppose there isn't a family tree in England that doesn't have some gallows-ripe fellows dangling from it? Only as the centuries roll on do those villains become quaint, rather than embarrassing, is that it? Especially if they brought fortune to the family. I understand. Your father hasn't been dead long enough for legend to gild his name. Well, if you feel that way, sir, I'm mighty glad I found out about it now. I was just going to introduce you to your great-grandfather, and he's a fellow I've been half in love with all my life. But now I see that that would be entirely too much for you."

Constantine turned slowly, and looked at her. "My *great*-grandfather?"

"Aye," she said. "He looks even more like you. But he was nothing like you. He's the one who made your family rich, my grandfather says, and he should know. Your grandfather was a quiet law-abiding gentleman, but my grandfather knew his father, and admired him, as did all hereabouts. You, however, obviously would not. Shall we go?"

"My *great-grandfather*?" Constantine asked again, incredulously.

"Yes," she said happily. "Captain Elijah the Cunning, the celebrated pirate, scourge of several seas and clever as he could hold together. Three nations offered gold for his head, two bid rubies and diamonds, and one, four elephants. But the captain kept his head on his shoulders and took their treasure galleons anyway, until he died at a ripe old age in a storm at sea, or from laughing at his victims, as some said."

"*My* great-grandfather?" Constantine asked weakly.

"Oh, yes!" she said with malicious glee.

Chapter 4

"Lord Wylde," Lisabeth said with sweet mendaciousness, as she looked up at the wall. "May I present your great-grandfather Elijah Wylde, the famous Captain Cunning?"

She held her lamp high, swept an arm out to indicate a portrait on the wall on the other side of the window from where the picture of Constantine's father hung. She ducked a curtsy that made the flame in the lamp sway and sputter.

A corresponding light seemed to flicker in the dark and dangerous eyes of the startling young man in the dark portrait above her.

Constantine stared. It was an old portrait; the years, and decades of wood smoke, had added darkness to a shadowy palette, but the forceful personality of the young man it portrayed shone through.

If Constantine's father had seemed to him to look like a mischievous boy, this man, his father's grandfather, was something altogether different. He seemed steeped in sin, as well as humor. The glint in his eyes, the tilt of his chin, the dark slashing eyebrows and the surprisingly sensitive mouth, even the invisible breeze that tugged at his flowing cape, hinted at a man of many parts. Most of them wicked.

The artist had not been a master. His choice of color was murky; his portrayal of the horse standing nearby his subject was amateurish. But he had perfectly captured a mood and a personality. The man in the painting was all fury and dash, and splendor. A strong breeze in the painting was blowing; a ship was waiting, wallowing in the swells of the dark sea beyond. Constantine's great-grandfather looked eager and restless, wild as the rising wind, as though he couldn't wait to dash off to another adventure.

Constantine now understood what Lisabeth had meant. He could certainly see how an impressionable girl could fall half in love with just the image of this reckless gentleman. She was also right about the resemblance to him. It was remarkable, and yet, even so, Constantine could never be mistaken for the man in the portrait. No, his great-grandfather was everything and nothing like himself. And for a wonder, for a moment, that made him sad.

He finally tore his gaze from the man in the portrait and looked at his hostess. She was still staring up, almost worshipfully, looking at the long-dead man who seemed so alive.

"And is there a portrait of my grandfather?" he asked.

That seemed to break the spell that had bound her. She turned to look at him. "No," she said calmly. "My grandfather said yours felt portraits were a vanity. Small loss. People without souls don't make for good portraits."

"He was an evil fellow, then?" Constantine asked, with dread. What other rotten fruit hung from his family tree?

She laughed. "Oh, no. Grandy said he was a dull dog, a conservative man without any romance in his soul. Poor fellow. And his wife was chosen for her bidability, as well as her dowry.

Poor lady. My grandfather only kept up a connection with him for the sake of the memory of his father, who helped him get started in his business, you see. And then, because of the friendship between his son and your father."

"How did they meet?" Constantine asked, fascinated. "I mean, my father and yours. Their upbringings were so different."

"Aye, chalk and cheese," she said promptly. "Day and night. But they met at school, and then years later one night at a tavern, and like called to like. Your father said he felt as if he'd been in chains all his life. My father said yours was a fine fellow, smart as a whip and not afraid to try anything once, twice, if it paid enough. They were kindred souls."

Constantine winced. "But your father didn't need money. Mine did."

"Defending him already?" she asked, smiling. "Good, good. My father was in it for the fun and adventure, and no excuses. And for all your father said it was for the money, he could have bowed to his father and kept his allowance until he'd saved enough to break free of domination. As heir to a title, he also could have found a nice dreary job of work, clerking or secretarying, or some such, couldn't he? No, they were a matched pair of bold bad boys, out for amusement and danger, and the devil take them, if he could."

Constantine swallowed hard. "Did my great grandfather have a home here? I don't understand how he could have hidden that from the world."

"He didn't," she said simply. "He was far too clever. He lived on his ship most of the time, and sent his booty to his man at law in London. That fellow sold the treasure, invested the coin, and then sent all the proceeds to your great-grandfather's estate. This village was his secret port. No one in London or Society ever knew he was the great Captain Cunning. Only those who worked with him did, and they were entirely loyal. And not just out of fear, mind. Fear fades when the man you're afraid of dies. But respect never does."

Constantine nodded. "I can understand why my uncle wouldn't want any reminder of that. Is that why your grandfather has the portraits?"

"No, your uncle wouldn't want any part of us. Your father brought his to us. As for your great-grandfather's, your grandfather only kept it because it cost money to create, and he never wasted a penny piece. That, and as a reminder to him of what he could become if he wasn't careful. But he was careful. He toed the line and never cast his net far. He never made money but neither did he lose any. He handled his father's estate wisely. The money may have been aquired by nefarious means, but your grandfather respected money, whatever its heritage.

"I'm afraid your father was a terrible disappointment to him. But not a shock, never that. Your grandfather always spoke of the bad blood in the family. Yet he respected the bounty that blood had brought him. Isn't that curious? Your uncle didn't warn you about this taint in your family? It consumed your grandfather. He threw away both portraits as soon as your father scandalized the name. My grandfather was happy to take them. You didn't know any of this?"

"As I said," Constantine said, "they kept it from me. I knew nothing of it." He paced away a step, and then looked back up at his great-grandfather. "And," he murmured, as though to himself, "if anyone else finds out about this, I'll be ruined."

"Ruined?"

He saw her confusion. "I'm known as a moderate man, I try to be a gentleman," he explained. "It's more than a title or what school one attends. It's a way of life. I belong to many clubs that I value, I have worthy friends and acquaintances and . . ." He closed his lips before he mentioned his fiancée. If her grandfather had told Lisabeth the whole story, then she already knew. If not, the less she knew about him, the better. He'd have to discover what she knew before he left this place. This wasn't the time for it, though.

"The point is," he went on, "they all think they know me. As did I, myself. But now this! Pirates? Highwaymen? Criminals lurking in my family tree? My fortune comes from crime and mayhem? It's outrageous. In some circles, I'd be immediately ostracized. At the very least, mocked." He shuddered. "I can picture the caricatures now, in every window in town. If it were to become widely known I might never be trusted again. Many people believe blood will tell."

"And you're one of them?" she asked curiously.

He shrugged. "I was. But now I think about it, I doubt it. Why, just look at my ancestors and me. I never felt the urge to command a pirate ship, I assure you. Nor would I ever hold up a coach on the public road, or a private one. I'm law-abiding and enjoy life lived moderately. No matter the financial need, those are just not things I would do, believe me."

She did. Then she sighed. "But look at the royals," she said. "If one goes back to the day they first sat on the throne, there isn't a royal line that wasn't

60

forever cheating and killing, murdering and stealing, and no one thinks less of them for that."

He shook his head. "I'm not a royal, thank God. I suppose a Viking ancestor could be excused. Even a murderous Norman. But anything closer in time to me—and you'll admit a father and a great-grandfather aren't exactly antiquity—would reflect upon me. Upon my character and my position. I'd rather these facts never left this room."

She laughed. It was an unexpectedly merry sound in the deep velvet quiet of the house. "But everyone here knows about your ancestors! They look up to your great-grandfather, and I don't just mean his portrait. He was generous to the villagers and to the men who worked for him, and that was fully half the men who lived here. He brought prosperity to a poor little fishing village. That prosperity lasted. Our men don't have to risk their necks bringing in perfumes and brandy from France if they don't choose to, because Captain Cunning had brought in jewels and gold long before the wars with France started. Why, when your poor father was shot, the whole district turned out for his funeral, and wept buckets, I'm told. The news got beyond this room ages ago."

Her expression grew serious. "Is it someone you care for whose opinion you worry about?"

He nodded, because if he didn't, and she knew about his plans for marriage he'd look like a fool, or a liar.

"Ah," she said. "Well, I can't understand that. We don't practice ancestor worship here, nor do we spend time blaming a man for what his father did. Or even for what he did. Most of the people here at Sea Mews have the most extravagant histories! Bloody awful, but a man can change and a woman must, as Grandy always says."

Constantine blinked. Ladies never said "bloody." Neither did gentlemen, unless there were no ladies about, and they were inebriated. But she said it casually and didn't seem to think a thing wrong with it.

"Take young Platt there," she said in a lower voice, tipping a shoulder toward the footman who stood near the hearth, still sleeping with his eyes open. "He's quiet and respectful, and his idea of a day off well spent is sitting by the river with his feet in the water, hoping he doesn't catch a fish because that would be a bother. His father was a drunk and a villain. Went through the family money, earned more seafaring . . ." A little smile appeared on her lips. "We prefer to call making a living from the sea that's not from shipping or fishing 'seafaring,' you see. 'Piracy' is not a happy word. I suppose because you're hanged for acts of piracy, even just for *being* a pirate. At any rate, then the fool came home and drank the roof off from over his head. Grandy gave his son, young Platt, a position here for the sake of his father and his grandfather, who were, though a bit hasty, and maybe a trifle flawed, still loyal men.

"Most of the people who work here have family histories. Many have interesting ones of their own," she said with a secretive smile. "One day you must ask Miss Lovelace about her past. During the day, literally, I mean. She's sober as a mouse until evening falls." She cocked her head to the side. "Does everyone in London care so much for what a man's family was? Rather than what a man is?"

"Yes," he said simply. "Well, at least, anyone who matters. And so if they knew about my father and great-grandfather, I'd be a figure of fun to some, one of pity to others, and considered a shady character by many more. I only wonder how my uncle managed to keep the thing secret so well."

"Well, I know your father was disinherited and cast out by your grandfather, and in turn, your great-grandfather had estranged himself from the family. *His* father was very moral, a friend of Cromwell, I believe." Her smile became wicked, reminding Constantine of the young man in the portrait above her. "So you don't have to fret. Wickedness seems to skip a generation in your family. The bad blood probably won't appear in you. You'll never pass a jewelry shop window and feel a sudden urge to break the glass and carry away the pretties, and any pretty lasses in your path. But your son, now . . . I'd beware if his infant playmates had silver rattles."

Constantine's eyebrows lowered. She was far too amused. At his expense. Her bright topaz eyes sparkled, her mouth curled up in a catlike grin. He seldom saw a grown female look so much like a cheeky boy, but it suited her. She was, he became aware again, a damned fine-looking young female, warm and soft-spoken. Standing this close to her, he realized the fresh wild scent of her reminded him of sun-warmed meadows of red clover and wild poppy, very unlike the intriguing, teasing French perfumes that the women he knew wore. But no decent woman he knew would be with him at this hour of the night, with only two inept guardians in sight, unless she was interested in getting him in her bed.

That thought didn't appall him, exactly.

She gazed up at him, studying his face, as though seeing things in it that he had never seen, looking as fascinated by him as she was by the portraits of his ancestors. The room was chilly, yet he felt the glow radiating from her and was drawn to it like a freezing man seeking a fire. It seemed to him that she'd drawn closer. It was dark and suddenly warm and they were alone in the wonderfully quiet darkness. Her full pink lips parted in a smile. Her head slanted. Her lashes fluttered down to douse the sparkle in her topaz gaze as his head dipped toward hers—until he realized he could see her eyelashes so plainly because he was moving closer.

His head reared up and he took a quick step back, feeling as though he'd stood too close to the edge of a precipice. A shudder ran through his body, whether because of his narrow escape or because his senses jangled from suddenly interrupted desire he didn't know. But he felt both relief and frustration.

Of course she was tempting, he told himself. He was a man and she was a lovely young woman, and more, she seemed free of all the constraints of polite society. He doubted she was a loose female. She was merely an oddity, as outrageous in her speech, candor, opinions, and likely also in her behavior, as any of his bizarre ancestors whom she so admired.

She was an interesting woman and a promising-looking one. But he had no time or reason to contemplate her. He had to ignore how appealing she was. He had a mission. He'd been assaulted by an impossible truth. Charlotte's father had had him investigated and never discovered any of this, he was sure, or he certainly wouldn't have been allowed to so much as approach her, much less become engaged to her.

But was his secret safe? Even in this little obscure village? Or might it one day escape and make his life miserable? He had to discover all, and mend all too. He must find out all about his wretched heritage, see how far the knowledge ran, stopper up what he could with money or charm, or promises, or threats. And then leave this place and his sorry history behind him, forever. Constantine put his hand on his vest pocket, withdrew his watch, and glanced at it. He stiffened. This place must have bewitched him. It was past midnight, and here he stood, as good as alone with an unmarried young woman, with only the chaperonage of a sleeping old woman and a comatose footman. And the young woman had a rogue of a grandfather who had already said he wanted Constantine as a grandson-in-law. Constantine blinked. Was he mad to have lingered so long in such jeopardy?

He bowed. "The hour is later than I could have

imagined," he said. "I'm sorry to have kept you awake so long. May we continue this conversation tomorrow?"

"Certainly," she said, as coolly as though she hadn't sensed the strange moment that passed between them. "I ride before breakfast. Would you care to join me?"

Constantine frowned. He kept town hours. "Perhaps," he said evasively. "But if not, then may we speak at luncheon, say?"

She laughed. "Say anytime all day. I have few pressing errands. Oh, there are visits to make to neighbors and chores to do in the garden, I love to garden. But we've not had anything as interesting as yourself here for many a day. And you are a guest. If you want me, just ask for me, and I'll be glad to bear you company. Good night. Young Platt will show you to your room. The house is enormous, and you could get lost in the dark. And Grandfather sleeps with his pistols under his pillow. Habit, I suppose."

Constantine repressed a shudder, bowed, and gratefully left, with young Platt trudging behind him.

"Well, well, well," Lisabeth whispered, as she looked up again at Captain Cunning on his dark windy beach. "Could you have guessed that you'd pass down your looks, sir, and not a breath of the life that was in you? The same wicked brows, the same beautiful eyes. Sometimes I think I can see a spark in them that had to come from you. But he's such a stick! Such a pity, what a shame."

The painted eyes seemed to sparkle.

Lisabeth's own smile returned. "No, sir," she said, with another curtsy to the portrait, "you are entirely unique, utterly without compare. And I'm grieving for it, disappointed and let down. I actually tried to see if I could discover life and fire in him. I thought I almost had. But you have more, even painted on canvas as you are. He was tempted, I'd swear to it. But then appalled. *Appalled!* Can you believe my folly? Now, that," she murmured to herself as she turned to go wake her old governess and steer her up to her bed, "is what comes from falling in love with an illusion."

"Nay, lass," Miss Lovelace said from behind her. "Not an illusion. You're right. There wasn't a thing wrong with old Captain Cunning, or his grandson, nor never was. Hearty lads, with heads and hearts in the right place, even if their actions weren't always proper, nor legal. But they weren't mean or cruel, and they didn't harm anyone if they could help it. Only," she added with a little sigh, "in their line of work, they often couldn't help it.

"You'd have loved either of them. And they, you," Miss Lovelace said sadly. "But that's not to be. Nor will your heart be broken. Heartache is what comes of trying to fit the illusion to what isn't there. I'm pleased you know it so soon. The lad looks like them, but he's nothing like."

Lisabeth tilted her head. "Lovey? I never thought! Did you know them?"

"I knew his father. Charming fellow. Bright and fun-loving. A rascal, in the nicest way, of course." She sighed. "They're gone now, all those bright, clever young men."

"His son isn't like him at all," Lisabeth said sadly.

"Yes. That's his tragedy. He was ruined by his uncle, I think. Brought up proper as a parson, with not a speck of life left in him. Too bad. But be kind to him, Lisabeth, for he'll never know what he missed, except in his dreams. And he's been trained to ignore them."

Lisabeth sighed too. "I suppose it's also because it skips a generation. All that wildness and courage." She grinned. "Now, maybe if I can stay unwed until Lord Wylde's son grows up—now there would be a man for me!"

"Nay, don't be foolish," Miss Lovelace said. "And blood doesn't skip. It races, it flows, and it may tell, if it isn't stopped up too soon. Lord Wylde's blood's grown thin and sluggish. He's got just enough to get him through the life he chose, but it wouldn't be enough for you, or any lass with spirit."

Lisabeth smiled at her beloved governess. Esther Lovelace was a scandal and a delight. She was well read, well bred, and had lived badly. She knew literature, history, art, and music, and even more about life. Lovey was small and busy, with snow-white hair, bright blue eyes, and a plump smiling face. She looked like a retired cook or nursemaid. But she'd been a governess in her younger days, before she'd met Lisabeth's grandfather. She'd been hired by him, as had many of their servants, both those who could still serve and those who now lived in this big old house in retirement. They'd taught Lisabeth loyalty, as well as how to wink at dishonesty if it was for a good cause. They were, for all their age, a lusty, lively crew. Lisabeth grew up learning how to speak well, and freely.

"Let be, my love," Miss Lovelace said. "You'll find a right mate, and a true love. And maybe both in the same man!"

"Amen!" Lisabeth said, laughing.

And giggling, they made their way up the stairs to their beds.

Chapter 5

~~~oOo~~~

Lisabeth got ready for bed slowly, not like hours earlier, when she'd gone through a wild scramble trying to dress exquisitely for her lofty company. She was a woman who only bothered to dress well for church or a neighbor's occasional dinner invitation, and she usually wore her day gowns until they wore out. Tonight she'd searched through wardrobes and sent the maids scurrying, looking for pins and combs and ribbons—for all the good it did, she thought grumpily.

She'd come in from the damp and was going to say hello to her grandfather, until she saw the stranger standing there in his study. Even though she'd met few gentlemen, she knew the visitor could be no other than the nobleman from London her grandfather had told might be arriving. She hadn't expected him so soon; she'd never expected him to look the way he did. Lord Wylde! He was really beyond her wildest dreams. He was the very opposite of his name. He was calm, contained, well mannered; well bred, handsome as he could stare, and seemed at ease in all company. Lean, dark, and elegant, he was nevertheless the image of his wicked ancestor; but also the perfect civilized gentleman.

Best of all, she'd thought, he was real, and really there! He must have actually been considering their fathers' mad pact. She couldn't believe her good fortune.

So she had rushed upstairs and bathed and dressed as though for a party. Her hair was dried, brushed till it crackled and shone, and then tied back behind her head, so it fell in curls on one shoulder. She'd worn her lucky golden locket at her neck, the one with a miniature of her mother's face in it, and had decided on a deceptively simple russet gown. It had long sleeves, for the weather, a low neckline, for fashion, and a high waist that she hoped made her look more statuesque. She'd looked in the glass and sighed. There was not much she could do about that. She was small. The fashion was tall. But they'd be sitting at dinner, and maybe he wouldn't notice.

That wasn't to say she had fallen in with her grandfather's ridiculous plan. She didn't even know the man, and had just recently been told about his existence. Lord Wylde might turn out to be a fool; he might be toplofty—she'd thought she'd caught a hint of that in his expression. Until he'd flashed that smile! It had been so sudden and so charming. Maybe too charming? she'd worried. He could even be a wastrel, looking for a way to improve his fortunes. She needed a man who was wise and considerate, *and* self-supporting. But her grandfather was wise. He wouldn't have invited a rogue to meet her, whatever sort of pact his son had made.

Whatever Lord Wylde was, he was the most exciting thing that had happened to Lisabeth since . . . forever, she guessed.

She'd rushed down the long stair to the study, where her grandfather always entertained before dinner. At least, where he always entertained those few important guests they'd had. Their life was simple, their visitors, the same. Her grandfather's many business acquaintances were merchants, often well-to-do, but seldom paragons of good manners. This would be, she'd thought, the first time they'd actually ever entertained an honest-to-goodness nobleman, a true *gentleman*. She'd paused at the door to the study, taken a deep breath, and walked in.

Their visitor had been standing by the hearth, talking with her grandfather. He'd been wearing simple black-and-white evening dress, but his closely fitted jacket was perfection, and his high white neckcloth gleamed even in the intermittent light. She saw a glimpse of his white shirt and a peacock-blue waistcoat, with a golden fob hanging at his lean waist. His legs were long and muscular. He was so splendid he took her breath away. This was the man Grandy wanted her to marry? She'd been half inclined to say "I do" instead of "good evening." How lucky could she be?

He'd turned, looked at her, bowed, and smiled, his teeth as white as his impeccable linen.

Her heart had raced. She'd curtsied. She hoped she didn't make any mistakes in speech or actions this evening. Lovey had taught her manners, but she'd never tried them out in such high company.

So she'd spoken. And so had he.

And it turned out he was nothing like the man she'd been hoping for. He was a stick, a priss, an arrogant muttonhead, more concerned with the proprieties than life itself. But he looked so much like the man she'd loved since childhood, Lisabeth felt confused and cheated. So now she slipped her night rail over her head, reached for a thick comfortable robe, tied it tight, opened her door and tiptoed down the stairs in search of comfort.

She found it where she always had. A light was still on in his study. She eased the door open. Now there was a fire in the hearth, and a lighted lamp on his desk. He knew. He always knew.

"Thought you'd be down here sooner or later tonight," her grandfather said. He gestured to a deep chair by the hearth. "Sit down and tell me about it."

She plucked a pillow off the chair, and clutching it in front of her, sank to the thick carpet in front on the hearth instead, as she'd done since she was a child.

"It's ridiculous," she said. "Impossible! But I know you meant well," she told him. "You always do. And so I thank you for your trouble, I do. Still, I have to tell you that though I'll be nice and I promise to be gracious for so long as he stays here, that's that. Can you forgive me? I don't mean to be unappreciative, I don't want to put you into a pet after all your pains, but Grandy, I have to be myself."

"Wouldn't want you to be less," Captain Bigod

said gruffly, his smile so tender it was slightly loopy. "I just wanted to give you a chance to meet him. Can't meet his kind out here in the back of beyond, y'know. Not that there's anything wrong with the fellas hereabouts," he added hastily. "And if you set your sights on one, I wouldn't stand in the way, 'less I had good reason to. But the truth is, you're two and twenty and you don't seem to love any fella at all."

"Except you," she said with a tender smile.

He didn't answer; he just gazed at her fondly. As she knew he would. He smiled, because he knew she was playing him like a fiddle, and even so, he appreciated her. She was his sunrise and sunset, and they both knew it.

She was such a pretty little thing, he thought again, as he had since the day they'd brought her to him, an hour after she was born, and placed her in his arms. Her ma had died producing her, and his clever, foolish son hadn't much cared about anything but seeking amusement after that. But at least he'd left his father that babe in his arms.

Now, of course, his granddaughter was grown, and in his eyes, even prettier. He knew no higher compliment for a woman, and he'd known all kinds of females in his time. Because in his experience, a beauty was a standoffish kind of female, as impressed with her looks as those looking at her were, and his Lisabeth surely wasn't that. In fact, she didn't think much of her looks at all! And a gamine was a lass who was perky but full of backtalk, and his Lisabeth wasn't that either. A handsome woman belonged on a coin or a locket, but not in a man's arms. He'd met Originals but all they ever wanted to do was run rings around a fellow and impress him with their wit. His late wife had always been described as a good woman, and he'd loved her dearly, but she'd been called that because her looks had never been more than passable. That had been good enough for him, but she'd lamented her appearance, and so ignored it, as he did.

As for the wenches he'd known, and he'd known many, he wouldn't even think of them at the same time he did his granddaughter.

His Lisabeth had them all beat. She had wit and looks and charm, and it all came naturally to her.

She had everything a man could want. She was small, but also just the right height to have to look up to any man of stature. She was well spoken and so kind that he'd never heard her talk down to any man. Even though she could, he thought, she was that well educated. He'd seen to it. There was nothing worse than an ignorant person in his eyes, man or woman.

She was perhaps too fetching. He feared for her when he saw the way men looked at that lush mouth, and then the lavish form beneath it. But they didn't dare look at her that way when he was there, and if they did, they never did again, not if he was there to see to it.

The trouble was, he was getting on, and he worried because he knew he wouldn't be there to protect her forever. She needed her own man; she needed a husband for that.

"I liked the cut of his jib," he said now. "He's a gentleman through and through. Not a bit standoffish or puffed up, like some I could name."

"Oh, Grandy," she said on a long disappointed sigh. "But of course he's standoffish and puffed up. That's the problem."

"Just getting used to his surroundings," her grandfather said. "Give him time. Some fellas need time to loosen up. He's smart, of course, well, his father was a clever fellow too. And his looks . . ." He stared at the ceiling of his library, as though trying to summon up the right words.

She laughed. "Yes, I know who he looks like, but he's nothing like him at all."

"Yes," her grandfather went on as if he hadn't

heard her, "like his father, the spit and image. And more like the great captain hisself, only more modern looking, o'course."

Lisabeth turned her head and studied the portrait near the window. She frowned as an awful thought occurred to her. "Grandy! You didn't threaten him in order to get him here, did you? Is that why he came? No wonder he was so stiff and unbending."

"No," he said with great mock offense. "I did not. What do you think I am?"

"I think you're devious, and determined to get what you want. But I know you'd never lie to me," she said. "So it was probably only a veiled threat, wasn't it?"

He didn't answer. She thought she detected the pink of a flush under the stubble of his beard. She laughed. "Aha. That might explain a lot. At least he's smart enough to be a little wary of you, and me. Well, a visit to us won't do him any harm. So you told him the tale and he came to meet me? Why? And he's seven and twenty, you said. So why is he still unmarried? Do you know anything about that?"

He shrugged.

"Well," she said. "I expect we'll find out soon enough."

He breathed easier. He'd hidden the London paper, so she couldn't learn more about young Constantine Wylde than what she might find in the *Peerage*. No need for her to know the fellow had promised himself to another. In his experience there was many a slip twixt a word and a vow. That could be decided, and discussed, later.

"Grandy," she said slowly, "please don't get your hopes up. I don't care for him much. But I'll try to at least be polite. As for him? He might have agreed to see me because he's a gentleman and it would be the right thing to do, especially because of what you said his father and mine wanted." She paused and looked at him suspiciously. "Although why you didn't tell me about that sooner I still don't know."

"Wanted to give you the chance to make your own pick," he said piously. "Since you didn't, I figured it was time to let you in on what your father wanted."

"Thank you," she said. "I'm curious about what my father wanted, and it may be that this Lord Wylde is too. But don't forget, whatever he is, he's a lord, and a rich one, and in London Society. I'm just a girl from the countryside."

"You're well dowered and well brought up, pretty as a picture and smart as a whip!"

"But we aren't Society. And he is."

"We're Society hereabouts!" he roared.

"Hush! Want to wake the whole house? We may be Society hereabouts, Grandy, but we also have a history that folks around here don't care about."

"They do too," he said. "They're proud of us."

"Maybe," she said. "But our family isn't one most gentlemen would brag about."

"Well, his family did worse," he retorted. "And I'll have y'know," he said in agitation, "none of *us* never died in no commission of a crime neither!"

"That's because they were never caught."

"Well, there you are. Nor never would be. Clever as they could hold together, all your ancestors, and lucky too, because luck counts, y'know. As for me, I made *my* money in business, good investments and such, missy, and don't you forget it."

"But your father didn't," she persisted.

"Well, neither did young Wylde's!" he said triumphantly.

She sighed. "All I'm saying is that I'll be polite. But I don't want *you* to expect anything else. I don't. What his father and mine wanted doesn't matter." Her eyes widened. "Unless you mean to hold me to it, whatever I think?"

" 'Course not!" he said promptly. "You don't have to take him if you don't want him."

She nodded. "Right. If I don't like him, you'd understand. So if he doesn't want me either, you'll have to understand that too."

"If he hasn't lost his wits after one look at you," he said, "why, I'll eat my own beard!"

She frowned. "I wish you would. Whatever possessed you to try to grow such a ratty-looking thing, anyway?"

He looked guilty, and stroked his ragged, grizzled beard protectively. "Well, I told you I went to see some old mates when I was in London too, and they wouldn't have recognized me without it. I wore one when I was a lad."

"So why don't you shave it off now? Don't tell me the widow likes it!"

"Her name is Mrs. Twitty," he said with awful dignity. "Ain't her fault her man up and died."

"She's been 'the widow' since I can remember." Lisabeth's eyes widened. "Oh! Of course! I'm sorry, Grandy! Does this mean you've decided to make it legal? That could explain your eagerness to see me wed and gone, because there can't be anything worse for a bride in a new marriage than an old flame in the same house, and some women look at any other female that has a claim on their husband's heart as that. This puts a new face on things. I'll find someone soon," she said quickly, "or try, and if I can't find anyone, why then I'll go live in London a while, I've always had a fancy to—"

"Now wait!" the captain bawled, holding up one hand. "Ain't nothing like that! In fact," he added more quietly, before she could scold him again, "she and me, well, we're sort of going our separate ways anyways. She's got her eye on Mr. Finn, the butcher, and good luck to them, says I. I never made her any promises, nor she to me, and she ain't getting any younger, nor am I getting any fonder, so that's all there is to that. I want you to find a good man so's I can rest easy, is all. And," he added slyly, "I could use a grandchild or seven playing about my feet in my old age."

She laughed. "Well, if you're waiting for your old age, I can put off meeting someone for at least another twenty years."

He smiled. She'd forgotten the beard, as he'd hoped. But how was he expected to throw the fear of God into a fellow if he came to him all neat and sweet and clean-shaven, as was the fashion these days? Not that he thought he'd scared young Wylde. But he'd certainly got his attention.

"So all I want is for you to be civil to him, even if he don't suit you."

"That jest I made at dinner was too warm, I knew it," she said, looking guilty. "I just wanted to see how he'd react. It *was* rude. I'm ashamed of myself. And I confess I did it to shake him up a bit, to see how much life there was in him. But see how he reacted? As though I'd waved a dead fish in his face. What I said wasn't *that* crude. He could have concealed his distaste. And he should have, being such a gentleman. Fact is, he's a prig, Grandy, and that's that."

"Early days," her grandfather said. "How was he to know you wasn't a prig yourself, just mis-saying something?"

She ducked her head so he wouldn't see her blush. Bringing her lips so close to Lord Wylde's hadn't been a jest or the work of a prig. It had been an overwhelming compulsion. Yet he'd reacted to the offer the same way he had to the jest.

"His father was a good man," her grandfather said. "Even if he was a foolish lad. But he would have grown out of it, if he'd lived. And his mother was a fine woman. His uncle is a bag of wind, and more impressed with his godliness than God will ever be. Pounding a Bible, spouting it all the time, and acting all holy never got any man into heaven. It's living right and doing good that turns the trick. An old pirate can get through the pearly gates easier than a parson, if he never done bad for the sake of it, and the parson only preached what he didn't practice. Or so says I. And so says your Mr. Beecham, I'd wager."

She shook her head. "He's not my Mr. Beecham. And he's not a parson, only a schoolteacher, and a good one, I might add."

The captain held his tongue. No one knew better than he did that criticizing something set a young person to defending it, and then loving it. Half the crews on pirate ships were lads still defying their parents. Of course, the other half were out-and-out villains who never had parents to defy, because in all likelihood, they'd crawled out from under rocks.

"You're considering him?" he asked humbly.

"You'd know it if I was. No. He's just pleasant to talk with. But I can't see him as a husband, at least not for me."

The captain concealed a great sigh of relief. Nothing wrong with young Beecham, except that he was a bore with no more money than spirit, which was to say, not any.

"Well, if there ain't nothing more troubling you, puss, I'm to bed," he said. "Got to get up early and talk to Ames. The lawns look weedy. Highborn folk like their grounds neat as pins. What are you planning for tomorrow? Hoped you could take young Wylde for a tour of the land."

"Of course," she said simply. "I may not like him, but I do know what a hostess is supposed to do."

"Good, good," he said. "Go riding or walking, or whatever. Get to know him before you condemn him to the noose. You might be surprised. Now, are you off to bed too, or is there anything else I can do for you?"

"You've done exactly what I needed. I'll go up presently," she said absently. "You know how it is with me. Once I'm up and my mind's racing, I have to cool down before I can rest. You go, though. And thank you, Grandy, for understanding."

"I always try," he said gruffly. He rose, as did she. They hugged, and then she watched him make his way up the stair to his bedchamber.

She waited until his footsteps had faded away before she walked up to the portrait near the window again. She cocked her head to the side, scrutinizing it. It had hung there for as long as she could remember, and she was fond of it, but she'd never studied it as she did now.

The young man was posed with a spotted dog, and a fine white horse in the background. Lord Wylde's father wore clothes fashionable in the last century. It looked like many another noble portrait of an English gentleman. The man was lean and dark, with a sly smile that made him look rakish.

But what most distinguished him from any portrait she had seen was that glittering smile. Devilish, charming, and bright. She'd always liked him.

She curtsied to the portrait and then drifted over to the dark one that hung on the other side of the window. She didn't have to study that one. She had it committed to heart. She'd loved it when she'd been a girl. The artist who had painted it hadn't been very skillful. She knew that now, but when she'd been a girl it hadn't occurred to her. It had been the drama of the portrait that had captured her imagination. It had a history as exciting as any fairy story she'd ever been told. This man might have been a gentleman or a rogue. He'd been both.

He too was lean and dark. But he had a thin mustache over his curling smile, and his close-clipped beard ended in a triangle below his chin. It made him look devilish and polished at the same time. He carried a saber, and stood with his head high, as though ready to take on the world. He'd been painted with the sea behind him. The artist who had created his image wasn't a fraction as gifted as the one who had limned his grandson, on the other wall, but even he had been able to communicate something of the man's personality.

It was a murky canvas, but the man's smile was a slash of white, his eyes sparkled, his high-booted feet were planted apart. He wore a red cloak that billowed in the invisible wind. In all, he looked like a cavalier from an even earlier day. He was so full of life he looked as though he were impatient to leap away from the sitting, stride down the beach, and board the many-masted ship that sailed the painted waves behind him.

Lisabeth had hoped to find him one day, in real life. She thought she had done so. But she was sure the painted gentleman wouldn't have let her lean in for a kiss and then hopped away like a frightened rabbit.

She sighed. So much for her hopes. The pattern of life here never changed. She'd wondered if the arrival of Lord Wylde would alter it. Much as she loved her life and enjoyed its sweet familiar patterns, still she'd found herself hoping it would. Even heaven must get boring sometimes, she thought. She'd hoped to find a cure for the odd restlessness that had consumed her these last months.

She didn't really want to marry, there wasn't a man alive she'd want to devote her life to, and that was what marriage was all about. She didn't like the idea of some man ordering her life either, and that was also what marriage was about. Because even though she might be a touch lonely here, now and then, she was entirely free, and had been brought up to value that. She didn't want to go to London either. Her life was here, at Sea Mews, as was her happiness. As well as her boredom and restiveness. She didn't understand it, but there it was.

Lord Wylde was beyond any living man she'd ever clapped eyes on. Well, but she'd only known sailors and farmers, fishermen, local merchants, and those who came down from London to meet with her grandfather. And local smugglers, of course, as well as some of her father's former associates. She liked some of them very well, but knew enough to avoid getting involved with any of them. Gentle, educated, boring Mr. Beecham shone in the usual company she kept.

The lord her grandfather had coerced into coming to the heart of Cornwall to see her had turned out to be a bore, and a snob. But at least, she decided, he was a new one.

She turned, and after bowing to the portrait, went up the stairs to bed.

Chapter 6

He'd never felt so alone. It was ridiculous.

Constantine had been alone when he came to his childless uncle's house when he'd been five, after his grandfather had died. He'd felt keenly alone even though his grandfather had seldom spoken to him, much less comforted him. But he didn't remember his father or mother, and the loss of his grandfather, and so too his home, had startled him. Uncle Horatio had a wife, and a staff of smiling servants, so he'd thought life would become better. It hadn't. But it hadn't gotten much worse.

He was used to neglect. His aunt was an invalid, his uncle a hard taskmaster, given to lectures and fond of doling out advice as well as punishment. Being neglected by them was actually a boon. Even though he'd recently told his uncle he hoped never to see him again, he couldn't feel that as a loss.

He'd felt alone every night he'd gone to a new school too, but had gone to so many he'd learned how to quell the terrible empty feeling, dam up the incipient tears, turn his head into a pillow, and go to sleep.

Now, it was absurd that he felt so lonely. He was a grown man, with friends and acquaintances, and a place in the world.

He thought it might be because he'd seen a picture of his father at last. He wondered whether it was because he'd met the woman his father had purportedly wanted him to marry, and knew he could not. Whatever it was, he couldn't fall asleep.

The bed he was in was wide and the mattress soft, the sheets sweet smelling and crisply clean; the temperature in the room was just right, and the house was silent. But his thoughts kept his head whirling.

He'd come here to meet the woman the bizarre captain had said he was supposed to marry. Because he'd already discovered the story was true.

He'd expected his uncle to say, "Ridiculous," after he'd told him about it, or at least explode in fury and vow to get the Bow Street runners on the case. Constantine didn't want that. Even a false rumor couldn't be allowed to be breathed to the *ton*. The matter had to be handled with care and discretion. Uncle would understand; care and discretion were what he lived for. Constantine told his uncle his tale, and then amused himself by privately wagering on what word he would say first. It was the way he'd learned to deal with his uncle years before, and the way he still did. After all, his was a household that dealt firmly and quickly with impudence or ungodliness.

Constantine had never been afraid of corporal punishment, even as a boy, but he'd been told, early on in his stay with his uncle, that infractions that were repeated would be corrected by banishment from the house, and from the family. He didn't love his uncle, but respected his firmness of purpose, and didn't doubt him. Being cut off forever from the last of his family would have been a terrifying prospect for any boy.

And so he behaved. But wagers made silently with himself was not gambling. Sins committed in his imagination could not offend his uncle's ears or eyes. And insolence spoken in the mind couldn't translate to a whipping, or exile. In short, an imaginative boy, he'd discovered early on that misbehavior in the mind was very satisfying, because that way he could obey and disobey at the same time. He didn't know that that was the time-honored way that slaves, clerks, governesses, and many married women coped with living with a tyrant. He only knew that it worked. Constantine had more lavish daydreams than his uncle or his friends could ever imagine.

"I never thought he'd do this," his uncle had finally muttered. "Or at least, I thought he would have the common courtesy to come to me first."

Constantine had blinked and sat up straight. "You *know* him?"

His uncle nodded.

"And what he said was *true*?"

His uncle nodded again.

Constantine had leaped from his chair as though it were red-hot, but his stomach felt cold. "My father was a . . . highwayman?" he'd exclaimed over the sudden roaring in his ears.

His uncle scowled. "No, he wasn't. He played at being one and it was the death of him. But he spent his life playing at one thing or another. He was light-minded and unprincipled, a rogue and a rotter, the bane of your grandfather's existence."

"And you never told me this?" Constantine had asked, amazed.

"To what purpose? We agreed that no one should know, and no one does, except for that old pirate. We thought he'd keep it to himself. What good would exposing your father do now, after all? Only great mischief. You say he wants you to marry his granddaughter? Never. Your grandfather would roll over in his grave. *I* forbid it. Put it out of your mind. He can't force you to do anything. Your father was a criminal and so any pact or agreement he made wouldn't bear upon you in any court of law. Rest easy, say no, forbid the fellow your house, and forget about it. Bigod doesn't want a scandal at his door at this time in his life any more than you do. *Especially* if he wants to see his granddaughter well established."

"My father," Constantine had said carefully, trying to listen to what he said so he could believe it, "was a highwayman and a cheat, and died in the commission of a crime, and not in the service of His Majesty? And I," he'd added more carefully, "was never told this because you and my grandfather decided to lie to me about it."

"For your own good," his uncle had said. "You had some mischief in you, we could see that. You were the image of your father, after all. He never saw you. Your grandfather threw him out of the house and disinherited him before you were born, and your mother was too near her time to join him. He wasn't allowed near her again. If they'd caught a glimpse of him, he'd have been thrown into prison and left to languish there, or transported . . . under another name, of course. Nor was your mother allowed to receive letters from him. But she never recovered fully from your birth, and when your father died, she followed soon after. It's over and done, and no part of your life now, so forget it."

"Bigod said that his son knew her, as well as my father."

Horatio Anstruther shrugged. "So he may have done."

"Why was he thrown out of the house?"

"Impudence. Disrespect. And impiety."

"But not for the commission of a crime?"

"No, that came later. I imagine once he had to earn a living for himself, he strayed down the evil paths his behavior had headed him toward."

"But my grandfather kept his son's wife with him and gave her a home? She wasn't even related to him. Why would he have done that?"

"He was, as I said, a godly man. His son was a great disappointment to him, but he knew the right thing to do. And her sister, my dear departed wife, was a gentle creature, and a model citizen, so he knew there was good blood in her family."

"How did you keep this a secret?" Constantine had asked incredulously. "I can understand why I never knew. But surely there were others . . ."

"Your grandfather paid handsomely to have it kept quiet. And he paid to have his threats made plain. Your father only dealt with villains toward the end of his life, and they feared the full weight of the law."

"And my father's career in the army?" Constantine had asked, grasping at one last straw.

"Your grandfather called in some favors, and the news of his son's dishonorable discharge was expunged from the public record."

"So, my father, finding himself cast out and about to become a father himself, may have cheated and robbed in order to survive, and to amass enough money to make a home and get my mother to join him again?"

His uncle's laughter had sounded like coughing. "Put as nice a face on it as you will. Who knows what goes through a criminal's mind? What I do know is that your grandfather was a good and moral man. Your father was not. I am not your blood, but I respected your grandfather and promised him that once he was gone, I would watch over you and nip all such tendencies in the bud. And so I have done."

Constantine had stopped thinking, and was only reacting, and so all the things he normally would have answered in his mind were spoken aloud. He'd been angry, confused, and determined to defend his long-dead father. He'd always been proud of the man he never met. For the first time he realized his father had died at about the same age that he himself was now. He'd suddenly felt a deeper sympathy with the real man than he ever had had with the idealized icon of the saintly soldier and war hero. That fellow didn't need defending. This new one he was learning about did.

"You threw out all his effects?" Constantine had asked. "There is nothing left for me to see of him?"

"Of course," his uncle had said.

Constantine was shocked, staggered, and slightly shamed. But also furious. "So you taught me to be moral with lies? Interesting."

"Lies are sins," his uncle had said, holding up one finger. "But a lie told to save a soul is another matter."

"And my father's soul? Was that of no account?"

"He was beyond help. Your mother was weak,

but then, she was a woman. We decided that you should be spared the pain of knowing their circumstances."

Constantine had stared at his uncle. "And so you, even disapproving of my mother and father as you did, nevertheless agreed to take me into your home and raise me as your child? Very noble, Uncle."

"Well," Horatio had said, "it was the least I could do, as a man of God."

"But my grandfather paid for it," Constantine had said carefully. "Didn't he? That makes sense. Because he was a very rich man, and had only his one son and then me, to leave it all to. I doubt he'd have wanted to leave the money from his estate away from it, since I inherited the title, and the manor, and the properties, and he set great store by blood, and name. And I don't doubt he'd have cut you off without a penny if you disagreed. So though you clearly deplored everything about my father and sneered at my mother, you nevertheless let their devil spawn into your home. Was that godliness, Uncle, or plain good financial sense?"

His uncle's face had flushed and darkened. "Aye, and see the thanks I get! You dare admonish me? Be glad that I took you in when your grandfather died, or doubtless you'd be with him and your father and mother by now. Who else would have housed you?"

"There were schools, Uncle. I went to enough of them. There were other respectable people who could have been paid to bear my presence. My grandfather's lawyers would have seen to it. I can't see how your act was particularly noble."

"I will have an apology sir!"

"Will you?" Constantine had asked. He'd found himself seething with anger. His quiet life had been shattered. He had been taught to worship propriety and reserve. But suddenly, nothing he'd known was so. And the fact that his uncle, who had expected him to be grateful all his life, was suddenly exposed as a liar, staggered him. The monster of respectability and piety was just as much of a cheat as his father supposedly had been. All the insolence that had stayed secure in Constantine's mind rushed from his mouth, and he exulted in it.

"An apology?" Constantine had said with a sneer. "Get one from my mother, poor soul, parted from her husband when she most needed him. Get one from my father, cast out without a thought, because he dared to have a thought of his own. But don't expect one from me, Uncle. I've been lied to since the day you set eyes on me, haven't I? Punished for things I never did, and warned of banishment you never meant to carry out, because although you didn't like me, you liked my money very well. Good day, sir."

"And you think that old pirate will tell you more truth than I have?" Horatio bellowed after him.

Constantine had paused at the door. "I think he could scarcely tell less truth," he'd said, and left the house.

He had not only left the house, he'd come here, to meet the odd occupants of this strange house. An eccentric who was a former sea captain of some sort; a drunken governess; a staff of aged or addled retainers; and a girl with the manners of a commoner and the mouth of a doxie, and the face of an angel. And he'd almost kissed her, and sealed his fate forever.

He had better leave this place while he could. And, he told himself, turning over in bed again, restlessly seeking a comfortable spot, he must remember that he was *not* alone. He had friends. Why, Blaise and Kendall had offered to come with him when they heard the story. He'd told them because he could trust them; they'd known him since school days and had always been true. Languid, amused, and amusing, Sir Blaise de Wolf was a landed gentleman whose lands had been conquered for him by his Norman ancestors, and who, to most people's knowledge, hadn't done anything to exert himself since he'd inherited his title and estate. Dark, intense Sir Richard Kendall, sportsman and Corinthian, an athlete who was more at home on a horse than in a parlor, who boxed, fenced, and rode to an inch, but never exerted himself to attend a *ton* party, unless someone there was rumored to be selling off his horses.

But they both exerted themselves for a friend, and Constantine was proud to be one.

"I have to go see for myself," Constantine had told them. "I've been unable to think of anything else."

"It is bizarre, if any man in England looks less like a villain than you, I don't know him," Blaise had finally said.

"Well, a man can be a rogue and look like an angel," Kendall had argued. "But, no. You don't look as if you have ever considered a shady deed, Con. If anything, you're prim."

"Yes," Blaise had agreed with a smile. "And proper. Now, there have been kissing highwaymen and singing highwaymen, and even that French chap, what-was-his name, the waltzing highwayman. But none who looked as though they were ready to read a sermon to their victims. The idea's absurd. The old man's running some sort of a rig. Girl must be a gargoyle. Go see your uncle and get the whole story. Then call on us. We'll jaunt down to Cornwall with you and help chase the big bad captain out to sea."

"I don't need help getting rid of him," Constantine had said defensively. "And thank you, but I don't need company while I'm doing it."

Constantine picked up his pillow and pounded it before he laid his head down again. He'd been wrong there. He certainly could use company now. He had tried to soften his words to his friends.

"I just wondered if you fellows had any insight into the problem," he'd explained. "And, I might add, I do not consider myself 'prim' although I certainly do attempt to always be proper."

"Don't have to try, you are," Kendall had said. "Never a breath of scandal about you. Never saw you in a caricature in the broadsheets, or heard a word to your discredit."

"Now he looks wounded," Blaise had commented. "Beware, Kendall. Keep damning him with such faint praise, and he'll tie a handkerchief around his face and go out and hold up orphans and widows, just to change the way we think about him."

Even Constantine had laughed at that.

"Still," Kendall had said thoughtfully, "if you run into any trouble, all you have to do is send word. I'll be there."

"And I, of course," Blaise drawled. "Town is rather thin of company now anyway. But, dear fellow, doubtless your fiancée will want you in constant attendance now. Newly engaged females delight in dragging the males they've caught to the firelight to show all the other women how well the hunt went. How will you explain your sudden absence to her, by the by?"

"I'll tell her that important family matters have arisen," Constantine had said. "She'll understand. She sets great store by family. As do I."

So his friends had agreed to keep their eyes on his fiancée, and dance attendance upon her at balls and parties to divert her from the fact of his absence.

Constantine now remembered that he was, after all, engaged to be married to Miss Winchester: an upright, intelligent female. He had a delightful life ahead of him, once he solved this present complication. He turned in bed once more, comfortable at last. So the strangely lovely woman his father had wanted him to wed was out of the question, and

103

the matter would soon be under control, and he would be free to go. But that scent, and those eyes, and those lips of hers . . .

Constantine sat straight up in bed. He saw bright sunshine outlining his shuttered windows and shining between their thin slats.

"My lord," his valet said, pausing by his bedside. "Did I wake you? Pardon me. I attempted to be silent."

Constantine rubbed his aching head. "No, Atkins. You could have been quiet as a mouse and I would've heard you. I didn't sleep well."

"First nights in strange surroundings are often thus," the valet said.

"Yes. My problem is that I don't know how many more strange nights we must spend here," Constantine grumbled. He looked up. "Have you had anything to do with the other servants here? Have you any impressions of them?"

Atkins, the soul of propriety, paused. "They are . . . unique, my lord. Friendly. Helpful. And loyal to a fault, if loyalty can be a fault. Many are unread and untrained, but they accomplish their tasks, keep the house clean, and are pleasant enough, and always ready to share a jest. Yet one may say nothing uncomplimentary about their master and mistress. Why, if there were a flood, one gets the impression that they would drown in an attempt to save them. If there were a fire, they would burn, if there were—"

"Enough. I get the idea," Constantine said, head in his hands.

"Did you overindulge last night, my lord?" Atkins asked solicitously, noting his master's distress. This was rare behavior for his lordship, but not at all unusual in the elevated ranks where Atkins had worked all his life.

"No," Constantine said. "It must be that I'm unused to being up so early. I think I'll wash and dress."

"Then you're in for a treat, sir," Atkins said. "The captain has installed the most modern conveniences in his house. He has rooms for the family and for guests, with marble tubs and running water. And conveniences, indoors, that flush. He even has one for his servants' use. The man is generous, all say, and rich as he can stare. But many men are rich and few are as beloved by their inferiors."

"Do they say nothing to his detriment?" Constantine asked. "No gossip . . . no matter how old?"

"None, sir."

"Well, then," Constantine said more cheerfully. "Lay out my riding clothes, please. It looks like a fine morning, after all."

Because, he thought, as he rose and padded over to the window to see the glowing morning, maybe the captain and his granddaughter were just being uncommonly forthcoming with him, getting him acquainted with his family, so to speak, and didn't usually discuss their odd history with outsiders. That would be fine. Better than fine. That would mean he could stop here a day or two to make a better impression, reject the old pact gracefully, incur no hard feelings, and leave his family's ignoble past behind for good.

He whistled as he bathed in the captain's truly luxurious marble bath, and then hummed as Atkins shaved him. It might all have been a tempest in a teapot. The night, and the odd sight of long-dead men who bore his face, had made him too anxious. They were gone, and probably forgotten by all but the daft old captain and his curious granddaughter.

She hadn't seem smitten with him; she'd said she wanted no part of their father's pact. In fact, he could distinctly sense her derision when she looked at him. That stung, but only because he'd never felt any female's censure before. And yet, and still, last night there'd been that strange, erotic moment. Maybe she wasn't as unlike her wild ancestors, after all. Still, whatever her problem with him, he was free of all obligations. He could go on with his life, moderately, as he had always done.

He dressed with care, in a well-cut blue jacket, dun breeches, white linen, a casually tied high neckcloth, ruby vest, and shining boots. He accepted a tall beaver hat that Atkins handed him, and after one last look at himself in the glass, left the room and took the long stairs down to the front hall as blithely as a boy.

Chapter 7

The footman showed Constantine to a dining parlor he hadn't seen before. There were many chafing dishes out on a sideboard, and the scent of ham, eggs, and sweet rolls was incredibly appealing.

Constantine saw his hostess at a sideboard, filling a plate with victuals.

"Oh, good!" he said as he strode into the dining parlor. "You haven't left yet."

Lisabeth turned and showed him a surprised and glowing face. And more. He stopped in his tracks and gaped at her.

"Oh, good!" she echoed, with a dimpling smile. "You're not a slugabed! Everyone said a London gent would sleep till noon, and only turn over when the sun got in his eyes. How nice that you keep country hours."

What she looked like froze him and left him speechless. Her conversation wasn't proper, but he couldn't concentrate on it. Of course a lady never mentioned a gentleman's bed habits, in any context, unless she was in bed with him. And then, of course, she wasn't a lady.

But he couldn't think about that while he looked at her. He could only stare.

She was dressed outrageously. She looked nothing like a young woman of birth or fashion. But she didn't look like a milkmaid or a servant either. She didn't look proper but she wasn't precisely improper. A tart would wear something fashioned to catch a man's eye. A slut would be half dressed. Lisabeth was fully dressed. But not like any female he'd ever seen.

She wore a man's riding breeches. They were old, but they fit well, that was the problem. He hadn't realized she had such a shapely little bottom, and such shapely legs. Female gowns were currently worn high at the waist, and flowed down to the floor, leaving a man to guess at what was actually beneath, unless, of course, there was a high wind blowing. But even if there were, any proper woman would have on a pelisse, or a shawl to cover over all.

Lisabeth also wore a smock sort of a shirt, tucked in at the waistband of her trousers. It neither showed off nor hid her high, buoyant breasts, but looked almost like what a pirate of old might wear, Constantine thought uneasily. That was, if a pirate had run mad and decided to disguise himself as a luscious young woman.

He thought she'd cut her hair, but then realized that she'd drawn it up and let down curls that ringed her head. In all, she looked adorable. Impossible. Scandalous. In a weird sort of way, she looked like a deliciously attractive . . . young boy. The thought unsettled him. Although, looking closer, he could see she looked nothing like a boy. That didn't settle his nerves at all. She looked too damned tempting. And utterly unaware of it.

He supposed there was a reason it was amusing to see men in women's clothing, in pantomimes and at the theater. Because they looked foolish in them. Females, he realized, didn't look amusing in men's clothing. At least, this one didn't. She looked incredibly more like a woman, curved and supple, and for all her lack of height, perfectly proportioned. Constantine was shocked and titillated, and didn't know where to look. He knew where he *wanted* to look. But, of course, he couldn't.

"Now, wasn't I right?" Miss Lovelace's voice said, from where she sat at the table, spooning up her porridge. "You've gone and scandalized the gent, Lizzie, my love. Best hop upstairs and put on a gown. He's proper as can be, and it's clear he doesn't know what to make of you. Lord Wylde may keep country hours, but he clearly isn't used to country ways."

"Oh, Lord Wylde," Lisabeth said, with a mischievous pout. "Never say you want me to put on a gown this morning? I assure you no one will see us who hasn't seen me this way many times before. Happens I have a fine riding habit, all amber velvet; it's a treat to see and cost the earth. But where's the sense in putting it on if we're going to go down dusty roads, and maybe even get caught in a sudden squall, as happens so often hereabouts? The habit would be ruined. After our ride, I'd come home smelling of horse, and covered with mud. But that won't matter if I'm wearing old clothes, made for rough use.

"Unless," she added, with a sly look under her lashes, "you actually are interested in honoring our fathers' bargain? Then, of course, I could see that you'd want everyone in the village to notice we're keeping company. After all, I suppose you want to see the village, the church, the inn, and such, don't you? If you're dressed as you are, and suddenly I'm all tarted up like a Christmas goose to go with you, everyone will suspect something's in the wind . . . But this is so sudden."

She placed a hand on her heart and fluttered her eyelashes. She also looked as if she might burst out laughing.

He was at a loss for words.

"I didn't think so," she said. "So, what say you, sir? You look fine as fivepence, by the way. No one here dresses like that unless there's a funeral . . . or a wedding." She grinned at him.

"I say," he said carefully, "that you should wear whatever you wish. Are those fresh-baked biscuits I spy? They smell delicious."

She smiled. "Yes. Let's eat, and then go delight the villagers."

He nodded, and hid his apprehension. He wanted to meet the locals, of course, and find out if any of them knew anything about him or his history. That was of paramount importance. This woman would keep her silence. He could tell she had pride as well as spirit. Still, even though she said she didn't want him, there was that odd moment last night to consider. What had she wanted? But he believed her given word.

Even so, no woman would be thrilled to let the world know he'd been offered her hand and turned it down. Although, he thought moodily, she might be thrilled to let them know she'd turned him down. What he had to do, he decided, as he put a hot biscuit on his plate, was try to turn her up sweet without making her like him too much, or too little.

"And where's the captain this morning?" Constantine asked a while later, after they'd had their breakfast and were walking to the stables.

"Grandy's out on his favorite boat," she said.

He strode along at her side. He tried to keep pace so he wouldn't have to see her walking in front of him. It was a sight to see, but he didn't want to be caught seeing it.

"He loves to watch the sun come up over the horizon and spread across the water," she explained. "He left the sea, but never completely. He says he's got salt water in his blood, and I think he does. We can see the sea from the top of the house, and there's a road that borders it that we'll take down to the village, if that's all right with you. It might be a bit windy though. Autumn's here, and the wind blows fiercely sometimes. I find it refreshing. But if you think you'll be too cold we can take the road through the wood, and then down to the village. Or maybe you want to go back and put on something warmer?"

"I won't be too cold," he said stiffly. It was one thing to be thought a fop—what else could be expected of a woman who knew nothing of fashion? It was quite another to be thought a hothouse flower.

Constantine asked a stable worker for his horse, and was cinching its saddle when he stopped short and stared. There, in the center aisle of the stable, stood his hostess. She'd thrown on a moth-eaten man's jacket, stepped on a mounting block, and swung herself up on a pretty roan mare.

"Something amiss?" she'd asked him, with a twinkle that told him she knew exactly what was.

"I don't often see ladies riding astride," he said stiffly. "In fact, the only time I have, I've been at Astley's Amphitheater to watch an equestrian performance."

She smiled. "Lucky you!" she said blithely, as though she hadn't understood the barb in his comment. "Oh!" she cried with sudden mock surprise. "Does my riding astride offend you? I do have a sidesaddle, but what use is it here, with only my old friends and a stray fox or hound to see me?

And you, of course. Our roads are steep and difficult. Riding the correct way for a lady might well be the most incorrect thing I could do—for my life and limb, that is. But if it bothers your sensibilities . . ." she said, raising her head and wearing a noble expression that made Constantine want to wring her neck. "I'll throw on a sidesaddle. After all, if I do fall, you'll be there to pick me up. If it doesn't get your lovely clothes all dirty, that is. I shouldn't want that. So if I'm lying in a muddy ditch, never fear. You can ride back and get someone to retrieve me."

She cocked her head to the side and waited. The stable workers hid their grins behind their hands.

"It is your home, and your choice," Constantine said coldly. Of course, it was also shocking; it just wasn't done. But as she'd said, who was there to see her but him? And he'd soon be gone from here, or at least, as soon as he could go.

Then she grinned, clapped a jockey cap over her curls, bent low, and gave her horse its freedom to run. But she knew the road. Constantine didn't. He followed more slowly. He was an excellent rider, but in that as in all things, a cautious one, and he didn't want to risk his horse or himself to an unexpected hole in the road. He felt a universe away from Rotten Row in London, and the tame and lovely byways of Kent, where his uncle's house was.

Fifteen minutes later, Constantine was gritting his teeth, trying to keep them from chattering. He'd lost his hat to the sea wind almost as soon as they'd come in sight of the beach. Now he could only hope he could keep his head on.

Lisabeth was riding like a demon.

He plowed on, head down, until he looked up to see that she'd stopped at the top of a hill, and was waiting there for him. Her cheeks were red, so was her little nose, her eyes sparkled, and she laughed out loud.

"Lovely, isn't it?" she cried.

He looked down to where she was pointing, and cold and winded though he was, he had to agree. A perfect little portrait of a country village lay at the foot of the hill beneath them. It was a glorious early-autumn day, and the few trees that could withstand the constant sea winds were bent into interesting shapes, their leaves already stripped from them, so he could see far and wide. From here, he could see the little village was close to the sea, and saw rough iron-gray waves beating against the strand. The colorful fishing boats he saw were safe, high on the strand and firmly secured to the sea wall. There was a village green, and the thatched cottages that hugged each side of the one street were neat and well kept. A classic Romanesque church, made of gray stone, one of dozens that the first Christians had erected all over Britain, stood at the end of the street and towered over the village. The graveyard behind it had lawns that rolled down to the sea.

"It is indeed a charming place," Constantine had to admit.

"Would you like to warm up with a pint first, and then meet the parson?" she asked him. "What he doesn't know about the village doesn't count."

Then he, at least, Constantine thought, would know of his irregular ancestors. He'd face that when he had to. It was his experience that a generous contribution to the church fund could buy a man anything, except, for all they promised, a valid ticket to heaven.

"A stop at the inn sounds fine," he said. "Will any locals be there this morning?"

"With this weather? Aye!" she said. "Our men don't have to go to sea unless they want to. So on a day like this they'll be at the inn, discussing the usual things: the weather, what the weather will be like tomorrow, and what the weather was like last year." She flashed a smile at him. "They'll be fascinated by you. We're off the beaten track here.

Why, I heard we're not even on some maps! So it's not often we get visitors, especially from London."

Good, Constantine thought. The less that his world knew of the place, the easier it would be to hide what had happened here. In fact, he wondered if any but the oldest residents would remember his notorious family at all. Wasn't everyone hereabouts said to traffic in smuggling and other illegalities? How much interest would a long-dead rogue, or two, still hold?

"Come along," Lisabeth said, interrupting his thoughts. "It's just down the hill; follow the road. If I get there first, don't fret. I know the way. So does my Misty," she said, smoothing her gloved hand over her horse's neck. "She loves a good downhill run. See you there! You can't miss it, there's a sign hanging in front: *THE GOOD CAPTAIN*."

Constantine frowned. " 'Captain?' " Still, it was an innocuous enough name for a seaside inn. Wasn't Lisabeth's own grandfather a captain? There must have been dozens of captains here. He chuckled to himself. He was behaving like a thief who'd just taken a wallet and was afraid everyone was eyeing him.

He watched Lisabeth put her heels to her horse and race down the hill toward the village. With a sigh, Constantine let his horse carefully pick his way down in her wake.

She was gone from sight by the time he reached the village. He rode down the long street, looking curiously to the left and right. He saw curtains twitch back from windows as he rode along. Finally, he came upon a modest inn, with the sign *THE GOOD CAPTAIN* blowing in the wind. He checked. The name was inoffensive. But the picture on the sign showed a black-visaged pirate, legs apart, a mug of foaming ale in his hand. Though crudely drawn, he looked suspiciously familiar.

A coincidence, Constantine thought as he slid down from his horse, and gave the reins to an eager lad waiting there. The resemblance was merely a chance one. He was bedeviled by the idea of pirates today. Many of them doubtless had dark flyaway brows. The detail was only to make the fellow look more sinister. After all, this coast was chockablock with villains.

He straightened his jacket, regretted the loss of his hat, smoothed his hair with one gloved hand, and then, carefully sidestepping manure in the road, pushed open the door to the inn.

He squinted because the place was so dim after the bright autumn daylight. As his eyes adjusted, he saw a veritable wall of eyes watching him. It looked like the half of the village that hadn't been peering out their windows were assembled here, gaping at him silently. There was a hedge of men, and some women, of all sizes and shapes, their only commonality their rustic clothing, and the way they were staring at him.

"God Almighty!" one masculine voice exclaimed. "Them at the house was right!"

"Aye," another voice said in awe. "Good thing it's broad daylight, or I'd be thinking he come back by moonlight to join us for a pint!"

"The spit and image," a woman's voice marveled.

"What sort of welcome is this?" Constantine heard Lisabeth ask scornfully.

"Aye!" came a roar from the back of the crowd. "Whatever he is, or whoever he be, he's welcome!"

"Good to have ye back, Captain!" another shouted, laughing.

"Three cheers for our beloved Cap'n Cunning, hisownself, whether he be ghost or not!" someone bellowed.

They cheered until Constantine's eyes rang. His head was spinning as it was.

"And three more for his grandson, brave Jack,

and may his killer rot in hell," another man offered, when the cheering was done.

And as Constantine's heart sank, the whole
motley crowd kept cheering for his long-dead but
obviously not forgotten ancestors.

Chapter 8

"Come in, come in, sir," the innkeeper cried, beckoning to Constantine.

The crowd drew back to make his way clear. The innkeeper plunked a mug of ale down on the tap in front of him, and then poured a generous shot of rum, and put it beside it.

"The good captain's favorite libation," the innkeeper said. "Or so my dad told me his dad told him. So hoist your glass, my friend, and be you himself, or his son, or his great-grandson, drink a toast with us to our beloved captain, our benefactor and friend. To Captain Cunning!" he cried, turning and lifting his own mug in a salute to the wall behind the tap.

The crowd behind Constantine did the same. With dread, Constantine lifted his gaze to the wall. The portrait hung there in a prominent place of honor. Not the exact portrait, of course. This one was obviously a copy of the one he'd seen last night. It didn't have the same murky atmosphere; the colors were instead bright and cheerful. Obviously the painter who had done the sign outside the inn had done this copy. It was almost a caricature, done in bold primary colors. The captain on the shore looked younger, more devilish, and a sight more cheerful, but in the way a demon would look as he prodded a sinner into the fires of hell.

Constantine sighed. It felt as though he were looking into some sort of distorted mirror. Because the features were his own, even though he doubted he'd ever worn such an expression.

"To the captain," he said hollowly, and tipped back the shot of rum. He never drank in the morning. This morning he needed it.

"To the captain!" the crowd echoed.

He felt a hand on his arm, and turned to see Lisabeth standing at his side. She had a smudge of foam from her mug of ale above her upper lip. She wiped her sleeve across it, and grinned at him. "May I tell them who you are?"

He shrugged, defeated for the moment. "I'd rather not, but doubtless they already know. I suppose everything that happens in your house is soon known everywhere here?"

"In about an hour," she agreed. "Gentlemen, ladies," she said to the crowd, "allow me to introduce my grandfather's guest, Lord Wylde!"

The room went wild with "huzzahs!" and yelps of joy.

Constantine felt dread. They obviously knew his name, which meant they must know who he was related to.

"Why dint you tell us you were here?" one old party shouted into Constantine's ear.

"Why, because I didn't know you were," Constantine said.

"Then let me tell you about your dad," the old party said. He paused, and then cocked his gray head to the side. "Here!" he shouted to the crowd. "Where's a toast to the lad's father? We should raise a cheer for that fine lad. He was a treasure, he was," he told Constantine mistily.

That toast was raised and many more, until Constantine's head hurt. It wasn't the shouting so much

as the stories he heard. His father had been a highwayman, successful, it seemed, until his last robbery. He was still held in great affection. He'd been
charming and witty, a good fellow all round, as
they were eager to tell him. As for his great-grandfather, he was considered something of a demigod.
Constantine had seldom felt worse. The only way
to keep this secret would be to burn the village to
the ground. Doubtless, he thought moodily, he had
some ancestor or other who used to do just that.

They cheered him, they toasted him, they began
to tell stories he couldn't understand because they
kept interrupting each other trying to correct the
stories. They were stories of hard-won battles at sea
and clever, successful land robberies. One thing
came clear enough. They worshiped his old pirate
great-grandfather, had adored his father, and were
thrilled because Constantine looked so much like
them.

"It's like havin' them back, all in one go," an old
woman vowed, a hand on her heart, the other
holding tight to her mug of ale.

Constantine tried to smile. But he was at an
impasse. If any of these people had relatives and
friends in London, and mentioned his presence, it
might slip out and become gossip in the places he

would most wish it never be known. He stifled a groan as the thought occurred to him.

"You're not happy, are you?" Lisabeth whispered to him a half hour later.

"Only a bit overwhelmed," he lied.

"Ladies and gents!" Lisabeth bawled, loud enough to make Constantine start, and the crowd become still. "His lordship's tickled to see you, but he's drowning in your praise. Throw him a lifeline! He never expected such an ado. I didn't warn him, see? Let me take him down to meet the vicar now. He'll be back tomorrow, or the next day. Give the poor fellow time to get used to us."

There was a chorus of "ayes!" and enough back-slapping to cause bruises as Lisabeth led an insincerely smiling Constantine out the door and into the sunlight again.

"They meant no harm," she assured him, looking up at him worriedly. "They just meant to pay tribute. Come, I'll take you to meet the vicar; he's something of an historian. He'll be thrilled to meet you too, but not so noisy about it. No sense in us riding, he's just up the street. No sense in riding most places here," she said as she strolled at his side. "Everything's all that close."

"Why do they love my great-grandfather so much?" he asked in wonderment as they walked.

"Well, he was a generous fellow. He gave employment to the village, and money to those too weak or old to follow him."

"Or too burdened with conscience?" he muttered.

"Yes, as a matter of fact," she said. "If a man didn't approve of the captain's doings, though most did, most of the people here were fed up with Puritanism and stupid laws. They'd had a bellyful of them. Still, some people were religious enough to have problems with the captain's profession. If they did, why then he saw to it that they didn't starve either. Grandy said that was because he was smart enough to know that a village full of people who loved him would be the best place to hide his doings. But I think it was because he also had such a big heart."

She stopped, and looked at him, studying his face, a slight frown marring her own as she did. "But though you're his image, you're really nothing like him, are you?"

He looked down at her. For a moment, he found he hated to disappoint her. She looked so appealing. Her eyes were glowing with sunshine, her lips were very near . . . and she looked so disenchanted with him. But he had to tell her the truth for her sake, and his own.

127

"No," he admitted. "I'm not. I'm about as far from my great-grandfather and my father as a man can be. The thought of piracy horrifies me. The thought of being a thief appalls me, and however dashing they were, that is, in the end, what they were. Thieves. Whether you call yourself a brigand and take a man's money at sea with a cannon and a vicious crew at your side, or call yourself a highwayman and hold people at the point of your pistol to pick their pockets, it's plain theft. And it's just not right," he added, somewhat weakly. Because what should have sounded noble came out sounding prim and self-righteous.

"I'm not prim or self-righteous," he added quickly. "I just try to do the right thing, all the time. I certainly wouldn't rob, pillage, rape, or steal."

She took a step back. Her eyes flared. "Your great-grandfather only took from those who had, and from enemies of the nation. And he never pillaged, as I understand pillaging. Why burn a ship when you can take it over and add it to your fleet? Why lay waste to a town when you can leave it standing for future use? Why kill a man if you can make him yours to command? Wasteful and uneconomical. As for rapine . . ." She took a deep breath. Constantine waited. She looked as though she might attack him. Then she raised her chin and smiled like a cat, which alarmed him even more. "It is said he never forced a female with his superior strength, but only with his superior mind, and his lips, both for what he said, and what he did with them!"

Constantine's eyes widened.

She sneered. "I suppose you're now going to tell me you never seduced a female?"

He thought a moment. "In truth," he said, as though to himself, as he considered it. "No. I never have." Then he recalled what an improper conversation this was. "But I've no intention of sharing that part of my life with you, young lady."

The sneer didn't leave her lips. He sighed. For some reason, that sounded worse than saying he'd seduced more females than Casanova had ever met. But he had never seduced a woman. He'd no idea of how to go about such a thing. The fact was, he realized, he'd either paid for them, or agreed to their proposals. That suddenly made him feel even worse.

Lisabeth marched silently at his side until they came to a small rose-covered cottage near the church.

"The vicar lives here," she said. "He'll give you a cup of tea, the plain truth, and no discourtesy or shocks. But you'll have to speak up. He's eighty, and though his wits are keen, his hearing is not. You'll like him."

Constantine suppressed a sigh. He supposed she would think he'd only like the elderly. It was a good thing, he thought suddenly, that she'd never come to London. If he were a fish out of water here, she would drown there. There wasn't a soul there that he admired that she'd like, or who would appreciate her in the least either. She was too plain-spoken, outspoken, really, and too unconventional for the *ton*. The only females who could act the way she did were royals, or extremely wealthy old eccentrics. He straightened his shoulders. So he was nothing like his great-grandfather or his father, except for his looks. What of it? That was no crime where he came from—quite the reverse.

The vicar's elderly housekeeper let them into a sunny salon, and before long, the old gentleman joined them. He didn't look eighty, he moved along in sprightly fashion, and took Constantine's hand in a firm clasp. He was slender, had shrewd blue eyes, a few tufts of white hair at the sides of his head, and a warm smile.

"Sit down, sit down, my lord," he said at once. "Would you care for some tea?"

Constantine began to sit, but paused, as Lisabeth answered before he could. "I already promised him some," she said. "I knew you wouldn't mind."

"Mind?" the vicar said. "I asked for it to be prepared when I heard you were heading here."

"So I thought," she said. "Now, the thing of it is that Lord Wylde is down from London, on a strange mission. Oh, I can tell the vicar all," she added in an aside to Constantine. "He's kept my secrets all my life. Now," she told the vicar. "Seems his father and my father made a pact years ago, promising us in marriage to each other—before I was even born! Folly, of course, but you remember what roaring boys they were. Well, Grandy believed in the pact though. He went up to London, and went to see poor Lord Wylde to find out why he'd never come to meet his future bride."

Constantine let out his breath. So she herself didn't know of his engagement. The clever old man had some scruples, after all. Or did he just know that she might have some?

"And," she went on, "turns out my lord here never knew a syllable about anything! He never met his father, nor knew anyone who would tell him the truth about him. But he came down to meet me because he is a gentleman. Well, the upshot is that chalk and cheese, is what we are. But that's not what's got Lord Wylde so down. He never knew about Captain Cunning either, until he came here! And to make matters worse, they told him his father was a decorated war hero who died in the service of his country. The poor man is very conventional, you see, and his head's in a whirl. I was hoping you could ease his mind. He just met half the village in the inn, and doesn't know what to think. He disapproves of crime, he hates pirates, and he's ashamed of the thought that his father was a highwayman. Well, it takes all kinds, you know."

Constantine didn't know if she was being sarcastic or not. But the vicar smiled.

"As for me," she went on, "I'm sure you'll excuse me if I do some errands, drop in on some old friends, and return when I'm done. You two will have a lot to talk about anyway. So, may I leave?"

"With all good will," the vicar said. "If his lordship doesn't mind?"

"Of course not," Constantine said, yet feeling every inch as old in Lisabeth's eyes now as that kindly old fellow.

"Well, good-bye for now," she said, and sauntered out the door.

Constantine sat again, and watched as the vicar slowly lowered himself into a chair.

"I daresay that all this is a great and unpleasant surprise to you, isn't it?" the vicar asked.

"Not all of it," Constantine said gallantly. "Miss Lisabeth is a charming woman."

The vicar's smile was knowing. "But nothing like any respectable female you've ever met, I venture to say." He waved a thin hand. "And she is respectable, never doubt it. Though I suppose you do. Don't bother to deny it, my lord. Lisabeth is an original. But she is, withal, in many ways more honorable than most ladies you will meet. Still, she is not at all suitable as a wife to a gentleman like you, and I can see she already knows it. Nor are you right for a free-spirited creature like her. It's a pity, for her, and I suppose for you, little though you may credit it.

"Still, she must be disappointed. She always worshiped the legends of the captain, and his jolly grandson." The vicar waved his hand again, this time at a portrait over his fireplace mantel.

Constantine stared. The man in the portrait stared back at him. It was another depiction of the rogue pirate who bore his face. This time the fellow looked more sardonic than demonic. He stood in front of a house this time, with his horse and a pair of hunting dogs. The painting was a little brighter than the one in the captain's house, but not so vivid as the one in the inn. The artist was obviously not as well trained as either of the others. But primitive as it was, nevertheless the portrait held more humanity.

"Captain Cunning built this house we are sitting in," the vicar went on. "He helped rebuild this village, restored the church and this part of the country at a time when protectors and kings were too busy tearing each other apart to care for the common man. I do not say he was a moral man, but he was at least as moral as some of the royals we have had, if not better than many. He wasn't greedy, he was generous, and he took care of his people. It's a thing that's been handed down in the family. His son, however, was a prig, humorless and joyless. I think that's why your father was such a wastrel in his youth. He was defying his father, and in a way, trying to honor his grandfather. Had he survived his wild youth, I've no doubt he'd have calmed down. But there we are, and if you follow the family tradition, I suppose that is why you're more like his father than your own.

"Lisabeth's family was associated with Captain Cunning. Her grandfather, a very wise fellow, used those connections and went into a more legal line of seafaring, which no doubt his son would have done. But alas, the fellow was in the petticoat line, lifted the wrong skirts, and paid with his life for it. In a way, your father's death was nobler, for he was only trying to get enough money to support his wife, and leave his father for good."

He leaned forward, and lowered his voice, although no one was in the room with them. He studied Constantine intently. "It would help if you tried to see your family in terms of the conditions that bred them. London is a great city, but here in the countryside is where England's lifeblood flows. While our regent gives grand parties and spares no expense in collecting great art and clever guests to his flowing table, there are parts of England, London itself, where the poor are starving to death. Your great-grandfather would never have allowed that to happen."

He paused. "And as for Lisabeth. She is unconventional, of course, but she's got pluck and heart and kindness in her soul. She's the way she is because of her unconventional upbringing. You know about the servants in the captain's employ?"

Constantine nodded his head.

"Well," the old man said with a shrug. "It's good and it's not. Because all the older ones come from . . . bleak beginnings, let us say. Another family tradition. Many of the footmen, the stablemen, the housekeeper, the maids, even Miss Lovelace herself, are unfortunates whom the captain took on as servants after their . . . interesting lives were done with. Many were jailed, many saved from the noose . . . No matter, they're all reformed now, not to mention too old to do harm. The younger ones, of course, are merely local, in need of work. However legal the origins of the captain's own fortune, he took some steps in your great-grandfather's footprints. It is a charitable way to live, if somewhat irregular."

"Miss Lovelace?" was all that Constantine could say, trying to picture some of the quavering footmen as cutthroats, the gardeners as brigands. But the old governess?

"It is her story to tell, and doubtless she will, after a few glasses of good wine. It is one of her pleasures, but not my story to divulge," the vicar said. "But I can see you'll need time to think about this. I hope you plan to stay a while and learn for yourself?"

Constantine was glad to see the housekeeper and a footman come in with a tray and the tea. There was too much to think about for him to respond immediately.

But after the servants had left, and he'd had his first sip of tea, he put his cup down. He leaned forward. "Sir," he said earnestly. "I'll try to learn more,

and to understand as well. But if I may . . . make a
generous contribution to the church, could I assure
myself that this fascinating history will go no further than it already has?"

The vicar looked at him as though he'd thrown
the cup of tea in his face.

Constantine was unused to disapproval. He
blinked.

"My dear sir," the vicar said slowly. "You do
indeed have much to learn. This is your story,
which is why I told it to you. I would not indulge
in such gossip otherwise. Perhaps you need more
time away from us, than with us, after all."

"No, no," Constantine said. "Please forgive me.
It was rude and insulting, and I beg your forgive-
ness. You're right. I've been too long in London. I
need time to acclimate myself, and understand
that life is indeed different here."

The vicar nodded. "Perhaps. But I can relieve
your mind about one thing. You don't have to
worry about Miss Lisabeth wanting you to agree to
her father and your father's strange pact. That's
clearly not in her mind, and to my mind, best for
both of you."

Constantine felt vaguely insulted.

They sat and drank their tea in silence for a while,
as Constantine decided that staying on for a while

was really the best thing to do. He had to try to keep these people, this village, as deluded and happy about him and his family as they had been when he arrived, so they'd have no hard feelings when he left. Happy people tell no ugly tales.

Then he'd make sure to never visit this part of the world again. Nor would he ever tell his friends, or his fiancée, about anything that he had learned here.

Nor could he insult Lisabeth or her grandfather. He would have to charm them, until he left. It would be difficult to be friends with Lisabeth without leading her on; she was a tempting piece. But since she didn't seem to like him, perhaps it wouldn't be so hard after all. He just couldn't afford to alienate her . . .

As he was thinking of her, she appeared in the doorway.

"Oh, good," she said, "I haven't missed tea!"

"You never could," the vicar said, with a smile.

Constantine smiled too. "Welcome back," he said.

She looked at him strangely, but took a seat.

And he kept smiling.

Chapter 9

Constantine and Lisabeth walked back to the inn when they were done having tea with the vicar. There, they had a few bumpers of ale, heard a great many stories, and laughed a good deal with the crowds of local folk who had come to see Constantine. Lisabeth was astonished at his behavior. He'd changed. He was charming, friendly, patient, and seemed entirely at home now with the people at the inn; it was almost as though he'd grown up in her little village.

The vicar, Lisabeth thought, must have had quite a talk with him. She was still eyeing him curiously when they mounted their horses and began the ride back to Sea Mews.

"What is it?" Constantine asked her amiably, after a few moments.

"What?" she answered guiltily.

"You're looking at me as though you've just seen me for the first time."

"Well, so I think I have," she said with candor. "I never thought you'd take to our local folk the way you did. After all, they're a long way from the people you normally rub elbows with."

He turned to look at her and raised one of those arced brows. "And who do you think I normally spend my time with?"

She shrugged. "Earls and dukes and such. Ladies of fashion and gentlemen of leisure. Certainly not anyone who works with their hands, hauls nets of fish, or sews for their livelihood, that's certain."

He laughed. "But that doesn't mean I don't know people who do. I spar twice a week at Gentleman Jackson's boxing salon. If you don't use your hands there, you'll lose your head. He doesn't care whether you have a crown on it, or not. Nor do any of the bruisers who regularly work out there. I go to the races, and if I want to bet on something with a chance to win, I meet with jockeys and stablemen to get the odds. I attend the theater and talk with actors and stagehands." He fell still, realizing he'd neglected to mention that he usually spoke with the actresses, but a glance at Lisabeth and the burgeoning laughter in her eyes told him she knew it.

"All right," he said, laughing. "*And* I talk with the actresses and dancers there too. I do communicate with my household staff as well, and regularly deal with people from all walks of life, all over London. What I'm trying to say is that no man in London can live in a gilded cage, except for Prinny, of course. And even he doesn't, but I'm not at liberty to tell you who he regularly chooses to speak and deal with."

"It may be true," she said. "But you're a changed man since you talked with the vicar. Did he lecture you?"

"On godliness? Charity, and love toward my fellow man? No. He just chatted with me and made me see that there's a different way of life here. And I realized it's one I'd like to get to know before I have to return to London." His eyebrow arched higher. "I thought you'd be pleased. I am trying to please you, you know. I was a bit stiff and off-putting after we met, I suppose. Well, my family history was a shock to me. Still, that's no excuse. You've been nothing but kind to me, and

I'm heartily ashamed of myself. Shocked or not, I didn't act like a gentleman, or even a very nice man. Forgive me? Please? And let me try to make amends?"

His smile was intimate, teasing, it quite transformed him, she thought. He looked more like his rascally forebears than he ever had before.

The sudden transformation in him was difficult for her to absorb—or maybe too easy, too long wished for, to take in all at once. She ducked her head to avoid the familiar and yet unfamiliar look in his eyes. "There's nothing to forgive," she said. "And no amends to make . . . But I'd be delighted if you dared to race me home!" She spurred her horse, and flew up the road.

He sat back and laughed. He'd no chance to catch her, and no way to do it. She knew the roads, she knew the byways. But he'd seen the color fly into her cheeks when he'd looked at her before she left him. And he believed he had a very good chance of catching her in other ways. Though he wouldn't of course, he reminded himself immediately. That would be folly. Still, catching her favor was no bad thing. Constantine nudged his horse, and rode back slowly, deep in pleasant thoughts.

* * *

The boy was gone. In his place stood a radiant young woman. Constantine tilted his head to the side when he saw how Lisabeth had dressed for dinner. Her face grew pink, which looked very well with the rose-colored gown she'd put on. Her grandfather beamed at her. Constantine raised an eyebrow.

She grinned at last, and only then did Constantine see any traces of the cheeky lad he'd gone to the village with this morning. Otherwise, she was transformed. Her gown wasn't the latest style. Constantine was very well up on that. But she was dressed in a very acceptable high-waisted gown of soft muslin that flattered her lush form. Her breasts were, he mused, remarkable, or at least it was remarkable that he'd forgotten them so completely when she was dressed as a boy this morning.

Her gown was sashed with apple green, and she wore a golden locket at her throat. Her hair was drawn up with a green ribbon, and left to tumble down in back to rest on her white shoulders. She looked, he thought, very young, and very enticing—and suddenly very shy with him. She stood near the hearth with her grandfather, and after Constantine entered the room, raised her gaze to his. She looked at him with her clear topaz gaze and then let her lashes flutter down over her eyes. He liked the effect. It made him feel more comfortable because it was familiar, and after all, how most young women reacted to him.

He'd passed a quiet afternoon writing letters to London. One to his fiancée, to say that the business he was attending to would take longer than he'd thought, but that he'd be back as soon as he could. And one to each of his two best friends, to tell them he'd learned much, needed to know more, and would see them when he returned. He was still too irked with his uncle to even let him know where he was.

"So, I hear the local lads are mad about you, my lord," the captain said, as he handed Constantine a glass of wine.

"I don't know about that, but I'm certainly taken with them," Constantine said.

"Cod's liver!" the captain said, laughing. "You? And the local lads? Nonsense. Wine and water. No, I only meant that you didn't put on any airs with them and they liked that. No man here expects you to be his friend! They know their places."

"But they were my father's friends, and my great-grandfather's too," Constantine said.

"Nay, that they never were," the captain said. "It wasn't the title, mind. Captain Cunning was their leader, and no man is the equal to his leader. As for your da—he was a lad suffering growing pains, eager to befriend anyone kinder to him than his father, and that would be about anyone."

"Too true," Miss Lovelace said unexpectedly from the depths of a deep chair. "Many noblemen roister in their youth, and with the most unsuitable characters. Why, just look at King Hal. He was a friend to every sot and criminal in the lowest taverns of England. Poor Falstaff," she said on a sigh, as she took an audible swallow of wine.

"He should have known better," Lisabeth said. "Royals just use people."

"Ah, but Falstaff tried to use Prince Hal," Constantine said.

"The pair of them were bloody fools," she countered.

The captain laughed. But Constantine was shocked again. He was spared the effort of a reply. He saw a bony finger raised from the deep chair, as Miss Lovelace murmured, "Now, now, my love. What did I tell you? The gentleman isn't used to females talking so freely."

Lisabeth gazed at Constantine. "True?" she asked him. "Are you offended?"

It seemed to him that she'd taken a battle stance. It looked odd to see a delicious young woman stand, legs apart, hands on hips, a challenging look in her eyes. Her back was to the fireplace, her gown was very thin, he could see how very shapely her legs were. He knew what he wanted to challenge her to, and was shocked again. This time, at himself.

"I am not offended," he said carefully. "I always consider the source. Obviously, you have had an unconventional upbringing, and mean no offense by what you say, while such an utterance from a young woman raised in the *ton* would be the reverse."

Constantine saw a flash of disappointment cross her face. He hadn't meant to rankle her. In fact, he was annoyed with himself now, not her. He'd sounded so priggish. But still and all, he was right. Even so, for the first time in a long time he found he didn't know what to say next.

"The gentleman is entirely right," Miss Lovelace said. "I failed you, my dear." There were tears in her voice.

Lisabeth hurried to her side, sank to her knees, and clasped her governess's hand between her own. "Never!" she said angrily. "You never did! Why, how would I know about Prince Hal and Falstaff at all if it weren't for you? You taught me well, Lovey, honestly, you did."

Miss Lovelace's voice was clotted with emotion.

She peered around the side of her chair, and looked at Constantine. "I had a fine education, my lord," she said. "That's true. But since my family lost all their funds, and I was orphaned young, I led a life of servitude, first working for distant cousins as a governess, and then forced to acquire positions I could find through employment bureaus. But in either case, I'd no life of my own. And so when I reached the age of five and twenty, I discovered I could no longer bear it. Well, no, that isn't exactly so. I didn't discover it alone. It was Roger, a footman in the house where I was employed, who helped me discover myself.

"We ran away, Roger and I," she went on dreamily. "We shipped out on a fair tide, to meet his friends in the Caribbean, where he said he could make a new start and become rich. The difficulty was that his friends were—how shall I say it? Oh, the whole truth, then. They were brigands. And Roger, while an excellent fellow, and gifted with a silver tongue, was not so handy with a knife."

Miss Lovelace heaved a long sigh. "And so I soon found myself alone, a widow without any benefits of widowhood, since Roger and I never exchanged vows, in a strange land, far from home. I refused to beg. I found a way to support myself full well. I took up a trade that I suppose I ought to be ashamed of now, but which at the time I found to be lucrative." She glared at Constantine. "Think what you will, my lord. But being under the . . . influence of one man at a time for half an hour was far more to my liking than to be under the power of one man for the rest of my life."

Constantine couldn't think what to think. Was this ancient woman confessing to prostitution? He was far out of familiar territory now. He shot an agonized look to the captain.

"That's over and done, Lovey," the captain said quickly. "Long gone and long since. Thing is, my lord, I was touring the islands one year, looking to my investments, and heard of this lady who could quote whole books, even in her cups! Well, I needed a governess for my Lisabeth, none had suited her, and if they did, they didn't suit me. My girl was always one to know her own mind, a handful she was. Then I met Miss Lovelace. And so there it was. I interviewed her, and in spite of her occupation, found her to be a gentlewoman, and eager to return to England and settle down."

"I was much older by then," Miss Lovelace said sadly. "Quoting Shakespeare held more of a chance for me to earn a living than my previous occupation. Men appreciate minds, you see, but only if they are presented in the proper casings."

The captain cleared his throat. "Well, there it is. Would you believe that just because of my rough exterior, there was many an educated lady who didn't want to work for the likes of us? But not Miss Lovelace. So I introduced her to my Lisabeth, and they hit it off right away."

"You were in the Caribbean?" Constantine asked Lisabeth.

"Yes, and on the Continent too," she said, lifting her head. "My knowledge doesn't come just from books, my lord, but because of travel, and of course, because of Lovey here. I never had the patience for formal learning, but Miss Lovelace had a way of getting me interested in reading and writing and such. I was a wild young thing, and she was the only one who could tame me."

"And not your grandfather?" Constantine asked, amazed.

She laughed, and giving her governess's hand a final pat, rose to her feet. "Grandy? Oh, he roars like the north wind, but he never frightened me."

"Too true." Her grandfather chuckled. "Oh, here's Mr. Bell coming, looking pregnant with news. Dinner must be ready."

Constantine took a deep breath. He'd thought he was a flexible fellow. But the closer he became to this odd family, the more shocked he was. It was obviously imperative that he learn whatever else he could from them. It was of paramount importance that he charm them completely, and then leave them forever, with no hard feelings. He thought he could do that. That was, if they could just stop astonishing him for a while.

"You don't have to do this, you know," Lisabeth said the next morning, as the sun rose.

"I know that," Constantine said. "But I have gone sailing. I don't get mal de mer. And I'd like to see this coast from the seaside. I'm very grateful your grandfather arranged this for me. But tell me. The men we're going to sail with. Who are they?"

They stood on the stony beach and waited for the light to rise. Just now, it only gilded the waters, far off. Again, Lisabeth wore men's clothing, but as she wore a thick oilcloth jacket, a sailor's cap, and high black wading boots, Constantine didn't find her distracting this morning. Still, even with her hair and shape covered, there was no mistaking her for a boy. Her fine features were feminine and pure, her mouth and cheeks were blushed by the cool morning breeze, and her eyes danced with sunlight and laughter. Constantine realized he was wrong. This morning he found her only a little bit distracting.

"Well, first," Lisabeth said. "It's not a sailing ship, as such. Grandy wanted you to see our world as the folk around here usually do. We don't have a pirate ship so we can't see it as your great-grandfather did, and Grandy's ships are all at sea, but at least you can get a glimpse of our world as your father saw it. We're going in a fishing smack. The men aboard will be William, Francis and Henri. They're bound to show off a bit. But don't worry, they're excellent sailors. And the weather bids to be fair. Good thing you borrowed the clothing Grandy gave you though. We'll be soaked, because that's the way of it."

And she smelled like freesias, he thought. Even though the air was redolent of sea and salt, standing close to her was like standing in a spring garden.

"Look!" she shouted, shielding her eyes. "Here they come!"

A fishing smack, its nets hung high near its sails, came scudding toward the beach, to them.

"Oi! Lisa!" a man's voice called. "Wade in, luv. We'll hove to, but there's only so close we can come."

She marched into the water. Constantine followed, realizing that the old waders he'd been lent had a hole in a toe. But he marched beside her until they came close to the little fishing smack, and then he saw two rough-looking men lean down and haul her on board. Another extended a hand to him, and he clambered aboard as well.

It was a fair day, in late summer, and it was bidding to become sultry. But he was thoroughly wet, and the small boat stank of fish and fish guts. He was appalled. But well trained. None of it showed on his face as Lisabeth introduced him to the roughly dressed crew: tall William, red-faced Francis, and handsome, constantly smiling Henri.

The boat turned, and they steered out into the open sea.

"We can pull in a mess of fish even as we show you the land," William said above the sound of the snapping sails. "No worries there. Lisa will point out the sights. We have to haul in the nets. We may get a storm later, so we have to make hay—or fish—while the sun shines," he said, guffawing.

But it was only William and Francis who threw the nets out and pulled them in. And only those two upended the nets and dealt with the showers of flipping silvery fish. Because Henri stood next to Lisabeth and caught her whenever the ship tipped, and smiled and looked into her eyes and not at the scenery or the catch, all the while.

This was nothing like any fishing Constantine

had ever done. He'd stood in silvery Scottish waters and cast for salmon, and in rough-running streams in England for hours, waiting to lure a trout. He'd thrown a line into turquoise waters in Italy, and watched dolphins racing with yachts he'd been passenger aboard. He'd never sailed in a rocking boat that was more of a skiff, getting salt water dashed into his eyes every time it dipped, sliding on fish blood and guts, and all the while, seething at how Henri kept closing in on Lisabeth, while she tried to point out interesting sights along the shoreline to her guest.

After what seemed an eternity, the boat turned.

"Time to get you to safe harbor, missy," William said. "And time for Henri to finally do some work. We did most of it, so now he does the scaling and gutting before we get to market."

"But my friend," Henri whined. "How can you be so cruel? Me, I am a Frenchman. You expect me to ignore a beautiful woman and concentrate on feesh? Bah!"

"I'll 'bah' you," Francis said. "We did our share, now you do yours. Pleasure to have had you aboard, my lord. Sorry we couldn't talk more. But they were running, and so were we."

"I'm delighted that you took me," Constantine said. "Thank you."

"There's manners," William said with approval. "Careful you don't slip on that slimy patch there. Here's where we leave you."

Constantine looked out. He saw a different beach, and a deserted shore.

"Good," Lisabeth said. "We'll go through the wood and be home soon enough."

She took William's hand, and stepped off the boat. She sank up to her hips and then marched toward the beach. Constantine sighed and then did the same, slogging through the water beside her. When they reached the shore, she turned and waved a hand in farewell at the fast-disappearing boat.

"Henri is a Frenchman?" Constantine asked, as he tried to stop shivering. It wasn't cold. He was just clammy and soaked.

"Yes," she said, as she sat on a rock, pulled off a boot, and tipped its watery contents into the sand.

"Your suitor?"

She laughed. "He wishes it were so, but no."

"Still, a Frenchman. We *are* at war," Constantine said as he too sat and tried to drag off his own leaking boot.

"Not with Henri," she said. "He's not a spy. The

men rescued him off the coast, near France. He was trying to get away from trouble. He always is. He flirts because he's Henri. But he's harmless, in all ways. They were done with guillotining people, but he only took the side that seemed to be winning, and the little emperor's men were after him. The English were shooting Frenchmen. But fishermen weren't hunting anything but a living, especially if some of their catch came in bottles with French markings. Henry is charming, but very careful of his neck."

She tilted him a merry look. "And as you know, cautious men don't appeal to me. By the way," she added, as he tried to decide whether to be insulted or not. "That little voyage didn't turn out the way I thought it would. You hardly got a chance to see a thing. But when the fish are moving, the men must move with them. Next time—if you wish there to be one, that is—we'll go out on a bigger boat and see things in comfort. Still, you were gracious, and I thank you for that."

He nodded. Useless to say he enjoyed himself. Although, right now, with the sun coming out and the warmth of the day drying him, it didn't seem as horrible as it had been. He watched as Lisabeth took off her hat and shook her honey-colored hair until it spilled over her shoulders, gleaming in the sunlight. Then she unbuttoned and pulled off her oiled slicker, and reached up to plait her hair so it didn't fly in her face. His eyes widened. She wore an old fisherman's sweater over a pair of breeches. His morning didn't seem at all unpleasant now. It was amazing how a ragged old sweater was transformed when it covered a lithe young woman. He thought he might have a word with some of the men he knew in the theater world when he got back to London. A man could make a fortune. A revue with females dressed as males would be even more titillating than the usual bits of gauze and gossamer the dancers performed in. Except, he didn't know if it would be allowed, because it might offend public morals. He was willing to find out.

"Oh," she said, rising to her feet and dusting off her hands. "Company."

A tall, rangy rider on a dark horse was picking his way down the strand toward them. The man wore a tilted hat, and proper riding garb. He was well dressed, Constantine thought, or at least better clothed than the usual local men. As he came closer it could be seen that he was also young, with a thin face and intense blue eyes. His dour face lit up when he saw Lisabeth, but the look he turned on Constantine was guarded, and instantly forbidding. His hand snaked into his jacket. When it appeared again, he was holding a pistol, and still staring at Constantine.

Chapter 10

"**M**iss Bigod," the lean man said as his horse came closer. He halted, doffed his hat, and shot a suspicious look at Constantine. "Is everything all right?"

Constantine drew himself up in annoyance. He wasn't used to being regarded as though he were a threat to any young woman. Then he felt his toes squelch in his boots. He remembered what he was wearing and what he must look like. He stood tall, nonetheless.

"Everything is fine, Mr. Nichols," Lisabeth said, laughter in her voice. "This reprehensible-looking fellow is no bother to me. In fact, he looks as he does because I just took him out on William's boat, with Frank and Henri, and I might add, all they were catching were fish. This gentleman is our houseguest. Lord Wylde, may I present our local revenue official, Garner Nichols? Mr. Nichols; Constantine, Lord Wylde."

The revenue official's expression didn't change. He nodded. "I'd heard you'd arrived," he told Constantine. "After all these years. Thinking of taking up the family business, my lord?"

"Hardly," Constantine said, "I came to learn about the family business. Captain Bigod invited me, and as someone who always had a keen interest in genealogy, I was fascinated by the tales he told me. Say, rather, *am* fascinated," he added, with a smile for Lisabeth, in order to annoy his interrogator, because it was clear that if the dour revenue man had any smiles, they were only for her. He saw Nichols's expression grow taut, and was pleased at his good guess.

"I had no dealings with your father, he was before my time," Nichols said. "But I grew up in the district and your family history is one of the reasons I took up my profession. Captain Cunning has become a great folk hero. But he was, begging your pardon, my lord, for all his swagger and bravado, only a thief, and woe to the innocent man caught in a web of his design. My own ancestor was one of those unfortunates, who just happened to be crew on a ship that your ancestor commandeered. If your stay with us is in the interest of research, you can drop in at my office, it's a few miles from this village. I'll have stories for you too. But they won't be as charming as the ones you've heard in the inn. That, I guarantee.

"Good day, Miss Bigod," he said, clapping on his hat. "My lord," he said with a curt nod, turned his horse, and rode off down the rocky strand.

Constantine stared after him. "That fellow might have hated my forebears," he mused, "but I believe he wanted to bite my head off just because I was walking with you."

"He's a good-hearted man," she said. "Only so serious!"

"About you, at least," Constantine said, looking down at her. "Revenue men and sailors? And how many others? I'd no idea you had so many suitors."

"Aye," she said, laughing, "I do. But sometimes a lot is not very much. As Lovey taught me, Good Queen Bess had many suitors too, only none suited her."

"And none suit you?"

"None have," she said with a shrug, and started walking up the beach.

"You don't worry about that?"

"Worry? Oh, that I might end up a spinster? No," she said, smiling up into his eyes. "One day I'll find a fellow I want. Then God help him, because I'll never let him slip away."

Constantine walked on at her side. At the edge of the beach, they entered a grove of stunted trees and shrubs. Nothing grew tall or straight this near the sea, because of the constant winds, but as they went on, the narrow sandy path turned to an earthen one, and the trees became more abundant. The day was growing warmer but they walked in leafy shadow, the sea and the forest combining to make a pleasant earthy scent of early autumn. There was a scent of spring in the air as well.

"How do you do it?" Constantine marveled. "You got as thoroughly splashed as I did, you were there with the fish as well, but I stink of fish guts and low tide, and you still smell of perfume. It's freesia, is it?"

"What? Oh." She laughed. "I suppose so. I've a friend who frequently travels to France, and he brings back such lovely soaps and scents for me. Yes," she said, turning to him with a wicked grin. "There is an advantage to having a slew of suitors,

I suppose. And there's another reason Nichols keeps his eyes on me. He's after something aside from my hand. Several others in manacles would make him just as happy, I think."

Constantine lost his smile. "And you condone smuggling?"

She looked at him wide-eyed. "My lord, we live by the sea, and from the sea. We'd fight like madmen against Napoleon, and in fact, many of our young men do, in the royal navy, the army, and on the waters of the Channel as they sail out for fish, and other goods. But free trade is a fact of life here. If it disturbs you, I suggest you leave us, and now."

He held up a hand. "Please don't take offense. I'm a proper fellow, not a blind or deaf one. All London trades in free trade. I'm not blaming anyone. I just failed to realize that the revenue man had good reason to stop me. He was only doing his job. Does he really think I'm interested in going to sea as a pirate?"

"No. Well, I don't know. But he knows your history; it's the talk of our little village. And it's his job to be suspicious. Don't worry. Next time I see him, I'll assure him that you're the furthest thing from a pirate on the land or the sea."

"You say that as though I should regret it."

She stopped, and cocked her head to the side.

"In truth," she said, on a sigh. "You look very piratical at the moment." He was mussed, his hair disarranged by the sea wind, his clothing appalling, and now his face was like the one she'd seen before she met him, and so as familiar to her as her own. And yet he wasn't the man she'd hoped to one day find in reality. She reached up and brushed back a lock of his hair from his forehead.

He couldn't stop his eyebrow from going up. Ladies of breeding didn't touch gentlemen they scarcely knew, not even with their gloves on. Her fingers were bare, and warm, and where she'd touched him his skin tingled.

She laughed. "But no. It's all in the eyes, and those eyes are in a portrait. Because it's not in your heart or mind. You're more a preacher than a pirate, and that's that. There's nothing wrong with that, but it confuses me at times. I suppose it confuses others as well."

"It confuses me," he whispered. She was so close, she was dressed like no woman he'd ever known, or wanted to, but she was so damned appealing. He found it difficult to understand why.

She raised her hand, put it on the back of his neck, reached up on her tiptoes, closed her eyes, and kissed him lightly on the lips.

He felt her lips, soft against his own, and his

arms went around her. Hers had been a light kiss, a query. His response wasn't. It wasn't thought out and it wasn't gentle. It was surprised for only a heartbeat, and then it was full acceptance. She tasted delicious. He pulled her closer and opened his mouth against hers. She gasped and he touched her tongue with his, and felt a sudden surge of desire for more of her. He ran his hands along the rough sailor's sweater, gathering her closer still, and feeling the warm, vital female form beneath. He slipped his hand up inside the oversized sweater and reveled in the ease of it as he felt warm flesh and the way her soft breast peaked as his hand cupped her.

She wriggled closer to him, her eyes closed. He deepened the kiss, suddenly aflame, suddenly lost to everything but his senses as they responded to the warm, willing female in his arms.

He lowered his mouth to her neck, and she threw her head back and shivered. He put his other hand under the sweater to caress her silken back. The bud of her breast hardened in his palm, and she gasped.

And then he remembered who he was, and who she was. It took every ounce of his control, but he was well schooled in control. He dropped his hands, and drew back, appalled at himself.

"Forgive me," he said in a shaken voice. "I'd no right."

"You did," she said in a voice no more steady. "I kissed you, remember?"

He wanted to apologize, but stayed still, shamed and chagrined, realizing that what he'd done was as good as a declaration. Her grandfather's scheme had worked. He felt cold, then hot, and altogether like a fool. Had he been lured to this fate? She had, after all, kissed him. His expression of contrition turned to one of horror.

She saw it. "You are not caught, my lord," she said, affecting unconcern. "Nor have I, or will I, ask for more."

His eyes widened, because he suddenly wondered if he might. "But we kissed," he said stiffly. "And more."

"So we did. And not much more. Anyway, it doesn't signify. This isn't London."

He was, at that moment, very glad of it.

She turned her back and began walking again.

"Can you forgive me, and forget it?" he asked, coming up beside her, and trying to see her averted face. "I will confess to your grandfather, of course. And beg his pardon as well and take whatever consequences ensue."

She wheeled around and scowled. "*That* you

will not! I've already forgotten it. He doesn't need to know. Be done with it, sir. It was an impulse, and a test. You passed with flying colors. You're an honorable fellow. Forget it."

He wanted to ask what sort of test, but didn't dare. Talking it out might lead to more. He certainly wished it would, but dreaded it at the same time. So he bowed, and walked on beside her, relieved, guilty, and confused. Her grandfather knew he was engaged to marry, but hadn't told her. Or had he? Was this a cleverer trap than he'd expected?

But, no. He'd swear she was no actress. She was, however, light and fire, charm and temptation. That made her a better snare than even her sly old grandfather could have fashioned. Did the captain know that? Was that what he was betting on? Time for him to go then, Constantine thought. Past time.

But he certainly didn't need to add to the infamy surrounding his name. He decided that he'd go back to her house, stay another day until he was certain the incident was well past, and then go home where he belonged, and trust to fate that his terrible history stayed here, where it belonged.

They walked on in silence; her head was down, watching her boots. He watched her.

"Are you in love with anyone in London?" she asked suddenly.

"No!" he replied before he could think. But "no," was the right answer, he realized. Love was never a part of his forthcoming marriage.

"Well, you did ask me about my romantic situation," she said, mistaking his abrupt answer for anger.

"So I did," he answered warily.

"So, tit for tat," she said. She glanced up at him. "Anyone in love with you?"

"No," he said more carefully. That too was true. "Still, I am rather . . . involved with a young woman at present."

More he would not say. He needed Lisabeth's good will now. It wasn't strictly the truth, but it wasn't an out-and-out lie.

"Ah," she said. And smiled at him. "You know why it happened at all, Sir 'Involved'? That kiss? Out here, in the forest, near the sea, dressed as you are—and likely never are—you look more like the man in the portrait than the fellow who came down from London. Want to go for some proper fishing tomorrow?" she asked suddenly, with another mercurial change of subject. "We have a grandfather trout the size of a whale, but he's clever and shifty as the pickpockets you have in London. If you do catch him, we'd appreciate it if you threw him back. Oh, you'll get the credit, but that way you leave something behind for the rest of us to try to attain."

"You fish?"

"Of course," she said, laughing. "I love to fish, in river, stream, and sea. I swim like a fish as well, I sail, I ride. I can dance too, and bake, and sew a fine seam if I put my mind to it. But I'd rather read a book."

Every word she said disqualified her more for the life of a wellborn lady of the *ton*. Riding and dancing was expected. Sewing was acceptable. But reading books made her a bluestocking, and baking was something a servant did, and fishing and swimming, not the sort of thing any lady admitted to.

They came in sight of the long meadow that led to the drive to her grandfather's house.

They paused. He was searching for something to say. She was staring at him. She grinned again, pulled his head down, gave him a quick peck on the lips, not enough to signify, but enough to make him want to pull her close again. But before he could, she danced away, and left him, with laughter, as she ran back to her house.

"Tomorrow," she called back over her shoulder, "we go for the grandfather trout. And if it rains, I'll bake you a pie!"

He laughed in spite of himself, and watched her run away, wishing he could chase her, because he was sure he could catch her if he tried.

They didn't catch the grandfather trout. They caught some others, got chilled to the bone when clouds covered the sun, and ran all the way back to the house, laughing, before the downpour soaked them to the skin. He tried not to look at her in her drenched clothing. She ignored him. Then they changed into warm clothes, and spent time in front of the hearth in the salon, listening to the captain's stories about fish he had caught, had heard of being caught, and wished he had caught. The old fellow was, Constantine discovered, very amusing.

Then they had dinner, and after that, he discovered that Lisabeth could play the pianoforte, and sing very well indeed. He was about to go to bed, when the captain proposed a hand or two of piquet, and Constantine discovered that Lisabeth could play cards even better than she could sing. And although he kept losing and watching the captain, it was a wink from the old fellow that indicated it was Miss Lovelace who was cheating like a bandit.

Lisabeth pursed her lips when she saw his expression and then laughed until she was breathless, but only after Miss Lovelace had gone to bed. The captain left soon after, leaving Constantine and Lisabeth alone before a comfortable fire. It was too comfortable for Constantine. He stood immediately. He'd been going to tell Lisabeth he was leaving the next day, but didn't want to remain downstairs in the night alone with her for any reason. Tonight she'd dressed like a lady, in something green and clinging, though he'd begun to realize it didn't matter how she was clothed. There was always something alluring about her. He couldn't decide if it was her attitude, and so something she did on purpose, or his own confused attraction to her. At any rate, he knew being alone at night with her was no way to find out.

He said good night and went up the stair to his bed. He'd decided there was no hurry about leaving. However he watched, and he did, Lisabeth didn't look at him with desire. That was reassuring. It was also mildly annoying. He went to bed, musing about it.

The next day they rode out and visited with several villagers, Constantine was filled up with stories about his father and his great-grandfather, along with lashings of tea, fresh home-baked buns, and fresh sweet cream. Dinner that night was tasty, but both Constantine and Lisabeth were too full to eat much of it. After dinner, they played a home version of the forbidden game of hazard, where Miss Lovelace again skinned everyone else at the table.

Days passed into a week. And then two. Lisabeth continued to attract Constantine, but he thought possibly not on purpose. He didn't attempt anything but light banter. That amused her. Time flew by. He was scarcely aware of its passing, though he felt as though something were loosening inside him. His tension about his secret family history had vanished; perhaps, he thought, because it was not only *not* secret here, but actually admired. He felt freer, more relaxed, even younger, perhaps, he thought, because of the fresh sea air and exercise and good food. And the good company.

Constantine discovered that Lisabeth loved animals, books, laughter, and wicked men. Lisabeth got him to tell her about his life as a boy, and he was shocked to see the pity in her eyes.

"Your uncle never let you romp free?" she asked one afternoon, while they picnicked on the smooth green grass on a rill near an ancient bridge that crossed over a rushing silver brook.

"No," he said. "I see now it was because he worried that my wild side, the side he feared, would come out if I weren't under strict control."

"But you haven't a wild side!" she said. "Poor fellow."

"Poor fellow?" he said, lifting an eyebrow.

"Well, when we met you were horrified by your ancestors. But now I think that was not only because you were afraid people in London would find out about them, but also because you were just a bit"—she held her thumb and her forefinger a centimeter apart—"afraid that such wildness lurked in yourself. Don't fret," she said. "It doesn't."

"You sound disappointed."

"In truth," she said, "I am. No, listen. You know how taken I was by Captain Cunning's portrait. Now I realize that was because I was a very lonely, imaginative little girl. Now I can see that your great-grandfather might have terrified me in person. You are, after all, everything like him, and nothing like him, and I find I prefer a mannerly pirate, after all."

"Lonely?" he asked, focusing his attention on that and trying to ignore the rest of what she'd said. Those were waters too deep for him to measure. Especially with her sitting in the sunlight, her hair sparkling with shifting rainbow lights, her bonnet still tied but resting on her back. He noticed that because the front of her was too dazzling to look at directly.

"Yes," she said, with a shrug that made him finally look at what he'd been avoiding all afternoon. "Grandy was always off on business. The village children were nice to me, but they had chores and duties. I spent most of my time with Miss Lovelace."

"An interesting choice of governess companion," he said carefully.

"Yes. But you mustn't judge her too harshly. I knew what she did to survive, she told me herself. That, I think, was her way of teaching me to never even consider such a thing." She fixed a direct gaze on his. "You gentlemen think prostitution isn't such a bad thing, well, if you didn't, there wouldn't be any, would there? But it's dreadful. It's what turned Lovey into . . . such an admirer of alcoholic spirits. She told me everything about the trade, with no dressing it up. Running away with a lover was one thing. That happens to both ladies and commoners, and is excusable, I suppose, if their love lasts. But selling oneself day after day and night after night to whoever has a few extra pence in his pocket? That's pure hell, whatever you gentlemen think."

Constantine couldn't speak. He could never discuss this with a lady. He could, though, he realized, and perhaps had, discussed it with a female who wasn't a lady. She was right, at the same time that she was utterly wrong to talk about it with him. And, he saw from her sudden smile, she knew it.

"Well, the sun is sinking," she said, rising and putting a hand over her eyes so she could scan the sky. "And the breeze is growing chill, but there's no rain coming. On the way here I noticed that the oaks are laden with acorns. The berry bushes are definitely ready to harvest. We make preserves and jams that are a treat with scones. So, your lordship, do you think you'd care to come berrying with me tomorrow?"

She was smiling at him as though she thought he was too straitlaced to go berrying like a peasant. He'd been about to finally tell her he'd be leaving. But he'd never gone berrying.

Lisabeth hid her smile as they rode back to Sea Mews. She hadn't been so happy for weeks, perhaps in her entire life. He'd changed. It wasn't just that he was no longer the immaculate gentleman of fashion. She'd been impressed at how handsome he'd been when he'd arrived at Sea Mews, like a picture in *The Gentleman's Magazine*. But the moment she'd spoken with him, she'd longed for him to be more accessible, more human, more the man she'd fallen in love with long before she'd met him.

She'd talked with Lovey about it. She hadn't dared confide in Grandy or he'd drag the poor fellow to the altar without further delay. Lovely had led a terrible life, but if there was one thing she knew as well as she knew Shakespeare, it was a man's desires. Even the most reasonable man, Lovey had said, might be ruled by his brain. But he was also steered by his body.

Looking at Constantine now, Lisabeth saw a handsome, athletic-looking gentleman. Even though his breeches had grass stains on them, and his boots were smudged, he didn't seem to care. Perhaps because he knew his valet would correct that. He was well read, he was cultured, he was perhaps still a bit of a prig, but he had a lovely sense of humor and he seemed a genuinely good man. The pirate, she conceded, might not have been. This Lord Wylde was a good deal more of a man than the vague outline of the dashing rogue she had imagined he might be. And for all his prudishness, his kisses and caresses had been sheer magic. She couldn't stop thinking about it.

And when Lisabeth did the things Lovey had recommended, such as flirting just a little, and wearing clothing guaranteed to make him notice her, or saying something off-color and then looking innocent, to put him off balance, she saw more of the man Lord Wylde might be. Because then, if she looked at him when he didn't realize she was watching, she saw a breathtakingly handsome rogue with the hot look of a devil in his eyes—if he was looking at her. He'd changed in more ways than that. She'd seen the prissiness melting off him, his distant manner thawing, as though the tight cage that had been built around his inner self were crumbling.

She didn't know if he knew it. She did though. He was becoming, day by day, the man she'd hoped to find. Now she just had to discover a way to keep him.

Chapter 11

It rained too hard for berrying the next day. But it was a perfect day to wander through Sea Mews, looking at portraits, hearing stories about the people who were portrayed, riffling through ancient logbooks and maps.

"Your family turns out to be far more moral than mine," Constantine finally told Lisabeth sadly.

She laughed, but by now he knew her well enough to know he wasn't being mocked.

"Not at all," she said. "The difference is that my family went about their business in less spectacular fashion. And then too," she added with a grin, "they were never caught. The family motto was caution. Your family did things in an extravagant way. Every other generation, that is. My people were more consistent. Aside from my poor foolish father, they became practically stolid as time went by."

"Stolid?" he asked, lifting an eyebrow.

She shrugged. "My grandfather is a pillar of the community."

He thought a moment. "I see. But you must realize that your community is different from most, and far different from mine."

She put her head to the side, considering this. "That's true. But now that you're here, can you honestly tell me that your community is so far superior to ours? I do read the London papers, you see. And it seems to me that there's much more scandal involving infidelity, drinking, carousing, even dueling, among the upper classes than in any class here. And as for damage to property and crime in London!"

Constantine went still. She read the London papers! Then she surely must know of his situation. Why had she kissed him? "You read the London papers?" he asked carefully.

"Yes, when I can get my hands on them, and that isn't all the time. Grandy gets them, a day late, of course, in order to follow business trends. If there's a paper that has particular news he wants to save, that's exactly what he does: he saves it. I tell him again and again that I'm too old for fashioning paper boats out of them anymore, but ever since I was six, and did that with an edition that had an article on sugar futures, he doesn't trust me. I must admit," she said, grinning, "it made a fine boat! Must have got all the way to Spain, or so I imagined then."

"Ah, I see," he said with relief. She obviously never saw his engagement notice. Now he remembered that the captain had brought it to London to flourish in his face when they'd met. "But you read the gossip and scandal sheets. I venture to say that if you had such items in your local paper, you'd read much of the same about your friends and other villagers."

She laughed. "I don't need a newssheet for that! I just drop down to the tap at the inn. You hear everything there. If it isn't spoken aloud at the inn, you can hear it in whispers, over tea in any parlor in town. And I promise you, there's never news of duels and mad bets on horse races, or of some poor fellow blowing his brains out because he lost his family home in a game of chance. There may be talk of someone flirting when they shouldn't, or even whispers about someone considering leaving his wife, or of a wife leaving her husband. If anything like that happened, it would spread across town in an hour. It seldom happens because the shame of it would be unbearable."

Constantine couldn't tell Lisabeth that London, apart from being bigger, had the same taboos. Because that might mean he'd have to tell her the reason for his visit here, how it had to do with unbearable shame too, and that he'd only come to prevent his ancestors' pasts from becoming gossip that might reach the ears of London.

"And yet your father and mine were considered heroes?" he asked instead.

"Aye," she said. "Because they were amusing. Everyone had sympathy for your father, and tolerated my father's follies. And too, everyone believed they'd grow out of such antics."

"But your household staff . . ." Constantine said carefully. "They have histories involving all that and worse."

"Ah. The vicar told you all," she said. "But the past is forgiven here. Isn't it so in London?"

"No," he said simply. Again he wondered when he should leave this place. Surely Miss Winchester must be wondering what was keeping him. He'd written to say he'd been delayed on business.

She'd written to say she understood. He hadn't heard from her again. But he'd been drawn to her in the first place because she was, after all, a sensible person. As he had been. He wondered if he still was.

Best if he told Lisabeth he'd be leaving by the week's end, he decided. He'd learned all he'd come here to discover, and she was, even with all her sauciness and strange upbringing, an intelligent, understanding woman. And she hadn't kissed him again, or even looked like she was going to. He knew that—he'd been watching, her lips most of all.

"It's going to be rain all day," she said, peering out the window. "How about a game of cards? Or dice? I can wake Lovey. She's almost done with her afternoon nap. If you think she skins you at piquet, you should see her at loo. Grandy will join us if he hears her crowing when she thumps us. Because he can beat anyone at that."

"Oh, can he?" Constantine said, raising an eyebrow.

"Oh, a challenge," she said. "That will be fun to see!"

The next day the ground was soggy, and a dense fog covered the fields. It was too damp for walking, but they rode out through the mists so Lisabeth could show Constantine how the fog was rolling in from the sea. They rode to the top of a cliff overlooking the water. They tied their horses to the stunted trees and waited, because she told him that by noon, the sun would be up and burn off all the mists.

"You know this?" he asked.

"I live by the sea," she said. "We know its habits and moods. We have to."

The sun burst through when it was directly overhead, slicing through the gray, sending down blazing rays like lighthouse beacons, giving the appearance that a heavenly decree was about to be announced from on high. The light highlighted every slate swell on the rolling sea, gilding the curl of each gray wave, and setting an aura around Lisabeth's glorious unbound hair. Constantine silently vowed he'd seldom seen anything so magnificent. The sea, he said aloud, was very beautiful too.

"Too?" she asked.

He gazed at her. He couldn't say what he wished to. He was an honorable man. He kept trying to remember that. But she wore men's garb again today, and he'd gotten used to it. Instead of appearing bizarre or scandalous any longer, she looked charming, and delicious, he thought. Her hair glowed, her eyes sparkled, and her lips parted in a smile as she looked back at him.

She suddenly rose up on her toes, leaned forward, and kissed him lightly. He froze, too conflicted to take advantage of the sudden, shocking, so-long-desired moment. Instead, he stood stockstill. She backed away immediately.

"Thank you for the thought," she whispered. Then she tipped him a grin before she turned and sauntered over to her horse. "We'd best leave for home. I have to change my clothing. Mrs. Fellows down in town is expecting us for tea. Remember?"

He nodded, too stunned and angry with himself for not responding. And too worried about what might have happened if he had.

That night, they played cards and dice.

The next day dawned fair and breezy. They went for a ride along the coast, and Lisabeth presented Constantine with a surprise. She'd arranged for them to go out on a sizable ship, owned by her grandfather's company. They sailed along the coastline, while she pointed out all the landmarks and sights that she said had been as easy to read as a primer for her father, and eventually his. The ship sped over the water and rolled with the swelling waves as its sails swallowed up the wind.

A day in the sunlight and wind brought high color to Lisabeth's cheeks in spite of the bonnet she'd tied on. She looked at Constantine.

"You begin to look more and more like the portrait," she said as they rode home again. "You don't turn red, you're becoming teak. You've the color of a pirate or a fisherman now. What will your London friends think? I hear it's all the thing to be pallid these days."

"Only if you're a poet, or a Tulip of the *ton* and I am neither," he said.

That evening at dinner, Constantine had to repress his yawns. He was exhausted.

"Sea air knocks a fellow out," the captain said, as he eyed his guest. "No shame in going to bed early. Seems to me gents in London get up to all kinds of rigs and nonsense just because they're too wide awake when they should be sleeping."

"Seems to me," Constantine said, with a smile at Lisabeth, "that pirates didn't lack for energy."

"Aye, they didn't," the captain said. "But you can bet that was because they slept snug in their berths every night."

Constantine laughed, and had to agree.

But it seemed to him, later that night as he lay abed, unable to sleep, that he was changing. It wasn't just going to bed when he would have been going out for the night in London. Or the increasing pleasure he took in the captain's company. Or even the disturbing, delicious, increasingly strong tug of attraction he felt for Lisabeth. It seemed to him that he was also becoming someone he had never known. London seemed very far away. He was, in spite of all he'd anticipated, very happy and relaxed here.

What was keeping him awake was that he didn't know yet if that was a good or bad thing. He'd come here to find out about his family's past. He was now discovering there was too much about his present he hadn't known either.

He didn't sleep for hours.

Neither did Lisabeth. But she wasn't alone. All her life, when things troubled her, she had conferred with her grandfather. When it was something to do with being female, she talked with Lovey. And when she did, she sat in the kitchen with her, discussing it over a mug of hot, honeyed tea.

"I care for him, yes," she told Lovey, staring down into the amber contents of her mug.

"That's naught," Lovey said, tipping another jot of rum into her mug, and then into Lisabeth's.

"You care for the vicar too. Do you *want* him?"

Lisabeth sighed. "Aye, Lovey, so I do. From the first. Though then it was because he looked so much like the Captain Cunning of my dreams. When I saw how stiff and proper Constantine was, I changed my mind. By the next day, I'd changed it again, because I swore I saw the man he might have been beneath all that starch. And then, little by little, he became that man. It was as if all the starch were washed away by our rains and blown away by our sea winds."

She looked up at her old governess. Her eyes pleaded for an answer. "Thing is, am I imagining him, or is he real?"

Lovey shrugged and took a swallow of her laced tea. "Only you can know that. Have you made love to him?"

"I only kissed him, and . . . cuddled, a bit."

"And did you like it?"

Lisabeth nodded.

"And did he?"

"I think so!" Lisabeth said. "But he pulled away just as it started to become wonderful. And the next time he got the chance, he didn't let it go that far."

"But he didn't say anything?"

Lisabeth shook her head.

"Then he's being a proper gent," Miss Lovelace announced. "And he thinks you're a lady. If he didn't want you, he'd say it. But he knows that if he starts serious canoodling, my love, he'll have to marry you. That's a gentleman's code. They'll swive any lass they fancy if they think she's beneath them. And that's even before they actually put her there," she added with a smile. "But they're proper as parsons with ladies of breeding. Until he decides to declare for you. Do you want him to? Or do you just want some pleasure before he goes away again?"

Lisabeth's eyes widened. "I hadn't thought of it that way."

"Well, you ought," Miss Lovelace said. "There's many a lad who's delightful in the night, and a bore when the dawn comes. There's many another who's charming in the day and a boor when night falls. If you want to test him, that's one thing. Then you mustn't expect anything from him. If you want him for all time, that's another thing entirely. Then you should be sure he returns your affection. Now, Liz, my love, you decide what you want. The gentleman isn't involved anywhere else, and you're free as the wind. Do you or don't you want to stay that way? Or just have some fun? That is the question."

"*He* is involved," Lisabeth said sadly. "He told me just that. But there's no love on either side. He said that too."

"Not unusual," Miss Lovelace said wisely. "At least, not so with gentlemen of title and leisure. If his heart's not involved, then he's free. How long he remains so is up to you, my girl. A woman gets what she dares go after, at least a woman such as you. And a gentleman never goes where he isn't wanted. So it's up to you to show him that he is. In the end, my dear, it's all up to you."

That was what Lisabeth was thinking when she came to her grandfather's study. She saw the light shining out from under the door, and tapped at it.

"Come in, Lisabeth," he said.

"How did you know it was me?" she asked, as she entered his room and settled in a chair opposite his, near the blazing hearth.

"I've been waiting," he said, neglecting to mention he'd been waiting every late night for a week now.

"So you know," she said.

Her voice suddenly sounded small and uncertain.

"Yes?" he said cautiously, waiting to hear what she'd really come to ask him.

"He said he's 'involved' with a woman in London. But that he didn't love her, and she doesn't love him. What did he mean?"

He sighed. "Could be anything. But if he said his heart was free, then believe him. He's an honorable fellow."

Her face brightened. "So I thought! Thank you, Grandy!" She danced over to him, kissed his forehead, and said, in a relieved voice, "Good night, and thank you!"

When she'd left he sat back, deep in thought. So, as he'd thought, Lord Wylde wasn't in love with his fiancée. And also, as he'd thought, anyone would love Lisabeth. He'd been watching Lord Wylde. The man was smitten, and in heat, and no denying it. The captain smiled. He'd hoped for just such an outcome, or he wouldn't have asked the new fellow here to his home, to meet his greatest treasure. Then he frowned. Captain Cunning's great-grandson had better be an honorable fellow, he thought. If he weren't, then he'd be sure to make him one—if he had to.

The next day dawned bright, mild, and clear. A perfect day for getting the last brambleberries, Lisabeth announced at breakfast.

"So if you want to come with me," she told Constantine, "you'd best dress in rough old clothing, and I do mean a thick sweater and breeches you don't care about ruining, high boots and strong gloves. The berries are the sweetest in the world, but the brambles are fierce. Still, nothing good is easily come by. Dress in the nearest thing to armor that you own, and we'll try to beat the birds to last of the bounty. We'll take buckets, and a luncheon with us. Are you agreeable? Do you want to chance it? Or would you rather do something less dangerous? As for me, I must get them today, or never."

"I will face the monstrous brambles," Constantine said, smiling.

"Good!" she said, as she rose from the table. "I'll meet you by the stables in a half hour. We'll take a horse and cart. The best berry patch is a long way from here, and if we're lucky, there'll be too many full baskets for us to carry back without it."

"I doubt his lordship has such a rig in his luggage," the captain said as he too rose from the table. "Old, rough, and tough? Where would he wear such stuff in London? I'll see what I can forage for him. Stay a moment more, my lord."

After the captain returned, and presented him with an armful of donated clothing, Constantine went back to his room to shock his valet.

"Surely, my lord," his valet said in a horrified tone, "one isn't going out-of-doors in such apparel?

One can understand the necessity of donning a seaman's garb for sailing, or fishing. But this!"

"One had better understand," Constantine said, as he admired himself in the looking glass. "I'm going to pick brambleberries. If I don't wear this, I'm assured that not only my clothing will come home in tatters. And I'm careful of my skin."

But he didn't look or feel like a careful man today. He wore a ragtag collection. He gazed into the glass and smiled at his image as he saw a tanned man in a baggy fisherman's sweater, long leather gloves, and old breeches tucked into worn scarred boots. This rustic splendor was topped by a dilapidated, floppy hat, the kind that serfs wore, he guessed, a century or two past.

He was humming to himself as he came down the stairs. He smiled at a footman, and went out to the stables.

"Fella's making a fool of himself for her," a young footman whispered to the butler as he closed the door behind Constantine.

"As he should," an old footman said, as the housekeeper passed by.

"I don't know about him," she said, as she went on her way to the kitchen. "I do know she deserves the best. He's a gent all right, but not all of them are good men."

191

"There's truth," Cook spoke up from a corner of the kitchen. "And her taking him untried? Not my idea of a good thing, is that."

"And pray what do you mean by that?" the housekeeper asked, nose high.

"Don't 'pray' me, Flossie, my girl," the cook said. "I knowed you when you was earning yourself a fine improper living in the islands. You know just what I mean! My first husband was a dear, but a sad fumbler when it came to pleasure. My second was just the opposite. What a lover the man was! But he couldn't earn a penny or keep one in his pockets, no more'n he could keep his breeches on when a likely female came along. Don't turn up your nose at me. You remember him. Didn't I blacken your eye over him, that time in Tobago?"

"A lucky punch," the housekeeper said with a sniff.

"Now," Cook said, "I've no man at all, but all my memories. And you know the man I think about? A fellow like my first in the day, and like my other in my bed. If Miss Lisabeth thinks she's found the two in one, more credit to her! But so far's I can see, and I watch, they haven't done the deed yet. I'd see it in their eyes."

"No wonder," a housemaid said sighing. "He's so high-toned, never a pinch for another girl, nor a wink, nor even an invitation, here or in town. True noblemen are a different breed, just like the fairy stories say. And so she's got to offer, and he's got to take. But he's such a gent, and she's so picky! Who knows if it will ever happen?"

"We'll see," the butler said as he peered in the door. "Now, enough gossiping. The captain wouldn't have let them go alone if he didn't trust one, or the other."

"Alone? Again?" the housekeeper asked.

"Aye," a scullerymaid said. "Miss Lovelace took to her bed, all headachy this mornin', she swears."

"Ha! She's no fool," the housekeeper said.

"*Captain's* no fool," Cook said wisely.

They laughed, and scurried back to their chores.

Chapter 12

"What a glorious day!" Lisabeth said.

Constantine, sitting beside her in the one-horse cart, wanted to answer with a witty compliment comparing the beautiful day to her. But he couldn't. She wore a wretched old overlong coat, boots, and a battered floppy felt hat to shade her face from the sun. The most he could see of her in profile was her nose. She looked like a beggar woman of indeterminate age. So he settled for a random compliment instead.

"Yes," he said. "The air is fresh and mild, just as you predicted."

He was mildly disappointed. She'd looked very fetching last night, in a fine close-fitting gown the color of apricots. She'd flirted with him outrageously, but subtly. It had been amusing, and enticing. So this morning, after he'd heard that Miss Lovelace was ill, and that no one else had been selected to come with them, he'd had random thoughts of what Lisabeth and he might accomplish, alone, in the fields. Those would be things one couldn't do in her grandfather's house, or on a ship filled with fish guts and lusty sailors, or even in a fine sailing ship manned by her friends and acquaintances.

Of course, he couldn't and wouldn't act on his erotic daydreams; he was an engaged man, and a gentleman. Still, he'd considered it. That shocked him enough.

But when he'd seen her this morning, all thought of exotica and erotica had fled. He'd been relieved and disappointed.

She shook the reins and the horse that was pulling their wagon quickened his pace. "We can pick the berries first, stow them in the wagon, with a cloth over them to protect them, and then have a lovely picnic," she said. "Did you ever think you'd be wearing donated rags in order to go berrying again?"

"Again?" Constantine asked. "No. Because I never have."

She shot him a look of sympathy from under her ridiculous hat. "Really? Poor fellow. What did you do on a beautiful late summer's day when you were a boy?"

He thought. "By late summer I was usually preparing to go back to school. When I had the time I walked, usually down to the river. If I had extra time, I fished, or rowed out a few miles. I wasn't encouraged to do anything strenuous or dangerous. But don't pity me. I made up for it when I went to university. I played at cricket, rode, raced, and boxed. I sailed, swam, and was an oarsman too. I think I was trying to use up all the energy I wasn't allowed to express when I lived with my uncle."

"Was he a tyrant?" she asked sympathetically.

"No. Yes. I suppose he was. I hated living under his thumb, but obeyed so I wouldn't be banished from the only family I knew. I didn't know then that he was likely only doing it to keep the wild side of my nature suppressed. He knew the family secrets. I didn't."

"Well, I don't think he should have bothered," she said. "You haven't a wild bone in your body, my lord. You're a temperate and cautious fellow, nothing like your ancestors."

Again, he felt vaguely insulted.

She saw his expression and laughed. "Lud! But that's what you want to be, isn't it? I know I'm wild to a fault, but I don't care. You care very much. Is that because of what we were born to be, or trained to be? It's certainly a mystery to me. I don't know if family traits come from blood or upbringing, but I was brought up to be a lady, and never quite attained it, and you were brought up to be a gentleman and you've achieved it, body and soul."

"Well, but your upbringing was hardly conventional," he commented.

"Oh. You mean Miss Lovelace."

"And others in your household," he said.

"I see," she said. "You've heard stories. But you probably didn't hear that Miss Lovelace's mother was a very pious woman, and though our butler has a violent past, his father was a deacon. I could name many others in our household who revolted against what they were taught. I didn't. I just am. And I'm sorry if that shocks or offends you."

"It does neither," he said truthfully. "Not anymore. There's nothing wrong with high spirits. In fact, joy in life is a wonderful thing to see. The ladies of London are schooled to be cool and blasé. I think they could benefit from taking some lessons from you," he said, as a sudden vision of his correct and cool fiancée popped into his head.

"Then what's got you frowning?" she asked, as she saw his expression. "Is it something I said or did?"

"Something I did," he said cryptically. "So where are these wonderful brambleberries?"

"They're down the road, but still on our property," she said. "They grow wild. I think someone, sometime, planted a berry patch there. Now, no one but me and the birds know about them. We'll leave plenty for them. Aha! We're almost there."

She pulled the horse up to the side of a long path she'd taken off the main road to Sea Mews. Then she leaped down without waiting for Constantine to help her, and tied the horse to a low wooden fence at the side of what looked like a field of ripening barley to Constantine's untrained eye.

"Come, take a basket," she said, as she hauled two old wicker baskets from the back of the cart. "Now see?" she asked, pointing down the thin ragged lanes that ran through wild bushes. "We walk down there, pick and plop them into the basket, the ripest only please, let the green ones be. You go that way, I'll go straight down this path, and when our baskets are full, we can meet back at the wagon."

He gazed at her. The last chance of fulfilling his forbidden daydreams, or even resisting them, as he should, shattered.

"Well, we'd waste time if we both went down the same lane, wouldn't we?" she asked.

He agreed, took his basket, and began to walk down another lane.

"Oh," she shouted after him. "Remember, you can eat all you want, but don't eat too many."

"I know," he mumbled. "The birds."

"No." She laughed. "You don't want to ruin your appetite for luncheon. And anyway, too many berries will give you the squitters, ah—I mean the summer complaint, you know, loose . . . blast! That's how sailors talk, and how we say it here in the country. How does a lady say that?"

"Ah," he said, "she doesn't."

There was a silence.

"Pardon me," he heard her say meekly after a moment. "I didn't mean to be vulgar."

"You weren't. An understandable mistake," he said. "And after all, if no one who lives here minds, you weren't exactly saying anything untoward, were you?"

"Very kind of you," she said.

Then he heard her muttering as she walked down her lane. He shook his head, and chuckled.

No delightful kissing games for him today, he thought, and thanked God for it. But still, he enjoyed her company. He mightn't be able to embrace her, but she certainly tickled him.

Constantine's basket was filled with berries, he was hot, itchy, and sticky, the sun had risen high, all the bending and stooping he'd done had made his back ache, and he was eager to put down his basket and sit in the shade. He marched back to where they'd left the horse and cart, marveling at how little distance he'd gone.

He left the berry patch and stopped in his tracks. Lisabeth was nowhere to be seen. Instead, he saw a lovely young lady in a light yellow gown, parasol on her shoulder to protect her from the glare of the sun, standing by the farm cart. She was looking into the back of the cart. Constantine suddenly hoped that Lisabeth had been right, and they hadn't trespassed. He wondered what the fine for pilfering berries would be.

The young lady turned. She smiled. "Oh, there you are," Lisabeth said. "I was hoping you'd turn up. Otherwise, I'd have to change back into my other clothes and go looking for you."

"You changed clothes?" he asked, feeling as

though the sun had made him slow and stupid. "Was I supposed to bring something decent to wear as well?"

"No," she said, laughing. "It's just that I wore this under those." She picked up the old coat and boots from the back of the cart. "I wasn't trying to impress anyone. It's just you and me. But I wanted something light and airy to wear for our picnic, since it bids to be a warm afternoon."

Constantine never wore the wrong garb to any occasion. Now he felt not only slow and stupid, but out of place.

She laughed. "I just threw the old coat over my gown and pulled on boots. But I knew a man couldn't wear two changes of clothes, breeches over breeches and so on, so I had your valet send along some comfortable clothing for you too. There's a spot I know near a lake, and there's a place you can change there. Do get back into the cart. We'll go there, and I'll spread out our feast in the shade of the trees while you change. If you want to, that is."

"I want to," he said fervently.

She smiled.

He noticed her mouth was vividly red.

She laughed, and put a hand to her lips. "Oh. I must have scarlet smears on my face. Too many

201

berries, and I was greedy. But weren't they delicious?"

"They were," he said. "I've never tasted the like. They were warm from the sun, and incredibly sweet. Have I any red on my face?"

"No," she said simply, as she took his basket and lifted it into the back of the cart. "You're a gentleman."

She untied the horse and, with Constantine beside her, drove the cart out of the field. "Sea Mews used to have many sheep," she said as they went down another narrow lane, "but now Grandy just keeps a few for clipping the far pastures to make them neat. So there's an abandoned hut the shepherds used to shelter in. You can change there. Poor fellow," she said, glancing at him. "You haven't any berry juice on your face, but you look very warm. We'll be there in a moment. You can even take a dip in the water, if you like, before you change clothes. I won't look." She crossed her heart and then kissed her little finger. "I promise." There was mischief in her eyes.

He was silent. Take off his clothes and bathe so close to her, when they were alone? Then change into other clothing, so near to her? And they'd be alone? Was this seduction? Or childlike innocence? She was no innocent, not from her conversation or upbringing. She obviously either trusted him or wanted him. There was little question anymore that he wanted her. It was astonishing how quickly attraction to her had become so urgent. He'd only known her a little while and his attraction to her had grown since the first moment he'd realized she was lovely. Yet he couldn't forget he was promised to another. He'd have to leave this place soon. And today, he'd have to watch his step—and not her.

The lake was clear and blue, decorated by a pair of swans and a few geese, surrounded by lacy-leafed willows, and farther away, larch and towering oaks.

"The hut's just down that path," Lisabeth said, as she hopped out of the cart and tethered the horse by a grassy verge. She handed him a neat bundle. "Just follow the stream that feeds the lake. Go up to the top of the rise. Bathe, wash your face, or just dip your toes. I'll lay out our luncheon. There's eggs and ham, bread and cheese, and Cook always adds surprises. And there's a crock of clotted cream for our berries. Go along. Take your time. I'll see you when I see you."

He bowed, and went up a slight hill by the side of the rushing stream. The water gurgled and leaped as it dashed down the stones toward the lake. And there, at the top of the rise, under the trees, was a neat thatched hut, looking no more abandoned than any other edifice at Sea Mews. The interior was swept clean; there was a straw-filled tick in an alcove on one wall, a table, a chair, a cupboard, even a neat hearth stacked with wood.

Constantine looked around, every bit of cleanliness and convenience making him feel uneasier. This didn't look like an abandoned site. And Lisabeth had joked about spying on him. Or had she? There was no way on earth he wanted to be trapped in this place with her. He decided to go right back, tell her he had a headache and had to go to Sea Mews, to his own bed, to lie down.

He shook his head to clear it. He was reacting like a virgin finding herself snared in a roué's silken lair. He was a man, for God's sake! And an experienced one. Why should he fear a slip of a girl? Well, maybe he should, or at least fear his secret desires for her, and so maybe he'd better leave Sea Mews tomorrow. But as for today? He could take care of himself.

He went back to the stream. There, behind a clump of fern, in spite of his determination not to let her joke bother him, he quickly undressed, and washed, blessing the icy chill of the water. Then, using his discarded shirt as a shield, he went back to the cabin, dried himself, and put on a clean white shirt, a neat pair of breeches, and his own boots. He didn't look like a gentleman now, he supposed, because he lacked a neckcloth and jacket. But he was cool, completely covered, and hungry. He resolved to enjoy this last day in Lisabeth's company.

When he returned to Lisabeth, she'd spread a blanket and laid out the contents of her basket. There were crocks and dishes, napery and glasses, and plates bearing loaves of bread and great wedges of cheese.

"There are some bottles cooling in the stream," she said, without looking up as he came near. "Right where it feeds into the lake, the shallow pool over there. Please go get them. We have good wine, but they have no tax stamps on the bottles, so don't tell Officer Nichols." She looked up, her eyes twinkling. "Don't worry, everyone round here drinks the best wines; half of them take casks and bottles regularly right from across the water, and no one looks for stamps but poor Mr. Nichols. His is a thankless task, because even if he succeeds, he fails. At least with us."

"You think I'd refuse because it's illegal? Do you think me so very proper then?" he asked, hands on hips, looking down at her.

She gazed up at him. "I think you want to be," she said.

He walked away to get the wine. She'd said truth. There was nothing he could say.

They dined on simple foods, flavored by dappled sunlight and fresh air. They drank fizzy wine, and got a little high on laughter. It was a beautiful place; Constantine was with a beautiful, witty woman. He was totally at ease as he sat on the blanket, though he was aware that some part of him was still wary, and he still felt threatened.

Even so, he thought, gazing at Lisabeth, she couldn't help it. She was so candid and free. Her face was charming, her figure delicious, she had such shining sweet-scented masses of hair. He was the one who had to keep his hands and his thoughts to himself.

He resolved that today before they left this sylvan glade, he'd tell her he was leaving tomorrow and why he was doing it. Somehow he had to find the fortitude to tell her that he was, after all, engaged to be wed. It was the honorable thing to do. He must leave her immediately—as friends, but platonic ones.

He knew he'd committed more sins of deception and lust in the past weeks than during his whole life. He'd tell her so. But he could right those wrongs. He'd confess. He must. She was bright and sweet and lovely, but never for him. If he weren't promised . . . No, he thought, he was what he was, and his life had been shaped to one end: marriage to a well-bred, mannerly, proper young woman. He might wish he'd known his wild father, but he himself was nothing like him.

And he had, after all, discovered all he could about his place and his father and great-grandfather. What was known here would remain here. He just had to be sure to never let his wife, her family, or his own eventual children come to this part of the country. And too, he had to be sure to leave everyone here with good feelings toward him, so no one would ever seek revenge—or, for that matter, ever seek him again.

Lisabeth sighed. "What a delicious meal! Do you mind if we wait to have the berries and cream? I'm stuffed."

She should have said, "I've had quite enough," he thought, and said, "So am I. It was a feast!"

"What fun," she said, yawning and then stretching her arms to the side, and then above her head.

His eyes arrowed to how that movement raised her breasts.

"We have had such a good time this past month, haven't we?" she asked languidly.

"Month?" he asked, the amount of time she'd mentioned diverting him from lecherous thoughts.

"Yes, a month and three days," she answered, sitting back again, her arms in back of her as she leaned on her hands. "Though I'll admit it does seem like less, doesn't it?"

He was staggered. He felt like Ulysses stranded among the lotus-eaters. He'd passed a month here?

He was appalled, until she smiled at him. He noticed her lips were still unnaturally crimson. They looked fuller too. Her eyes were on his as she leaned forward. He held his tongue and his breath. He could see that the bodice of her gown gaped as she came closer. The skin at her breast was blemish free, white as Devonshire cream, and softly rounded. Her gown was fitted so that as she bent toward him he could glimpse the whole of one sweetly curved breast, even the rosy tip of it. And she smelled of flowers.

One last kiss, he thought, as she came to him and he bent his head to meet hers. It would only be one, and it would be the last.

But she reached past him to collect his empty plate and then drew back in order to put it in the picnic basket. He blinked, suddenly feeling cheated, angry, and desperate for her touch. And then he reached for her, caught her in his arms, and kissed her.

She drew in her breath, opened her lips, and clung to him.

Her mouth was hot and tasted of sweet fresh fruit, her skin was soft, and her breast, in his hand, tempted him to taste it too. But first he had to slake himself at her mouth, and it seemed to him that he couldn't. One kiss led to another, he breathed her scent in and held her close to his own body, and found that though her thin gown was as nothing beneath his touch, still he needed it off her.

He drew it off her, as she gazed into his eyes. Then he laid her down on the blanket and held her head in both hands as they kissed, and for a wonder and a delight, she kissed him back with equally frantic desire. She only paused to pull up his shirt so that her heart could beat against his naked chest. He reared back for a moment and flung off his shirt before he bent to her again. Now the tips of her breasts were hard, puckered and felt white hot against his skin, and his lips.

All the while he knew he had to stop. But it seemed he could not, and that she would not let him go.

His hands learned her body, his touch made

her gasp; he dared raise her gown and feel her warm smooth thighs, her rounded bottom, and then the very core of her, hot and damp as she writhed against his hand. He was surprised and shocked, but all his wariness had fled. He was overwhelmed by her responsiveness.

He knew enough of women to know she was as ready for him as he was for her. And so he rose again, cast off his breeches, and came back to her, pausing only for a moment to ask her what he must.

"Are you sure?" he managed to say.

"Oh, yes," she said, as she dragged him back.

He parted her legs, and came to her, entered her, and then stopped. She was so tight, and he'd heard her gasp.

"Please," she said.

And so he pushed forward into the depths of her, and then, it was too late to stop, although in some still sane part of his mind he knew he should. Because now she didn't writhe with him, she didn't rise to him, her eyes were shut, her face tight, but not with passion anymore. But he couldn't stop. He was schooled in control, but there was only so much control in the world, and this was beyond that.

It didn't take long. His emotions and desires

were too tangled. He would have been embarrassed, but was too horrified to feel anything but confusion and regret. He'd been in ecstasy, but that still sane voice inside his head had called him back to reality. He pulled away and fell to her side.

"Oh," she said, stroking his face, his hair, his chest. "Constantine. I do so love you."

He caught his breath. He rose up on one elbow and looked down at her, and then at himself. The stain on her thighs and his member was redder than the berries he'd picked.

And then it seemed to him that his heart stopped.

"It was your first time," he said dully. "Or is it," he asked with sudden hope, "your time of the month?"

"No," she said, still smiling sweetly.

"Oh," he said. "Did I hurt you?"

"Some," she said. "But I knew that would be inevitable, of course. It won't be so bad next time, I know. That's what I've been told."

His blood felt cold in his veins.

"But why?" he asked. "If it was your first time, why did you allow me . . . ?"

"Because I love you, of course, silly man," she said, reaching up to touch his face, her eyes glowing with happiness. "I waited and waited for the right man, all this time. And then you came to me, and I knew. At first, I didn't. You were so cold and distant. But you warmed up soon enough."

Her smile was tender. She brushed back a stray lock of his hair from his forehead. "Why should I simper and tease?" she asked. "Is that what fine London ladies do? I don't. I wouldn't. That wasn't how I was brought up. I was taught to find the man I wanted, and when I was sure he wanted me, to play no games. I didn't want to mislead you. After all, you didn't mislead me. You were only going to stay a week, yet after you found out about your ancestors, you lingered here, with me. I knew what I wanted soon enough, and when I saw you did too, there was no reason to pretend anymore. It was because I love you. Why else in the world would you think I'd make love to you?"

He sank to her side again, without words. He drew her close, held her, and closed his eyes. His future had been remade in the last moments. His heart felt like lead in his breast. If he could have, he would have wept the tears he thought all virgins did after their first experience: tears she hadn't wept. He'd been the experienced one. But she'd seduced him.

No, he thought in all honesty. He'd accepted what she offered, without thinking. But she was obviously telling the truth, and with all he was, he was, after all, a gentleman. He knew what he must do.

The life he'd thought to live, the plans he'd made, the safe, secure life he'd envisioned for himself had vanished. He could not in good conscience lie with a wellborn virgin and then desert her. Whether or not she'd tempted him on purpose didn't matter. Not marrying her now wasn't an option; it wasn't a moral thing to do. At least he wouldn't do it. It was a surprise; he would be talked about. He dreaded that. It would also be a complete change in his life's carefully chosen pattern. And if in some part of his soul he rejoiced for it, in another he deeply regretted it.

Chapter 13

"And so," Constantine said, "I wish to ask for your granddaughter's hand in marriage."

The captain sat back in his chair and studied Constantine. "Aye. Because you find her intelligent, you say, and beautiful." He leaned forward, his grizzled eyebrows lowering. "That ain't the half of it, laddie, and don't think I don't know it. Did you have your way with her?"

"I wish to marry her," Constantine said firmly. "There is no more you need to know."

"As if I didn't," the captain mumbled. "She

comes home blushing and singing like a bird. You look as though someone dropped a brick on your head." Then he peered up from under his brows. "And what of your fine fiancée, my lord? Thinking of polygamy, are you? That might be all the go in some parts of the world, but not this one, I'm thinking."

"I see that my marriage to Miss Winchester would have been a mistake for me and for her," Constantine said stiffly. "I'll go to London and speak with her, end the connection, and then return to marry your granddaughter. Unless you don't trust me, and in that case I'll marry her before I go to London."

"And have a lawsuit brought against you?" the captain asked. "Because engagement is no small thing and you have to free yourself from one female before you pledge to another. I won't have Lisabeth's name smeared, that I will not. I thought one day I'd host a party to end all parties when she got engaged to marry. But now, I'll not even talk about it at the inn until I'm sure of the way the wind's blowing."

The captain scowled, then fixed Constantine with a hard stare. "Listen, my lord, I'm not happy about this and don't think I am. If you'd gone back to London, broken off with your fine lady, and then come back claiming love for Lisabeth, I'd be throwing rice and buying a drink for every soul in the village, I would. But you come to me with a face like grim death and ask for her hand like you was asking the hangman to get it over with quick and clean, and what am I supposed to think? I don't have to," he said, waving a hand at Constantine before he could reply. "I know. Some things are too tempting to resist. But I'm disappointed in you, my lord, that I am.

"Now listen, there's something you better know," he went on, shaking a finger as though Constantine were a naughty boy he was lecturing. "My Lisabeth is clear as water and constant as the tide. She wouldn't have the time of day for you if she hadn't decided to give her heart to you, and for all time. Aye, she was brought up irregular. Mistress Lovelace taught her languages and letters better than any other did. But she also taught her about life as she knew it, as did the rest of my crew that was here while Lisabeth was growing up. And I admit, that's my fault. But so long as she was happy—and she was—I never thought to change things. Maybe I ought to have, but now it's too late. So my Lisabeth doesn't play coy or cute. She doesn't know how. But never think that makes her easy or sluttish, for it don't."

Constantine had blamed himself for his bad behavior through half the night before this interview. He was tired of feeling guilty. "You invited me here knowing I was an engaged man," he said, putting his hands on the desk and leaning forward. "You didn't tell Lisabeth that."

"Did you?" the captain countered.

Constantine moved back.

"Thought not," the captain said with a scowl. "I invited you here because I hoped you'd get to know her and see for yourself what a fine lass she is. You did. And I thought you were a gentleman. Had you gone back to London and freed yourself and then come back, all would be well. But you went about it arse backward. Now, in ordinary times, I'd refuse you, because I don't believe you're doing this with your whole heart. But it's clear you've ruined her. And I won't have that. Still, remember, I'll be guarding her wherever she goes, and I won't see her mistreated."

"I would never mistreat her," Constantine said.

"Marrying her without loving her would be mistreatment. Tell you what, my lord. You go to London. You talk to your fine lady. And now I'm telling you the truth with nothing fancy about it. If my Lisabeth has her normal courses come next month, I'm not at all sure I'll let you marry her. Unless you can convince me it's really what you want to do, and not just what you have to do. If she don't . . ." He shrugged. "Then it's the parson for you two, my lord, but I won't pretend to be happy about it."

"What about Lisabeth?" Constantine asked.

"She'll grieve if she don't marry you. She never gave her heart or her body, and it isn't a small thing for her. I know that. But in the long run, she'll be happier. Because if you're like the rest of your family, the wild side of it, she'd be better off without you."

There was nothing Constantine could say to that. He no longer knew what he was like. He turned to go.

"One more thing, my lord," the captain said. "I think it would be better if you tell Lisabeth about your fiancée before you leave. It'll be hard, but you've got the words, and she's inclined to believe everything you say. I'm not. But let there be some truth between you at last."

"I'd rather you had asked me for that from the very beginning," Constantine said, pausing, his hand on the door. "Then things may not have turned out as they have done." The captain's eyes blazed. Constantine didn't see. "But then," he murmured, as though to himself, "they may have done.

She really is unique, I never lied to you about that."

"Aye, but had I told her she'd not have thrown herself at you, that I grant," the captain said, deflated. "I trusted you to be a gentleman. But she is what she is, and you're only human. Be that as it may—we all sail the course the winds allow."

"I'll tell her the truth," Constantine said, turning to face his host again. "And I'll do it so she never blames herself. The truth is, mine was not a love match. Surely you know that. Now she will too. And then I'll leave as soon as I may, go back to London and put things right." He bowed, and left the captain's study.

The captain was still frowning. Lord Wylde had said that his first engagement wasn't a love match. But neither did he say that his proposed match to Lisabeth was.

She twirled around her room, dancing with the dust motes she kicked up as they rose to float in the sunbeams coming through her window. Lisabeth had never felt so happy, so content, and so excited, all at once. He loved her! She loved him. The dream that had begun years ago in a musty old portrait had come to exquisite life. Her friends were all already married. She'd turned down local lads, and friends of friends, honest men and scoundrels, waiting for the man of her dreams to come along. He had.

So he wasn't a daring pirate bold, or a highwayman on the high Toby, courageously and dangerously trying to win enough money to rescue back his beloved wife. Constantine was actually a bit prim and very proper, but his lovemaking had been as wild and wonderful as she'd ever dreamed. Once she'd been in his arms, his composure had vanished. He'd been ardent, gentle, thorough, oh, most deliciously thorough.

She sank to a chair and grinned to herself. She was the one who'd been courageous and bold. He hadn't known how frightened she'd been, how unsure and anxious. It was a wild and desperate thing she'd done, but she'd come to realize he was too much of a gentleman to ever make the first move. So she'd steeled herself, and done it. It wasn't as though he weren't interested. He'd signaled his desire a thousand ways. He'd said he was staying for only a brief visit, and had remained at her side for over a month. He gazed at her when he thought she wasn't looking, he watched her every move. She knew he wanted her as much as she'd wanted him.

So, although terrified of making a fool of herself, she'd finally decided to tempt him to the limit. She'd forgotten her fears the moment he'd caught her up in his arms. She'd known what to expect, after all. Hadn't Lovey told her about it a thousand times?

But she'd never guessed how much more wonderful it really was. To be so close to him as to be part of him. To feel his pleasure and know she was the one who provided it for him. To experience all those new sensations, to stroke his naked skin, to hear his breath in her ear, to hold him and wonder at his utter loss of control, because of her. She couldn't wait to do more with him, try more, feel more.

Now, she'd have the rest of her life for that. Would they live in London? Here? He had an estate. Would they go there? She wanted to stay here, and be there, but above all, to be with him always.

Now her only problem lay in what to do next. She hadn't told Lovey yet, only because her old governess was taking an afternoon nap. She giggled, just thinking of Lovey's reaction when she found out. For once, she'd acted on her own. Now, what would Lovey think of that?

She was tired of waiting and too keyed up to sit down. She stood. Should she go downstairs and wait for him? He'd said he was going to speak to Grandy. She sat. Should she wait for a summons? She rose again. She couldn't sit still and she couldn't go anywhere yet. How did one greet a man one had just made love with? Surely not with simpers or uneasiness. And yet surely not with cries of love, or by clinging to him either. He was, with all they'd done, still a reserved man, a gentleman, a fellow who observed the proprieties. She wished she knew what they were in this instance.

She'd cleaned herself up and changed her clothing once again. Her smile grew tender as she remembered how he'd helped her wash in the brook before they'd come home. Now, she'd washed again, dressed in a fine long-sleeved cof-fee-colored gown, and arranged her hair. She couldn't look better, so now she'd wait. At least another five minutes.

"Miss Lisabeth?" her maid said, appearing at her door. "Lord Wylde's waiting downstairs. He wants to see you."

Lisabeth stood, walked to her door, and with the greatest restraint, resisted the urge to slide down the long banister, and instead, only flew down the stairs to meet Constantine.

He was waiting in the hall. He looked ill at ease, but so very handsome, she thought. He'd dressed in correct afternoon wear. Not correct for a warm afternoon in the countryside, but for a gentleman paying a call on a lady in London town. He bowed when he saw her. She thought that was quaint, and absurd. Surely they were beyond that by now? Shouldn't he have literally greeted her with open arms, picking her up and twirling around with her in exultation? Saying something like: "You're mine, at last!"?

But that was the stuff of her old daydreams. This was the real Constantine, Lord Wylde, after all. And she supposed he'd put his best foot forward for Grandy.

She bowed to him and then raised her head, and an eyebrow, in inquiry.

"I spoke with the captain," he said. "He gave me permission to marry you . . . with some reservations." He saw her frown, and added quickly, "But these are things we can resolve here and now." He offered her his arm. "Will you come for a walk in the gardens with me?"

She put her hand on his arm, and paced out of the house and into the gardens with him in silence. They walked to a rose arbor with a bench beneath it. He waited until she sat, but didn't sit beside her. Instead, he stood, looking down at her.

She admired the way the sunlight lit his hair,

the way it showed the glow of his eyes, the way it outlined the whole cut of the man.

"I haven't been completely honest with you," he said.

She caught her breath. "I've been completely honest with you," she replied.

"Have you?" he asked, raising a winged eyebrow.

She lowered her gaze. She'd flung herself into his arms and hadn't told him she'd never done such a thing with any man before. She'd never know if he'd have made love to her had he known that. Or if he'd have volunteered to marry her if she'd given herself to another man before.

"May I?" he asked, gesturing to the bench she sat on.

She blinked. They'd shared their bodies less than three hours past, and now he was asking permission to sit beside her? "You're married," she said flatly.

"No," he said, shaking his head. He sat beside her and turned to look at her. There was a rueful look in his eyes. "I was engaged. Still am, that is, at least, for now. I came here on your grandfather's invitation. He read of my engagement in the newspaper and came to see me in London. He was outraged. He waved a pistol at me and told me I was already promised in wedlock, to his granddaughter. You," he said unnecessarily.

She gasped; her hand flew to her neck.

"Then he told me about my father and my great-grandfather, all things I'd never known. I came here straightaway to find out more. I met you. And . . ." He paused. "And I was captivated."

"Now there's a false note," she said, standing. She felt hot, cold, and empty. They'd been so close, now she'd never felt further away from him. His protestations were warm; his voice was cool and even. "You were seduced, my friend," she said. "Don't put fine feathers on it."

"I was captivated," he said, standing and looking down at her. "As I said. My engagement was not a love match. It was time for me to marry, Miss Winchester was an appropriate match, she found me to be the same, and so we made it a bargain."

"So coldly?" she asked, searching his eyes.

He nodded. "I knew no other way." At last, a faint smile made his lips curl, in wonder or in distaste, she couldn't say. "I never kissed her as I kissed you. I've never actually embraced her. That engagement must be unmade now. I want to marry you."

"And my grandfather's conditions?" she asked.

"That I tell you about my engagement," he said.

"And nothing else?"

He sighed. "He thinks I've ruined you. He no longer approves of me. He said that if you are not . . . eventually encumbered with the consequences of our actions, he might not allow our marriage."

"And you?" she asked, and waited.

"And I want to marry you," he said. "Whatever the consequences."

She cocked her head to the side. "Consequences?" She considered the word. "A poor reason for wedlock. Even so, how do I know what you say is true?"

"You don't want to marry me?" he asked as answer.

"What I want doesn't matter just now," she said angrily. "You were engaged. You were seduced. If I am not with child, why should we marry?"

"You make love to all your guests?" he asked softly.

"With none," she snapped, "as you know. But I won't take charity or sympathy."

"How can I prove my sincerity to you?"

She looked at him. He stared back at her.

He reached out, took her into his arms, and kissed her. "This way," he said roughly, when he lifted his head.

"I'll need more convincing," she said breathlessly.

"Oh, good," he said.

They walked back to the house slowly, arm in arm and in silence.

"I'll go to London, and end the matter of my engagement," he said, "and then, after a few weeks, I'll send for you. We can marry there or here, it's your choice. But I want the world to know who you are. There'll be no hole-in-the-corner ceremony for us. You and your grandfather and whoever else you think necessary will come to stay with me, or if you prefer, we can rent a house for you until the banns have been read and the invitations to our wedding sent out. I've cut ties to my uncle, or I'd have you stay at his home, though I don't think you could bear him. One day, he and I will thrash things out—not literally, of course. And then we may be polite acquaintances, if never friends. Our children may find such connections important."

"Will you lose your friends and your reputation because of this?" she asked.

"I don't think so. It will be done so that Miss Winchester is the one to end the relationship. That is the customary way to do such things. I have only to tell her about my family to accomplish that."

She stopped and stared. "So she'd have ended it anyway?"

"No," he said. "If I'd left here promptly and never returned, she'd never know. I didn't want to do that."

"But you did, once," she persisted.

"Once upon a time," he said. "Before the princess's kiss woke me from my sleep."

"Coming it too strong," she said.

He laughed.

"You're sure you don't want me to come with you to London?"

"No," he said. "Let me make arrangements, so you don't have a moment of unease."

She looked up into his eyes. "All right. But one thing, my lord: be sure, be utterly sure. If you find that when you get back to London and your proper lady, that she *is* the one for you, I'd rather know it sooner than later. I do have other beaux, you know. And here in the countryside we are more liberal, I think."

"I want to be more liberal, Lisabeth," he said. "I want you."

She smiled, and they went slowly back to Sea Mews.

They were met in the hall by a beaming Miss Lovelace. "We have company!" she trilled.

"What?" Lisabeth said. "Who?"

"Two dashing gents," Lovey burbled. "Top o' the trees! Tulips of the *ton*, or at least one is. He's so fashionable, dust wouldn't dare settle on his boots. The other is manly and athletic, a Corinthian, a sportsman par excellence. I'd bet my breeches on it. Friends of Lord Wylde, they said, coming to inquire as to his welfare and whereabouts, since they hadn't heard from him in a long while. The captain was surprised and then delighted to meet them. Handsome as they can stare, the pair of them. Mannered, mannerly, and charming. Why, I wouldn't be surprised if you didn't lose your heart to one of them or both, Lisabeth, as I've already done. Why does age come upon us so quickly?" she asked sorrowfully. "Just when we know all the rigs and roundabouts, we're too old to use them. Ah, me. Oh, well."

She finally focused on Lisabeth and Constantine. "Why, you two already look fine!" she cried. "Were you expecting them? Fie for not telling me! Come in, and greet them."

"Their names?" Constantine asked.

"The fascinating dark one is Sir Richard Kendall, the glorious blond is Sir Blaise de Wolf," Miss Lovelace said dreamily.

Constantine grinned. "Yes, they are good friends.

And they came all the way here to be sure I was doing well, they said? Trust me," he told Lisabeth, "it's gossip they're after, not reassurance. My letters were vague; I stayed longer than I said I would. I'm not known to deviate from my schedule. They must be dying of curiosity as well as worry about my welfare. But either way, you'll find them amusing. And they mean nothing but well."

She hesitated. Now her experience of his world would begin. Would she fit in? Would she make him proud of her, or embarrass him? She'd been so foolishly sure of herself. She hadn't thought it through, or considered an aftermath, after love-making, aside from dreamily imagining clutches of children who looked like him. She'd simply thrown herself at this man, and after a second of surprise, he'd succumbed. And though he'd sworn to wed her, he'd never said he loved her. Only that he wanted her.

He smiled now, had held her close and kissed her, but she didn't know him well enough to know what was going on behind his eyes. She hadn't known even when they'd kissed just moments ago. All she knew was that she wanted more.

Most of all, she could not forget, in slow and deadly detail, that when they'd made love, his ecstasy had ended at the precise moment he'd realized she hadn't shared it. Not because he'd failed her as a lover. But because he'd realized she'd never had a lover before.

Lisabeth composed herself. It was done. He was a proper gentleman and would do the right thing. Now she'd have to meet his friends and discover his world, and more than that, find out if by her entering his life, she would end his pleasure in it. His friends' reactions would tell her much.

She drew a deep breath. She didn't know if she could live the rest of her life doing the right thing, with the wrong man. Or the wrong thing, with the right man. But she'd been raised to trust her instincts, and she couldn't stop now.

"Lead on," she told him, placing her hand on his sleeve. "I'm eager to meet them."

Chapter 14

"**E**nchanted," the faultless Sir Blaise said as he bowed over Lisabeth's hand.

"Pleasure to meet you," Sir Kendall said as he took her hand in turn.

Lisabeth curtsied. She couldn't think of one word to say to these two gentlemen. Sir Blaise was beyond handsome. He was slender and exquisitely dressed; his immaculate clothing didn't bear a speck of road dust, although he'd just arrived at Sea Mews. His golden hair was brushed back from a pale and noble brow, his eyes were blue; his face looked as though it should be carved on a priceless cameo. Sir Kendall was gruff but polite, dressed like a man about town, handsome in an intensely masculine way, and obviously fit as a fiddle.

They bowed to her, and then looked at their friend Constantine. Who looked, she thought, as though he were in his element for the first time since she'd met him. Her heart sank.

"Fell in on you," Kendall told Constantine apologetically. "But worried about you, y'see."

"Lord Wylde is an old friend," Sir Blaise explained smoothly to Lisabeth. "And since he's usually as predictable as a mantel clock, we began to fret when he didn't return when he said he would."

"I sent you letters," Constantine said.

"The post," Blaise said with a shrug of one shoulder. "I daresay it's not that promptly delivered between here and London. Be that as it may. We see you breathe, and we are content. We'll leave."

"Won't hear a word of it," the captain said. "You'll stay to dinner. And for as long as you like after that. We have more bedchambers than guests, so please make yourselves at home. Daresay you two have been round the world, but I'd wager you have never explored our part of the world, have you? Well, you're welcome to do it from here. That is," he added, with a challenging look to Constantine, "if your friend Lord Wylde agrees?"

He wants to know if Constantine will tell his friends about his new wedding plans, Lisabeth realized. It was a rude and crude test, and maybe even insulting to Constantine. But she didn't say a word. She needed to know too.

"I'm delighted to have them stay, thank you, if it's not too much trouble," Constantine said.

"Wouldn't have asked if it was," the captain said.

"Maybe we can take them out on that delightful fishing boat Lisabeth's friends took me on?" Constantine said innocently. "And perhaps you fellows would like to go berrying too?"

Lisabeth hid her smiles. Sir Blaise looked astonished, Sir Kendall, horrified.

"We've much more to see than berries and fish," she assured them. "Good trout fishing, excellent sailing, good riding, breathtaking views from the cliffs, and a fine inn, down the road."

"But first, if I may, I'd like to show them my family: my father and my great-grandfather," Constantine said, "the fellows I discovered when I came here. Captain, would you mind?"

"Be proud," the captain said.

"And Lisabeth," Constantine added, "would

you mind narrating their rich histories for my friends?"

She smiled so broadly she was sure she glowed. "I'd be happy to, my lord," she said. "But first, surely, they wish to refresh themselves. You are staying on, gentlemen, aren't you? I'd like to pass the word to Cook, so she can try to outdo herself."

Constantine's friends looked at him.

He nodded.

"Be happy to," Sir Kendall said.

"Delighted," Sir Blaise said.

"Wonderful," Constantine said. "What a good idea. My long-lost relatives are best seen by moonlight anyway."

His friends looked puzzled.

Lisabeth laughed.

It was the last time she would laugh aloud, and mean it, for some time.

"By God!" Kendall exclaimed that evening, as Constantine held the lamp up to the portrait of his great-grandfather. "The spit and image of you, Con. But then again, he's nothing like you."

"Exactly," Blaise commented as he scrutinized the portrait. "He's dashing, Con. Charming and moral you are. But dashing? *That*, you never were. It's the eyes, I think," he said as he stared up at the picture. "His eyes hold wicked secrets that delight him."

Con? Lisabeth thought. She'd never heard him called that, nor had he encouraged her to use that name. But his friends had used it all through dinner. She'd kept still. She'd had nothing to say but inane polite things to his guests anyway. She didn't really know them. Now she wondered if she really knew Constantine.

Dinner had been pleasant; the gentlemen from London had taken it upon themselves to keep the conversation going. Blaise was obviously used to entertaining the company at dinner. Gruff Sir Kendall was positively loquacious when the subject turned to horses, hunting, fishing, or riding, and Constantine turned it that way whenever conversation lagged. It seldom did. Dinner had been very entertaining. Except that Constantine himself said little, nothing about her, and not much to her.

He didn't even look at her fondly. He was cool and collected, once again the stiff, formal fellow she'd first met. Was this the man who had made such passionate love to her? Was he the one who had asked her to marry him just this morning?

Constantine told his friends his family history

with never an apology or a defense. Her grandfather had kept silent, watching his friends as closely as she did. Sir Blaise and Kendall were by turns shocked, amused, and fascinated. And yet, Lisabeth thought, Constantine had claimed that knowledge of his ancestors' wicked past would ruin him.

But Blaise and Kendall seemed to enjoy the stories, and then enjoyed discussing them over a glass of port with the captain in the salon. Then they excused themselves.

"Tired as the devil after a day of traveling," Kendall said.

"All that fresh air!" Blaise said in horror. "I need a night to recuperate from it. Then too, Con has also told us we must be up early, as he's going to go riding with us to point out the sights. So good night, Captain, and good night, ladies. We'll see you in the morning."

They bowed, and left the salon. The captain went off to bed, and that left only Lisabeth and Constantine, and Miss Lovelace, snoring in her favorite chair by the hearth.

Then, at last, Lisabeth rose, and looked at Constantine with inquiry. "What's the matter?" she asked him quietly, her eyes searching his. "Have

237

you changed your mind? I'll understand. So will my grandfather. But I must know what's going on."

He turned a surprised face to her. "Going on?" he echoed. "Nothing. Why do you ask?"

"You didn't tell them about us," she said.

He smiled. "How could I? Remember, my dear, I am nominally still engaged to Miss Winchester. I want your name to be left out of any gossip until the day I am free to tell everyone."

She nodded. "I see," she said. "But it's more than that. You—you've changed. You're cool with me. You don't look at me the same way, or speak to me the way you used to do, even just this morning. It's as though a mask has come down over your face. You're the way you were when you first came here. Cold, mannerly, and . . . slightly superior. I don't recognize you."

"You obviously do, if you remember how I was," he said with a slight smile. "No, I'm just joking now," he added when he saw the anger flare up in her eyes.

He walked to her and held her by her shoulders, but at arm's length. He sighed. "First," he said. "I can't make love to you anymore, not here, and not now. It would betray your grandfather's hospitality. It also might become known by my friends. It wouldn't do your name any good, or mine. I'm not a scoundrel. You're not . . . an easy bit of muslin I chanced upon."

"I was," she said stonily.

"Once," he said. "If that. Whatever happened was my fault. I lost my self-control. Listen, Lisabeth, I'm not yet free, not in the eyes of Society. I will be. On that day and from then on, everything will be out in the open. Until then I must play at being the man I was before I met you. And you have to understand, I still want you. I can't forget our time together. But this is a new time, one in which we must keep this a secret between us."

"Are you going to tell Kendall and Blaise?" she asked. "They *are* your best friends."

He thought a moment. "Yes. Tomorrow, when we're out riding. I won't tell all, but I'll explain that I've changed my mind about Miss Winchester, and that I want to marry you. I'll ask for their help in anything that might arise, and I know they'll give it to me. But I won't say anything that might reflect on you. There's no need for them to know everything. Believe me," he said on a slight smile, "knowing that I've changed my mind will be enough to shock them senseless."

Her eyes searched his. "No kisses?" she asked softly. "No physical contact at all?"

"I'm not a cad," he said gravely. "I lost my head once. I won't do it again, even though I dearly wish to. Now, go to sleep. I'll stay on a week or so more with my friends. Then, we'll ride for London. Within a week, I'll settle matters with Miss Winchester and then see it appears in the newspaper. Then I'll send for you and announce our pledge for the world to see. Please understand. Please wait."

She nodded. "I will." But then her chin rose. "But only for a few weeks more. And if you find when you return to London that you've returned to your senses, I'll understand." She poked a finger into his cravat. "Understand that."

"And if our one moment of forgetfulness proves fruitful?" he asked. "What about that? Would you expect me to forget that too? I promise you, I would not."

She shrugged. "Then you'd remember. I can't stop that. But I'll never wed where there is no love. Not for the sake of a child, or myself. Be easy. I understand that there's not much likelihood of that. After all, it only happened once."

"But you'll tell me?" he persisted. "As soon as you know?"

She cocked her head to the side. Her smile was not merry. "Yes. No. You'd never know. Forget it for now."

"I can scarcely forget it if time is of the essence," he said.

"So far," she said, "it is not. Don't look for trouble. Go on and do what you must, and understand that I'll do the same. Good night, Lord Wylde."

He caught her hand as she turned to go, his expression angry. He pulled her toward him, stared into her eyes a moment, then bent his head and kissed her. Their kiss was long and fervent, and they clung to each other. Then he drew back.

"See?" he said in a shaken voice. "I've already gone back on my word. I'll leave in a few days. I can't trust myself for much longer than that."

"I wouldn't mind if you forgot yourself," she said, touching his sleeve.

"I would," he said. "Good night, Lisabeth. Trust me. I'm leaving sooner because when I'm with you I can't trust myself."

"But I don't care," she said.

"I do," he said. "I can't help that. If you want me, understand that this inconvenient morality of mine is as much part of me as my eyes or my nose. It is what makes me what I am. I'm not my father or great-grandfather. Don't marry me because I

241

remind you of them, marry me in spite of what I am."

She nodded.

He bowed, and left her.

"He's a good man," Miss Lovelace said into the silence of the room. She yawned. "Too good for the likes of me. But he'll never give you a moment's worry when you're finally wed."

"He never said he loves me, not once," Lisabeth whispered.

Miss Lovelace rose from the chair slowly and with difficulty. "Well, that's a gentleman for you."

"Yes," Lisabeth said bitterly. "He won't lie."

"Didn't say that," Miss Lovelace said on another huge yawn. "He won't say 'bip,' not he, until he's free to say it."

"He did things he wasn't free to do," Lisabeth said.

"He's a man. He's not a saint, or a man milliner. You wouldn't want him so straitlaced and proper he didn't sometimes give way to temptation, would you? Proves he's human. Now, what's the matter? You look as though you're going to cry."

Lisabeth shook her head. "How will I ever know how he really feels about me? Especially if I don't get my courses? I don't want to lie to him but I don't want him to marry me just because of one mistake."

"He wouldn't be the first or the last to do it. But you're making the stew before you've caught a fish. Wait and see. Now, give me your arm, I'm to bed, and so are you. And it's a lucky thing your young man isn't the type to go creeping up to your chamber by night. Morality will keep him in his whole skin. The captain keeps a loaded horse pistol by his bedside. Why, one night I remember, he heard a creaking below stairs, and he was up and out of bed and down the stairs in the altogether two seconds later. Had he not seen it was a cat in time, there'd have been cat all over the dining chamber wall."

"Lovey!" Lisabeth said, eyes wide.

Miss Lovelace patted her hand. "Not to fret. Many a long year ago, that was, when both he and I didn't look so bad in the altogether. Nor did either of us have a reputation to win or lose. That's over and done. Now, there's not a soul I'd let see me like that. Save for the doctor, of course. I'm not a prude. Only a prune." She laughed. "Now, let's go to bed."

Constantine went riding out with his friends the next morning, and Lisabeth, waiting for him, was so anxious she could not stop pacing.

"He's telling them now, is he?" the captain asked as he came into the front salon and saw her walking to the window and back again.

"So he said," she muttered.

"Doing it by the book," the captain said, nodding. "The lad's got manners. Lizzie?" he asked, in a voice she hadn't heard from him in a long time. "You sure of this? He's handsome, rich, and well mannered, I grant. But is he the fellow for you? You're not conventional; we didn't raise you as such. Right or wrong, I wouldn't want you to try to change for someone else's sake. There's nothing wrong with propriety, but it can make you feel tight-laced if you act like that to make someone else happy. Is he worth it? Marriage is a long time, God willing. And don't talk to me about my great-grandchild coming, unless you're sure, and then we'll discuss it. But even if so, you know how we live here.

"There's many a likely lad who would take you to wife with three brats at your skirts, and thank heaven for the chance to do it. Oh, people gossip. But everyone round here judges a lass by her heart and her brain, not her past. All I'm saying is that you're worth ten other females. So don't do anything because you think you must."

"What do you really think of him, Grandy?" she asked, stopping to study his face as he answered.

"He's not his father, nor his great-grandfather," the captain said with a sigh. "Sometimes I think I see a glimpse of them in him, trying to get out. But he was brought up strict and proper and he never rebelled, like they did. So I don't know. Thing is," he said, lowering his eyebrows, and studying her expression from under them. "If you were sure you loved him, I don't think you'd ask me that. You plain wouldn't care."

"Right," she said sadly. "And I didn't care, before. But now . . . ? When he's with his friends he's different."

"I know. Make sure you know what and who he is wherever he is before you post the banns or exchange one vow with him," her grandfather cautioned. "Because afterward, it will be too late. Oh, not for you to come home! You can always come home to me. But for you to be free to find another."

"Thank you, Grandy," she said. "I know that. I'm not stupid, you should know that too."

"You think you're in love," he said. "That makes anyone stupid."

She smiled. And then her smile faded. "But not he," she said softly. "That's the problem."

"Aye, I know it," he said, and then they both stood and looked out the window, waiting for Constantine and his friends to come back.

Chapter 15

"*Marry* her? Well, this is indeed news," Blaise said carefully. "I can certainly see the attraction. Miss Lisabeth is charming, quite lovely, an original, in fact."

"Aye, so she is," Kendall said. "But you're already promised. What are you going to do about Miss W.? She'll be mad as fire."

"She'll be wounded," Blaise said, correcting him.

"*Wounded*, you say?" Constantine asked. "Do you have a *tendre* there yourself?"

Blaise shuddered, very theatrically. "Never. It's only that I have sisters, three. And so I pride myself on understanding the female mind. A lady mightn't want a fellow, but as soon as it looks as though he doesn't want her, you can wager she'll change her mind and desire him, madly. Though, admittedly, that's hard to see in a female as reserved as your fiancée. Ah, that is to say, your soon-to-be former fiancée. As for Miss W., at least I can say it at last: she's far too cold for me. I may not have enough money to marry where I would, but I have enough care for myself not to marry where I wouldn't even if I had to."

They sat in the sunlight at an outdoor table in back of the inn, where they could speak without being overheard.

"Miss W. will want your head if she doesn't get your hand," Kendall persisted.

"I doubt she'll care," Constantine said. "That is, if the disengagement is done with discretion and made to look as though it's her idea."

Blaise tapped his fingers on the wooden table. His expression grew serious. "Con? We'll support you, as ever. But you're far too flippant about it, in my opinion." He spread his hands. "Yes, I know I'm usually the flippant one. But all jokes aside, I can't see Miss W. giving you up. Not for another female. Not for anything short of a direct assault, which we know isn't your style, or we wouldn't be friends. You set too little store in her pride. Why in the world should she let you go? She's already been congratulated by her friends, the date's been set, I don't doubt she's already gotten some fine wedding gifts."

Constantine took a deep breath. "Have you forgotten the reason I came here? Not just to meet the woman the captain said had been my fiancée since birth, but to find out about my family history. I did. I was shocked at first, and then in a way, strangely proud of the bold old monsters. Me, the descendant of a pirate, and a highwayman? Do you think Miss W. will be proud, or even amused? No, gentlemen, she'll be glad to wash her hands of me."

"But you also wanted to be sure the *ton* never discovered any such thing," Blaise persisted. "Have you changed your mind about that?"

"Yes," Constantine said simply.

Blaise and Kendall exchanged a troubled glance.

"If you want to challenge me to a duel for saying this, I will meet you, though I'd think it a waste of time," Blaise said. "We are equals, at least with pistol and saber. Kendall here has the edge in fisticuffs. But . . ." For once the glib Blaise seemed at a loss for what to say. He exchanged another look with Kendall. "You want to be free of Miss W.? We can see that," Blaise went on. "But you live for propriety, old man. And now you say you don't care?"

"What he's trying to say is that this is so sudden," Kendall blurted. "What we want to know is if your hand's being forced. You aren't a sudden sort of fellow. It looks like a 'compromising position' sort of thing. Don't scowl. Makes sense. After all, you stayed here longer than you intended, and in their house. The girl's clear as rainwater, or so it seems. But we know you. Moral as a monk in chains. Now this! Thing is, one look can tell you that the old captain is as shrewd as he can hold together. If you're caught in a trap, we want you to know we'll help spring you."

"Just so!" Blaise said with relief.

"It's a trap of my own making," Constantine said.

His friends looked at each other.

"And you both know my engagement to Miss W. was never a love match."

"And this one is?" Blaise asked.

"And this one," Constantine said carefully, "is something I never expected to experience. But no one is forcing me to anything."

"Well, that's a relief," Blaise said, sitting back. "And you know? I think you can pull it off. We'll help. We can make sure no one casts the first stone. After all, many in the *ton* have not only skeletons in their closets, but a veritable symphony of old bones rattling on their family trees. We can remind anyone who disparages you of them."

"A lot of bones still with meat on them too," Kendall said. "What you're going to do isn't so terrible. Been done before. Isn't like you're abandoning a wife, as many do. Breaking off an engagement's not so terrible. Especially one with Miss W. Having interesting ancestors isn't so terrible neither, except to the very highest sticklers, which I grant you were, Con. And I admit I like you better this way. But as for others? It wouldn't be a tragedy to anyone except for those with their noses so high in the air they can't smell their own stench."

"Yes," Blaise said, warming to the subject. "My own father was a gambler, he was famous for how much he could lose in a night. Which is why I have to marry to keep the ancestral roof over my head. But I'm welcomed everywhere."

"Had a grandfather who was never seen sober after he passed his thirtieth birthday," Kendall said. "Well-known fact. Yet I can go anywhere I want too. You'll do, Con. And if you don't, Blaise and I can dig through the *ton* and find some newer bones to chew over. No one will shun you. We'll see you through this."

"Drinking is a gentleman's leisure-time activity, the more leisure, the more drinking," Constantine said on a sigh. "Your grandfather was a drunk, Kendall, but all he did was ruin his own constitution. And gambling is positively necessary to prove blue blood; losing was your father's only crime, Blaise. But robbery, rapine, and defiance of the king's law? Not many people have pirates and highwaymen in their background. I suppose I could weather it, but I don't know if I want to expend the effort. It's a good thing Lisabeth doesn't care about such things."

"Her family must have been knee deep in villainy," Kendall said, looking around to make sure the barmaid wasn't within hearing distance. "Wouldn't doubt it. The captain's a rare old rogue."

"Yes, but a crafty one," Constantine said. "He never was caught or convicted of anything, though I don't doubt he dabbled in those trades, and smuggling too. But in fact, Lisabeth's lineage is much cleaner than mine. Her father was a friend of my father's, and a loyal one, but he never was caught at a crime. He only chased women and was killed by a jealous husband. My father chased stagecoaches and was killed by a guard on the king's mail. But Lisabeth doesn't care. The reverse, in fact. I suspect she was drawn to me because as an inventive and lonely child she heard the stories, saw the damned portraits, and formed an imaginary attachment to my dashing ancestors."

"Uncanny," Kendall said. "You do have the look of them, you know. Almost funny, you being such a proper fellow."

"And," Constantine added, "she's had a unique upbringing."

Kendal and Blaise exchanged another look.

Constantine waved a hand. "Yes, it's an odd household, filled with retired villains. You get used to them. Now, since you two villains are hell-bent on helping me, here's how you can do it." He leaned forward. "Would it be too much to ask that you both show Miss W. some interest when we get back to town? At parties and such? Not enough to get you caught, but enough to bolster her confidence?"

"She won't want to catch me," Blaise said. "I'm a fortune hunter. Everyone knows that. But I am an ornament in Society. I'll do the pretty with her, if you like."

"She won't want me," Kendall said. "I'm too rough for the likes of her. But I'll butter her up one side and down the other, for you, Con."

Constantine smiled.

"Never approved the match," Kendall said as he drained his mug of ale. "Always thought you two were too alike. Ice meeting ice only freezes harder. You need a fire, someone to warm you up, Con, and that's a fact."

"Indeed? You say that with such emphasis. Have *you* an interest in my Lisabeth yourself, so soon?" Constantine asked him.

"Well, I would, if I could," Kendall said. "She's mighty good to look at, acts like a lady, and looks like a lass a man can talk to. You're a lucky fellow."

"And how do you want us to act toward Lisabeth?" Blaise asked.

"Hands off," Constantine said, and sketched a bow to their blossoming smiles.

They were alone at last, in the garden. Constantine's friends were in the house, playing a game of cards with the captain and Miss Lovelace. Lisabeth and Constantine said they were going out for a breath of air. No one at the card table so much as looked up. Miss Lovelace was cleaning out their pockets.

The garden was cool, and smelled of grass and night-blooming flowers. Constantine and Lisabeth didn't speak at first.

"I leave tomorrow," Constantine finally said.

She stopped and turned to him, eyes wide. "You never said."

"I didn't know. But we've entertained my friends royally this past week. I should have left days ago. I suppose I dragged my feet because I was loath to leave you, if only for a little while. This has all been like a dream of contentment. But it can't stay that way; I'm too tempted to wrong you again here. I have business to finish up in London. I must face it. I don't want to leave, but I have to go, for our sake."

She couldn't think what to say. She didn't have to. He took her in his arms and kissed her until she moaned. Or he did. Neither of them knew, but both cared. It ended the moment.

"I can't go on like this," Constantine said in frustration against her hair. "Your scent, your warmth, your laughter, all inspire me to hold you close. But I shouldn't, and neither should I meet you in secrecy. This is no hole-in-the-corner affair; I want you for my wife. It's best for us both that I'm going to London tomorrow. When we meet again, I'll be free. You'll come to London and we can see each other freely and openly. Then we'll only have to wait a week or two, for courtesy's sake, to announce our wedding plans."

"Courtesy?" she asked.

"To my former fiancée, and so as not to make it appear that we marry in haste."

She looked up at him. "But what if there's reason to move faster?"

There was a smuggler's moon; enough to see by, but with enough shadow to fuel imagination and conceal realities. Here, in the shadowed garden, Constantine looked more like the dashing man in the murky old portrait than he'd ever done. The scant, fluctuant moonlight showed up his dark winged brows, the planes of his cheekbones, and the sudden slash of his white smile, but she couldn't read his expression.

"You still don't know?" he asked.

She shook her head and lowered her gaze, embarrassed to talk about womanly functions and humiliated because she had to.

"Well," he said, "if there's reason for haste, then, of course, we'll go to the altar sooner. But we can't announce it any sooner lest too many people guess at the reason for a rushed wedding. I won't have any slurs on your name."

"Or yours," she whispered.

Now she did see his expression. He looked pained. He stepped back.

"Remember, whatever happens, you don't have to marry me," she said suddenly.

"Ah, fallen to Kendall's blandishments, have you?" he joked. "Or is it Blaise? I've never seen the two of them so smitten."

She grinned. "And they've never seen a lady who can ride out a sudden storm on a small skiff without swooning or casting up her accounts. Or one who could catch a bigger trout in a stream than they could, or bring it up with her own hands. And I'll wager they never met a lady who could race them down a beach and . . . almost win." Her smile faded. "Of course, they mightn't consider me a lady at all because of that . . . and other things."

She felt his hands close tight over hers. "I've told them nothing private about us," he said. "Nor will I. Not that it would matter. Do you know how many fine ladies have sudden weddings and premature babes? It's common. You're not. They admire you; there's the truth. Stop worrying. I'll leave in the morning and send for you as soon as I can. Then you'll meet the *ton*, and then after we marry it can be your choice how much time you wish to spend with them."

"How much time do you want to spend with

them?" she asked, aware that this was something they ought to have discussed long before this.

"That hardly matters," he said. "We don't have to live in each other's pockets."

She went still.

He dropped a kiss on her forehead, and moved into the darkness. "I'll see you in the morning," he said softly. "Good night, Lisabeth."

She stayed in the garden until the damp dew forced her inside. And then she stayed awake in her bed, watching the sickle moon fade into gray dawn.

This morning Constantine bowed over her hand.

This morning Constantine, Lord Wylde, was immaculate, cool, and calm. Nothing like the man she'd kissed last night, little like the man she'd made such passionate love to in the grass, infinitely far from the ghostly devil of a fellow in the dark portrait who had first seduced her.

Lisabeth realized that she herself was nothing like the woman who had kissed him last night either. She measured him with her eyes now, and not her heart. She'd decided, in the hours before dawn, that she might never go to London to see him. She'd realized that loving two men, one nonexistent, might be too much for one heart.

And if there were a child, she would have the raising of it, and he might never know.

She *wanted* to live in her husband's pocket. She wanted him to live in hers. She didn't want all the trappings of a society marriage. She wanted a friend, a companion, and a lover. He'd been that.

And yet, even now, when he was with his old friends, he reverted to his old ways. He became collected, stiff, and formal; a perfect, languid, mannered gentleman. London was filled with his kind. She didn't deceive herself any longer. Once returned to his native ground he would revert to what he'd been before he met her. That wasn't the man she'd fallen in love with. In fact, now she no longer knew who she'd made love to that rare day. She hadn't seen him again, and didn't know if she ever would.

One thing she'd resolved. She'd wait and see about many other things.

The drive in front of Sea Mews was filled this morning with bustling servants, and all the preparations for departing guests. Kendall was mounted on his horse, Blaise was on his, bending down to have a last word with her grandfather. There was a carriage for their valets and their luggage, but the gentlemen would ride before it, unless a heavy rain came down.

"One last word with you, alone?" she asked Constantine now.

His dark brows lowered. He looked around, took her hand, and they walked to a shady spot by the front door.

"Yes?" he asked her softly.

"Constantine," she said as softly, looking at her slippers, the coach, the sky, anywhere but at his face. "I've been thinking. I think it would be best if you didn't break off with your fiancée immediately. If it chances that we don't have to marry in haste . . . why don't we leave things as they are until we know? It won't be long until I do know. Why rush things?"

He stood straighter, his expression grew tight. "Because we are not talking about fertility, but decency. Not only did I deceive and dishonor my fiancée, but I dishonored you. I have to make matters right."

It was what she'd dreaded during her long vigil in the night. "I am *not* ruined," she said, glaring at him. "Maybe I would be in your circles, but the point is that I don't travel in those circles."

"You will," he said. "I made love to you. You

were an innocent. I was not. There's only one right thing to do, and believe me, I intend to do it. The question is not if I should but when I should." His voice gentled, his expression softened. "I rue it, but I know I'm a stick, a prude, and a puritan in some ways. Hypocritical ways, to be sure," he added, "like most men raised to be 'gentlemen.' But with you, I'm not. When I'm with you, I get a glimpse of what I might have been had I been able to choose what I would be. Don't send me back to the stocks, Lisabeth. I realize I was never comfortable there. I like who I am when I'm with you, and I want to be the man you thought I was. Except," he added, "please don't ask me to commandeer any sailing ships, or hold up any coaches. I know I'd make a mess of it."

She smiled.

He raised her hand, and kissed it again. "I have to go now. Write to me. I'll send to you, and then for you. Take good care of yourself, and please, for my sake, stay far from Henri, and the good customs officer, will you? Remember me."

He bowed to her, turned, strode to his waiting horse, and mounted it. He saluted her, and then, with Blaise and Kendall waving back at her, began to ride away.

She stood and watched him go. She couldn't

help the tears in her eyes, nor the fact that once he was gone the tears trailed down her cheeks.

"Ah, lass," her grandfather said as he came to her side, "don't despair. He's a man of his word."

"I know," she said.

"Then why are you blubbering?" he asked.

"Because of what he didn't say."

Her grandfather frowned. "He never said he wouldn't return, did he?" he growled.

She shook her head. "No." '

"Nor never said that he wouldn't marry you?"

"No," she said, as she wiped her cheeks with the back of her hand. "He's said all that's right and proper. But he never said that he loved me."

"Oh, well," her grandfather said. "But he's a gentleman."

"And not a liar," she said.

He didn't know what to say to that, so he only took her hand, and walked back to the house with her.

Chapter 16

Miss Winchester was delighted to see him. Constantine saw her smile as she took his hand.

"Back at last," she said with satisfaction, looking him up and down with approval. He'd dressed with care for this morning call, and could tell that his correct attire pleased her as much as his arrival.

"You remained longer than you'd said you would," she said, "but I expect that the business that was occupying you is finally done, and done to your satisfaction."

He bowed over her hand. Her welcoming smile made him feel terrible. They stood in her front parlor, alone together with not a chaperone or even a maid sitting stitching in a corner, because they were engaged to marry. He'd left the door open after he'd been shown in, because he knew that what he had to say would change things forever. He didn't know what he'd do if he found himself honor bound to marry two women.

"Now we can accept all the invitations that have been gathering in the front hall," she went on. "It's been vastly inconvenient telling people that you were called away on family matters. Now the only question is whether we ought to have a ball to celebrate our engagement, or go to all the fetes we've been invited to first. And Father reminded me: where shall we post the banns? At your church near your home seat, or the one near mine, or perhaps right here in London?"

She looked very well today, he thought. Dressed in ice blue, her hair pulled back, a cameo at her neck, she was a tall, slender, perfect figure of a lady of fashion. Her smile was cool, but it had never been warmer. He couldn't remember what her laughter sounded like; he didn't know if he'd ever heard it. He didn't know why he'd ever pro-posed marriage to her.

Whatever she was, she was a woman who had no patience with nonsense. He'd have to get straight to the point.

"We have to talk," he said seriously. "Things have changed. I went because of family matters, true. And now I think, from what I've discovered, that you may not wish to go forward with this marriage."

She blinked. "Indeed? Then won't you have a seat and we can discuss this? Or would you rather go to my father first?"

"What I have to say is to you," he said gravely. "I'd wish that you would keep it in confidence, if not from your father, of course, then from all oth-ers. That's all I ask of you, except for your forgive-ness. But I didn't know myself, until now. My uncle did, but he kept it from me."

She chose a chair by the window, and sat straight-backed. She motioned him to take the chair oppo-site her, and clasped her hands together. "Tell me," she said.

He did.

"I see," she said when he was done. "Your great-grandfather was then a notorious pirate?"

He bent his head and nodded.

"Then why have I not heard of him?"

He looked up at her. That hadn't occurred to him.

"You yourself had never heard of him," she went on, "so he cannot be that famous, can he?"

"He was," Constantine said carefully. "And still is in that part of the world."

She nodded. "But we are not in that part of the world. And your father was a highwayman who was killed while committing his crimes? But that too is unknown to me, as it was to you. I thank you for your candor, my lord. Your honesty and morality are well-known, and what I prize about you. But I cannot think any of this matters now. It was well concealed for all these years, and there is no reason to think it will not continue to be. I see no reason for us to change our plans, though I thank you for considering my feelings in the matter."

He repressed a shudder. She spoke of feelings and it seemed to him she had none. Why hadn't he seen that before? Or had he been so frozen himself that the slight upturning of her thin lips had seemed like a true smile to him before? He thought of the vibrancy and laughter of the woman he'd lately left, and realized how much he'd changed since he'd left Miss Winchester. Still, that wasn't her fault.

"Miss Winchester," he said carefully, "it's only a matter of time until such rich gossip leaks out. I found out because of the announcement in the newspaper; it awakened an old acquaintance of my father's to my continued existence. His interest was only curiosity," Constantine lied. Truth he would tell her. Just not all of it.

"Others have seen the announcement, or will," he added. "My ancestors left enemies as well as victims, who will doubtless be eager to seek revenge or repayment. And too," he added, looking down, because lying came hard to him, "there are many who believe bad blood will out." He thought a silent apology to his father, who had turned to crime only out of love and desperation, "And obviously, bad blood runs in my veins."

That got her attention. She rose, and went to the window. "My father will certainly think so," she said thoughtfully.

He breathed a sigh of relief, and rose to stand beside her. "And why shouldn't he?" he said. "So I come to you to apologize and ask you to free me of our bargain. I know I'll never find another like you, but I also know you deserve much better. Now, would you like to explain to your father? Or shall I?"

"I'll put the notice in the paper," she said absently. "No need to make you look like a jilt."

He felt terrible again. She was doing what he wanted, but so nobly that he felt like a low cur.

"Or have people asking why you decided not to marry me," she added. "That would give rise to all the wrong, unwarranted sort of speculation about me."

He felt much better.

"Of course," she added, "I shouldn't like being known as a jilt either. And it will reflect upon you, you know."

"I should think it will do wonders for your reputation, making you seem like the wise and discriminating female that you are," he said. "And I can take care of myself."

"But I suppose it's far better in the long run," she mused. "That is, should anyone ever discover the truth about you."

"Exactly," he said, bowing.

"We should not avoid each other in public after the news of our decision not to marry is known," she said. "Nor gossip about each other either. A simple statement that we saw we would not suit will do."

"Precisely," he said.

"And I shall tell Father. He will be angry that his investigations didn't find this, but relieved at my narrow escape. I thank you, Lord Wylde, and wish you the best in future. The announcement will be in the papers tomorrow. Good day."

He bowed, clapped on his high beaver hat, and strode out into the hall and then out the door, restraining himself from whistling like a boy. But once he strode a street away, he let himself grin, ear to ear.

"So she took it well?" Blaise asked.

"And with relief," Constantine said, stretching out his legs, and blowing a cloud of smoke from his cigarillo.

They sat in his study that night, swilling brandy and smoking.

"Bad blood indeed!" Kendall snorted into his goblet of brandy. "Horses and dogs can have bad blood, but not men. Men think, and can overcome it."

"Men *think* they can overcome it," Constantine said. "To tell the truth, I don't know. When I looked at the old portraits and then when I rode the waves, even in that stinking fishing smack, on that turbulent sea, I swear I felt something stirring in me."

"Seasickness," Kendall said.

"Idiot," Blaise told Kendall fondly. "Your blood stirring?" he asked Constantine mildly. "She caused that, you fool. Your Lisabeth would stir a dead man's blood."

Constantine said nothing. He was too busy remembering Lisabeth, especially those dazzling moments in the grass with her that he couldn't forget. He'd never made love in the sunshine before. He'd never felt such profound lust. She'd lain beneath him, her hair spread out like a shining corona behind her, her lovely face glowing with blushed color, her shining eyes on his as her lips parted for him. He'd felt the rise of her body against his, and realized that the man he'd thought himself to be could never have come to her as a lover. That had to have been the wild blood thundering in his veins, set free at last. It had both shocked and delighted him. If that was bad blood, he was glad of it. He'd felt alive as he'd never felt before. But since then, sometimes he wondered what else was lurking inside of him, just waiting to be set free.

"So when are you sending for her?" Blaise asked.

"After the announcement in the paper is old news," Constantine said, called back to reality. "After the gossip about my aborted wedding with Miss Winchester has died down. Let's give the *ton* a chance to chew over something else for a while first. I don't doubt Miss Winchester will be engaged to another lucky fellow soon. Something about one man wanting her and then being thrown over by her will make her more desirable to all men."

"You've become a philosopher," Kendall muttered.

"I don't know what I've become," Constantine said truthfully. "I do know I don't want Lisabeth embarrassed. And I dislike getting up at dawn to fight fools in the morning mists. I'm sure you two wouldn't want to be rousted up that early in order to be my seconds either. There's bound to be some unwise words said and overheard after a thing like this. Those words are usually said by a drunk or a fool, and that means man to man."

Blaise laughed. "Whatever you've become, you've become more clever, Con."

Constantine sketched a bow from his chair. "Speaking of clever, I can fight men, but women are cleverer than we are; they deliver cuts so sharp they aren't seen until they're bleeding. Why should Lisabeth be victim to that? Or just imagine if her grandfather heard of it and responded in his own inimitable fashion? Now *that* would be a tragedy. I'm going to let things calm down. Then Lisabeth can safely come to London at last."

"I'd think you'd be longing to see her, come what may," Kendall said.

So had Constantine. But now he felt infinitely tired. Much had happened. He'd changed; his world had changed. He couldn't quite believe what he'd done, or know what he wanted to do next.

Of course he wanted to see her. He wanted to hold her in his arms, hear her laughter as well as her sighs of pleasure; have her to himself once again. He'd thought of little else—except for the future, and the consequences of doing what he wanted.

Could he live in London with Lisabeth? Would she even like the life that he led or the life she'd be expected to lead? She was an original, a rare handful; the prize of her grandfather's eye and doted upon by all the people in her little village. But it was only a little village. Could she cope outside of it? Would she care to? She'd surely miss her home. Could they live on his estate, or near her grandfather, instead? Would he feel cheated of all he'd previously enjoyed? If so, could they live apart for part of the year?

Miss Winchester had never expected more of him. He'd seen Lisabeth's expression when he'd mentioned it, and knew she would.

There were a great many things to sort out. As much as he longed for Lisabeth, he also needed time to see his way clear again. She'd enchanted him. But the increasing miles and living in London town again had woken him from that enchantment. What he'd done with her had been glorious, but the intensity of his reaction to her had shocked him. It had perhaps even alarmed him. He didn't know the man who had made such passionate love. Or did he?

He was, indeed, a new man. He had to learn how to live as one. And so he needed his wits together now. One foolish commitment to a life with a stranger had been ended. He needed some repose in order to plan before he took up life with another. But how much of what he'd felt for Lisabeth was raging lust and how much was love? Or were they the same? He'd never really experienced either.

Whatever his real feelings, there were two

things he knew. He knew he had to marry Lisabeth. And he knew he wanted to make love to her again. He just didn't know if their marrying was wise, sane, or sensible, for him or for her. And he'd always been sane and sensible.

"I long to see her," Constantine said honestly. "But I want things to go easily for her and for me when I do."

Kendall exchanged a look with Blaise.

"Bloom off the rose?" Kendall asked.

"Does distance lend disenchantment?" Blaise queried.

"Fools," Constantine said amiably, as he closed his eyes and laid his head back on the back of his chair. "A thing this important needs time and careful consideration. I have time for both now."

"Another letter from Lord Wylde?" Miss Lovelace asked.

"Yes," Lisabeth said.

"Lord, the man uses up paper. So, when are we leaving to meet him?"

"As soon as we choose," Lisabeth said, folding her letter again, and again.

Miss Lovelace clapped her hands together. "It's about time! It's been weeks. Why hasn't he sent for us before this? It's not just me prying. Your grandfather's started to boil about it. You know what that means."

"I do," Lisabeth said. "Constantine just wanted to be sure I'd be safe from spite and gossip. He hasn't changed his mind."

"No, dearie, that's true. But he ought to have been clamoring for you to join him. Three weeks, it's been." Miss Lovelace looked around the small salon, making sure no one was dusting, sweeping, or lingering nearby. "Have you told him yet?"

"It's not a thing to put in a letter, so no," Lisabeth said.

"Has he asked?"

"Constantine is very proper. He wouldn't," Lisabeth said in sadder tones.

"He should be dying to know. I dislike this, luv, I really, truly do."

"No need," Lisabeth said. "He's sent for me. He hasn't forgotten."

"He'd better not," Miss Lovelace muttered. "Or nobleman or not, your grandfather would have his bollocks hanging on his belt."

"Lovey! That's a terrible thing to say!" Lisabeth ruined her expression of disapproval with a giggle. "But Grandy would, wouldn't he?"

"Aye. It's pride and worry about you that would have him haring off to London armed to the teeth if your grand lord ever left you here to face things alone."

"There's nothing to face, and I'm never alone. Lovey?" Lisabeth asked softly, "what shall I do when I do go to see him?"

"What do you mean?" Miss Lovelace said, frowning.

"Well, the thing of it is—I'm no longer sure I should marry him."

Miss Lovelace stood dumbstruck.

"What?" roared the captain as he strode into the room. "What's this you say? Not marry him? Have you run mad?"

"You've been eavesdropping," Lisabeth said.

"Of course! How else will I learn anything round here, what with everyone being so ladylike and fancy all of a sudden. What's this you say? Not marry him?"

"I've been thinking," Lisabeth said. "Hard. You said I didn't have to marry if I didn't want to, but when you said that, I was sure I wanted to. Now? I don't know. Constantine was everything I ever dreamed about." She sighed thinking of him. But now, though she could never forget how they'd made love in the sunshine, that glorious incident was fading from her memory, becoming indistinct, like some wonderful erotic dream she'd had about his ancestors in the deep of the night. None of it seemed real to her anymore.

"He was smart and worldly, clever and kind," she said. "And yes, very like Captain Cunning in his looks, and like his bold father too. But he was prim and proper, and that was amazing to me since I'd never met anyone like him before."

"He warmed up fast enough," the captain growled.

"So he did," Lisabeth said. "But see, I don't know now which man was the real Lord Wylde and which the one I wanted him to be. There's a big difference. I'm not cut out to be a Society lady, Grandy."

Her grandfather and her old governess looked at her, standing in the sunlight that was coming through the windows. She wore a bright peach-colored gown, and she glowed, from head to toe. It was only her expression that was sad.

"I've read about the *ton* in the newspapers and periodicals. Miss Lovelace told me about them too. The gentlemen are charming. Look at Lord Blaise, and Lord Kendall. They're different in many ways from each other and from Constantine, but there are similarities."

"Aye! The very thing," Miss Lovelace cried. "They both were smitten by you, and I think you could have either of them if you wanted."

"I don't, Lovey," Lisabeth said. "If I wanted any gentleman, it would be Constantine. The point is that their expectations of a wife are the same, I think. But I don't want to go to parties and balls every night. I don't want a husband who needs a separate bedchamber, or who goes out every night never saying when he'll return; one who expects to live a separate life from his wife. I'd kill a husband who took a mistress, and I hear it's all the thing in circles of the *ton*. In short, I'll never marry where my heart doesn't lead me."

"It led you into enough already," her grandfather muttered. "Time to let your brain do some work."

"It has, it is, that's why I'm no longer sure." She looked at him imploringly. "How can I be sure?"

He scowled.

Miss Lovelace frowned.

"Can never be sure," her grandfather grumbled. "Can be married twenty years and still sometimes wonder if you acted too fast, and if you acted aright. I loved your grandmother, God alone knows, even though we bellowed at each other most of the time. She was the one for me. But still,

I'll tell you, when the wind blew in from the east sometimes, all perfumy, I remembered . . . Never mind what. What I'm saying is that you can never be sure. You just go where your heart tells you, I suppose."

"Well," Miss Lovelace said, "there are ways, little tests. Not that I'm qualified for giving such advice, for I never loved again, not after . . . well, that makes no matter. What I would do, love, is bring up the subject your grand lord is too prim to write about, and you're too afraid to put in a letter. Then watch his face carefully. If he's relieved, then you know there might be something wrong. If he looks sad, then you know he loves you truer than you do him. After, it's up to you to decide what to do."

"And if you don't want Lord Wylde," Miss Lovelace said, "you'll be in the perfect place not to want him. We'll stay in a fine hotel, you'll have new stylish gowns, and you can finally wear all your jewels and meet fascinating new men."

"Aye," her grandfather interrupted, "you have a fortune of jewels to wear in your hair, on your neck, round your waist. They've been sitting in trunks too long. Some of them are from princesses and queens, that's sure. And don't worry, no one's going to ask for them back, because they've been in the family for generations."

"So if you decide Lord Wylde's not for you," Miss Lovelace said, "you can pick and choose from all the gents in London town."

"And if I don't want any of them?" Lisabeth asked sadly.

"Then any lad from hereabouts," her grandfather said. "It's time, don't you think, my girl?"

"I do," she said, sighing.

"And don't worry," her grandfather said, "I'd never push you to anything. Fact is, I don't know what I'd do without you here."

"I see," Lisabeth said, her hands on her hips. "Then why did you go get Lord Wylde to come here in the first place?"

The captain's face turned ruddy. "Never said I'd be averse to grandchildren," he said.

She laughed, stood on her tiptoes, and kissed his cheek. "Whatever else I do," she said, smiling, "I'll try to give you those."

"Aye, grandchildren," he repeated, "whose mother's got a wedding ring on her finger, mind."

Chapter 17

The gentlemen were eyeing her. They were two exquisites, paragons of fashion and credits to their valets and tailors. One actually held up his quizzing glass to study her, the other simply goggled. Lisabeth looked straight ahead.

"If they don't stop that, I'll go over with a few choice words," Miss Lovelace told her. "It's a pity your grandfather isn't here."

They were sitting in the lobby of a fine hotel in the center of London, waiting for Lord Wylde. Lisabeth was dressed in the most elegant clothes she'd ever worn. Her village might not be a patch on London; in fact, she realized her entire village, ancient church included, would probably fit snugly on two, maybe three, if you included the village green, of London's long streets. But the seamstress at home was a French émigrée, and Lisabeth believed there was no finer dressmaker in the world.

She wore a dashing new dark crimson walking dress, with a tiny fetching little mockery of a hat tilted on her high dressed hair, a gold shawl over her shoulders, new half boots, and an antique gold chain and locket at her throat. She was ready for London.

London seemed to think so too.

Lisabeth spoke through tightened lips as she avoided the eyes of the impertinent gentlemen. "Do they think I'm a tart?"

"With a chaperone sitting next to you who looks as tough and tight as an overcooked duck?" Miss Lovelace asked, fingering the white starched lace collar of her simple black walking dress. "I didn't want to look like a madam, that's why I put on this terrible thing. But maybe that's the style now for a Covent Garden abbess. What do I know? I've been away from the trade a long time. In my day, procurers overdressed to get attention. Maybe now they underplay it. Any rate, I'll wager they're ogling you because you're beautiful, you're new, they don't know me, or you, and so they don't worry about who your father or your husband or your protector is. If they did, they'd slink away. Shall I tell them?"

"No, pay them no attention," Lisabeth said. "When Lord Wylde gets here, he'll deal with them."

But Constantine didn't. He came through the door of the hotel, glanced around, saw Lisabeth and came straight to her. The two gentlemen saw that, and left, promptly.

Lisabeth had eyes only for Constantine as she rose to her feet. If possible, he looked even more elegant than she'd remembered. His dark hair was brushed back; he wore a dark blue jacket, dun breeches, his linen was dazzling, his boots shone, his only ornament was the gold fob at his ruby-colored waistcoat. And his smile outshone all else.

The gentlemen she'd seen coming and going in the hotel this morning all seemed overly pomaded and overdressed by comparison. Lisabeth was delighted, proud, and a little frightened of Constantine. Again, she wondered if she knew this man, even considering all she'd shared with him.

He took her hand in his gloved one. "Lisabeth," he said, "welcome."

She looked into his eyes. He seemed sincere.

"This is no place to talk," he said, looking around. "And it would cause talk if I went to your room. Certainly even more if you came to my house right now."

Lisabeth's spirits fell. If they were soon to be officially engaged, what did it matter? It only would matter if he had something to say that he couldn't put in a letter. He'd asked her to London, and never said more. Had she misjudged him? Might she have gotten it the wrong way round? Could it be that he was too much the gentleman to end their relationship from a long distance?

"Good afternoon, Miss Lovelace," he said, when he finally noticed the aged governess beaming at him. "Forgive me for not greeting you at once. Would you mind if we took a walk before luncheon? There's a lovely park nearby, just down the street. The weather is clear, for now, and that way Lisabeth and I can have some privacy."

"Aye, nothing is too far for young bones," Miss Lovelace said sadly, putting a hand to her back. "But I'm not as young as I used to be."

"I'd send for my own carriage but there's a line of hacks for hire out front. That's faster," he said. "We'll take an open carriage, and when we get to

284

the park we can find you a bench in the sun. Does that suit you?"

Miss Lovelace smiled. Lisabeth hid her own smile, as well as her exasperation. Lovey could walk the legs off a woman half her age if there was gossip waiting at the end of the road. She just wanted to be able to hear everything that was said.

They began to walk out of the hotel, but were stopped by the sight of a gentleman coming in through the door. He was an older man, with a wrinkled face and bright blue eyes, and he was correctly, if soberly, dressed in black. He carried a fine ebony silver-headed walking stick, and swung it as he walked jauntily toward them.

"No!" Lisabeth gasped. "Grandy! You look . . . well, grand!"

"Had better," her grandfather said, stroking his smooth chin. "Had me a shave from the best London barber this morning. And a haircut, by God. Though there was more to take off on my chin. Got myself dressed to the nines too. I decided to surprise you. Well, now that I don't have to threaten anyone anymore, I can play at being one of the nobs."

Lisabeth blushed. Her grandfather seemed oblivious to his implied insult to her and to Constantine.

So did Constantine. "You look very much the thing, sir," he said. "You wouldn't frighten anyone. Not that you ever had to, or did," he added, smiling. "Now, what we can do is go to luncheon. The hotel sets a fine table. Would you care to join us?"

As the captain and Miss Lovelace eagerly agreed, Constantine bent his head and whispered to Lisabeth, "We can talk later," he said. "We must."

They had a superior luncheon. At least, Lisabeth thought so. The food was delicious, though she hardly tasted it. She feasted her eyes, instead, on Constantine, and she was filled with happiness.

They were eyed by other diners, but never stared at. Constantine nodded to a few acquaintances. He and his guests laughed and spoke of many things, but nothing remotely to do with an upcoming wedding, a canceled engagement, or plans beyond the next day.

"I thought to take Lisabeth to the theater tomorrow night," Constantine said at the end of the meal. "Should you like that, Lisabeth?"

"Yes," she breathed.

He looked at the other two at the table. "Should you care to come with us?"

"I have to," Miss Lovelace said repressively.

"I would," the captain said. "Haven't seen a good knockabout farce in a long time."

"It's a production of *Hamlet*," Constantine said.

"Good, I can get some sleep," the captain said. "But there's always a farce before or after, am I right?"

"You are," Constantine agreed. He took a deep breath, and then leaned forward, and spoke, low. "But before that, Captain, what I'd really like is a chance to speak with your granddaughter, alone. How can we do that? It's a mild afternoon; the sun's still bright. I was thinking that if we all went to the park, you and Miss Lovelace could keep us in sight, but Lisabeth and I might be able to speak freely for the first time in a long while."

"Well and good," the captain said, putting both hands on the table, so he could rise.

They were getting up when a bright-eyed gentleman with lacquered hair and a curling smile, dressed in the height of fashion, or maybe a bit above it, stopped by their table.

"Lord Wylde," he said with a bow. "Well met. How are you this fine day? And please," he said with a hand to his heart. "Can you introduce me to these two devastatingly attractive ladies, before I *positively* expire? *Everyone* at my table," he added, shrugging one padded shoulder over to a table of gaping gentlemen, "keeps asking who they are. Could you, would you, please enlighten me?"

"Sir Carroll," Constantine said smoothly, "allow me to introduce an old friend of the family: Captain Bigod; his lovely granddaughter, Lisabeth; and her charming companion, Miss Lovelace. They're here visiting London, and I'm showing them the sights. Captain, Lisabeth, Miss Lovelace, allow me to present Sir Carroll, who will perish if he doesn't know everything that's going on in town."

Everyone murmured greetings, Lisabeth dipped her head in a sketch of a bow. But her heart was troubled. She was being introduced only as an old friend visiting the city? She didn't look at her grandfather; she didn't want to see what expression he wore. She could swear she felt the vibrations of his growl.

In a few minutes, the foppish Sir Carroll bowed himself away and went back to his table to enlighten the men waiting for him.

"He's the biggest gossip in England," Constantine explained as they walked to the door. "I didn't want him announcing our engagement before we do."

"Oh, well then, aye," the captain said, sounding mollified.

Lisabeth said nothing. She really did have to talk to Constantine, and alone, whether it was here or in the park, or in a closet, and before much more time went by.

They took a hack to the park, and true to his word, Constantine parked the captain and Miss Lovelace on a bench, took Lisabeth's arm, and strolled away with her. They walked round and round an ornamental fountain, always in plain sight of their chaperones. It was a mild late summer's day, and the park was crowded. The only privacy they had was when they made the turn around the fountain until they were exactly opposite her grandfather and Miss Lovelace. Then the water spouting from the stone dolphins playing around a marble Neptune provided a curtain of mist and spray, and hid them from sight. But even then, they weren't completely alone. There were children frolicking around the fountain, trying to sail boats, or dip their fingers into the water, their busy nurses and nannies running after them.

"I'm free now," was the first thing Constantine said to her.

Lisabeth looked up at him. He didn't seem elated, or sad. He was just reporting the fact to her.

"Was she angry? Were her feelings hurt?" she asked.

"Not in the least. As I thought, when I told her about my ancestors, that did it. Miss Winchester's very proud of her family and her position in Society. She was glad to be rid of me and my bad blood. At least, once I dropped a few bad names, she agreed at once and I didn't see a hint of regret in her eyes. The notice of the end of engagement has already appeared in the paper, no excuses given. It's her right to announce it that way, and she did. I'm surprised your grandfather didn't show it to you. I wouldn't have sent for you if it hadn't already appeared."

"I suppose he wouldn't have come here if he hadn't seen it either," Lisabeth said. Her grandfather always had at least one card up his sleeve. He must have had his reasons for not wanting her to know about it before she saw Constantine.

"And so now I can take you around London, and then," he said on a slight smile, "we can announce our engagement when we wish." He paused a moment, and looking into her eyes with an unreadable expression in his own, he added, "That is, if we have the time for 'then.' Otherwise, we can do it immediately, though I'd prefer to have a space of time between ending one engagement and announcing another. And it would be better if we had some time between the announcement and the

wedding. There'd be less gossip that way. I suppose
we can delay another month, but that's the limit.
We won't be the first to marry with cause," he murmured. "There'll be people counting on their fingers, but let them. Needs must when the devil
drives."

He was so cool, so calm, so unimpassioned. She
wanted to kick him. She wanted to shake him. This
languid, proper, so correct gentleman was not the
man she'd fallen in love with. Was it the London air
that changed him? Was it that he'd come to his
senses? Or had she entirely lost hers that day when
she'd lain with him? Lovey was always saying that
the older a woman got, the more lust began to look
like love, and that a spinster's excuses for lovemaking grew with every birthday that came to her. She
hoped that wasn't true of herself, but began to wonder. He was still as handsome. But it turned out
that he was still as heartless as he'd seemed when
she'd first met him.

He'd as much as asked her if she was with
child—his child. She wanted to shout: "You're free,
damn you!" and then leave him standing there. But
she had loved him, and she hated to give up on
him as easily as she'd given herself to him. She
reined in her temper and concealed her disappointment. She counted to ten. She might not want to

marry him anymore, but she deserved something, if only ten seconds' revenge, for all her trouble.

Ten reached, she hesitated, opened her lips, and then remembered Miss Lovelace's sage advice. So Lisabeth kept her eyes on his as she assembled her thoughts.

He looked apprehensive.

She was delighted. But nothing good lasts forever, she thought, and she sighed. "I'm free too," she said. "There are no lasting consequences resulting from our . . . meeting."

She watched him closely and saw the vast relief wash over him. He smiled, and visibly relaxed. Now she wanted to push him into the fountain. She clenched her fists and waited to hear what he'd say. *Then*, she decided, she'd push him into the fountain.

"That's as well," he said, nodding. "Now there'll be no gossip. No one can challenge our association, and in time, we can announce our engagement and there'll be no undue talk."

She stared at him, resolved now to end it. She wondered how he'd feel when she told him that not only the idea of her being pregnant was over, so was their plan for marriage. Would she see disappointment or more relief in his eyes? Her own heart felt sore.

"I confess," he added softly, his gaze on the toddlers playing at the fountain's edge, "that I feel a bit cheated. You know? After a while, the idea of our child became very attractive to me. I began thinking of names, and wondering if he'd be lucky enough to look like you. Well, that will be another day. For now, we have time and leisure to do things right, and our wedding won't be a scrambling, embarrassing affair. You deserve so much better. And Lisabeth? When in God's name am I going to have you alone for a few minutes, to be able to kiss you again?"

She stared at him. And then she laughed. In that one moment, she'd caught a glimpse of the man she'd fallen in love with. "We'll find the time. After all, as you said, now we have it. And surely," she added with a grin, "an experienced man about town like you should be able to find a way for us to be alone."

"I wish I were that," he said fervently, taking her hand. "I led a misspent youth trying to be as trustworthy and moral as my uncle decreed. I succeeded, too well." He looked down at her with entreaty. "Help me find myself again, will you, Lisabeth?"

She tried to see his expression, but couldn't make it out because his image kept shimmering as her eyes filled with unshed tears of joy. He made a sound of exasperation, pulled her to himself, dipped his head and kissed her.

"What's this?" the captain roared from across the fountain. "I can't see clear because of the damned water, but it looks like . . . what's he up to now?"

"Hush," Miss Lovelace said comfortably. "It's naught but a kiss. Sealing their bargain, I believe."

"What's to do with that girl?" he asked, sinking to the bench again. "One minute she's going to renounce him, the next she's snuggling with him in public."

"She's in love," Miss Lovelace said. "Poor, fortunate girl."

Later that night, in Lisabeth's room, as she was brushing out her hair before going to bed, and smiling as she did so, Miss Lovelace came in to talk to her.

"He passed the test, did he?" Miss Lovelace asked. "Or was it just that you can't resist him? No harm in that!" she added quickly. "Though if that's so, it would be better if you never told the captain that's why you made up your mind to marry the fellow."

"Oh, Lovey." Lisabeth sighed. "He passed, and for all the right reasons! He was glad that I wasn't having his child, and you were right, I could read the relief in his eyes. But you were wrong too. It was only because he didn't want people to gossip about us, and thought I deserved less of a scrambling sort of wedding. But you know?" she asked in wonderment. "He was genuinely sad because of it too. He said he'd begun to daydream about our baby, and had got quite used to the idea. Then, when I said *I* wasn't sure I wanted to marry him— he kissed me. In public. He forgot everything but how much he wanted me. Isn't that wonderful?"

"It is," Miss Lovelace said. "But I'm surprised. I'm usually always right about men. I can't understand it. This means I'll have to think about my test some more. I didn't know there'd be any loopholes in it."

"There was," Lisabeth said. "Lucky me. Imagine. The great Lord Constantine Wylde, that paragon of propriety, kissing me right there and then, in the sunlight, in the heart of London town, without a care for whoever might see us."

"Tosh!" Miss Lovelace said. "Who was there to see but for some infants and nurses, and your grandfather and me? And we could only see outlines through a veil of water. What are you worried about? Why shouldn't he have been bold enough to kiss you in public? Squirrels and pigeons don't gossip. And no one else was there to see."

But again that day, though she didn't know it yet, Miss Lovelace was wrong.

Chapter 18

He got her alone in the shadows at the side of the theater as they were leaving it. They kissed, and then, as Lisabeth leaned into his arms, reveling in the warmth and heat of him, Constantine drew back.

"No, we can't," he said.

"Why?" she asked him in confusion, as she stood alone, suddenly chilled.

"Because we must kiss and run," Constantine whispered angrily. "We have to go now because it's not yet time to announce our intentions, and I will not shame you."

They'd sat in a box to the side of the stage, some of the best seats in the place, as Miss Lovelace had exclaimed with delight. "You can see the line where the makeup on the actors' faces doesn't match their necks," she'd added with great satisfaction.

Lisabeth couldn't. She'd turned her gaze to her right side, and watched Constantine more than the play all through the evening, wondering at the hard, handsome attractiveness of his face in the shadows, lit by wayward torchlight from the footlights that flickered at the foot of the stage. He looked so like his portrait—his father's and his grandfather's portraits, she corrected herself—that she vowed her first wedding gift to him would be to have his portrait painted to hang beside them in their home.

She missed most of *Hamlet* wondering where that home would be.

When the farce was presented, she reveled in Constantine's laughter more than anything going forth on stage. She'd been smitten, bitten, magicked by him: she knew that. And she didn't care.

So when he'd drawn her away from where the waiting carriages were lined up in front of the theater, because they'd lost sight of her grandfather and Miss Lovelace in the crush of exiting theatergoers, and he'd taken advantage of the moment to kiss her again, she lost all sense of time and place. She just wanted to stay in his arms.

"Tomorrow," he'd said to her when he left her off at her hotel.

But the next evening they'd seen Kendall and Blaise again and had had an uproarious dinner with them at a renowned restaurant. Constantine had no chance to get Lisabeth alone for so much as a private word with her.

The week wore on, and if it wasn't that they were out in the broad daylight in company, it was that they weren't left alone again by day or night. The captain and Miss Lovelace seemed to be taking their chaperone duties very seriously during their stay in London.

"Why?" Lisabeth had finally demanded one night as she paced her room before going to bed. "We are getting married soon, you know."

"No, we don't," Miss Lovelace had said blandly. "Not I. And not the captain. When's this wedding to be? Where was it announced? Where is it to be? Aha!" she'd said triumphantly. "You don't know yourself. So there's to be not so much as another stolen kiss until you do."

She fanned her face with her hand. "Thought we couldn't see it, did you? Ha. That would be the day. But we allowed it because then we thought you'd come to us full of plans for the wedding. You didn't. You were almost filled with something else before we came to London, and that won't happen again! Almost died of the pip when we thought you were with child, didn't we? Yes, you could have gone it alone, and your grandfather, God bless him, would have stood beside you through it all, and so would I, but we don't want to have that again. If you do have a babe, and I pray you do in time, it's to be legitimate, and that's that."

She shook a finger at Lisabeth. "Your lord may have wild blood in him, but you don't, remember that, missy. Get a time and a day, and a notice in good black ink for the world to see, and you can canoodle with him much as you like, we say."

"We?" Lisabeth asked.

"Your grandfather mightn't like to scold you, but he threatened to toss me overboard if I let you out of my sight for more than two minutes together. But you should know better, my love. What's happened to you? You're flightier than the parson's pointer in heat. Use your head, love, not your heart or other intimate parts. Get a ring, and a date, and then do whatever you want. It's not as though I like playing watchman," she added with a sniff.

"Have I been that bad?" Lisabeth whispered.

"Yes," Miss Lovelace said.

"I'm sorry. You're right. It's just that seeing him again, being so near to him and yet always having to stay so far, is just about killing me," Lisabeth said, sinking to sit on her bed. "I never knew I had such hot blood! I *am* acting like a fool. Well, no more of that. He'll get not so much as a kiss on the cheek from me until we settle matters.

"Because, in truth, Lovey," Lisabeth admitted shamefacedly, "I never asked him how long he expects us to keep company before we make the announcement, and that's just stupid. It's been a week. What does he want? A month? Two? Three? He's never said a word, no more than I have." She made a face. "If he's not ready, then I'll go home with you, and come back when he thinks the time is right. Because," she said sadly, "I don't think I could hold out for that long, and it's just foolish to expose myself to such temptation. Like keeping a fish on a plate on the table and telling the cat not to touch it." She grinned.

Miss Lovelace didn't. "You're not a cat," she said. "You used to be a sensible chit. I don't want to wound you, you know I never would. But you have to find out if he's even sincere. It's all very well for a gent to protest his love. After a while, he has to prove it. You think about how well you know him, and *then* you speak to him. Because your grandfather and I have noted that though he's charming, he's not the same man he was when he was staying with us. He's more distant, even when he's smiling. In fact, he seems to have starch in his soul now, and that's a fact."

Lisabeth nodded. It was true. Oh, he'd been merry with his old friends, but he didn't introduce her to new ones. He said it was because it was too soon after his breakup with Miss Winchester. But Lisabeth wondered. He was a different man now, and not one she wanted as a husband, until he kissed her. Then her wits went flying. After Miss Lovelace left the room, Lisabeth sat in her bed with her chin on her bended knees, pondering.

It was better to go home now and wait for him to send for her when he thought the coast was clear. She didn't understand his world, and didn't know when that could be, or if she'd want to live in his world, that is, once some time went by. He too might be having second thoughts. She'd made a mistake, a terrible one in his world, too common a one in her own. She'd been brought up to love freely and without stint, once she knew her love. But she hadn't really known him, had she? Maybe that's why Society insisted on virginity for females of breeding—so they wouldn't start breeding the second a girl saw a handsome face, Lisabeth thought, with no humor at all for her play on words, as she hid her face in her hands.

Tomorrow, she vowed, she'd talk to him. The next day, she'd go home. She'd leave the next move to Constantine, and if he never made it, she wouldn't be surprised. Devastated, yes. But not surprised.

She laid her head down on the pillow at last, and started when she heard a light tapping on her door. Her maid was sleeping. Everyone in the hotel must be sleeping, it was very late. She sat straight up. Could it be Constantine? Had he thought of some daring, dashing way to finally get her alone? She was both thrilled and terrified. If it was he, how could she resist him? It was such a bold thing, the sort of action a buccaneer or a highwayman might take.

She slipped out of bed, slipped on a dressing gown because there was only so much daring she could cope with, and cracked open the door. Her smile slipped too.

"Grandy!" she said. Her eyes flew wide. "What is it? Are you ill? Do you need a doctor?"

"Hush," he said as he came in the door. "Want to wake the world? No, I'm in fine tucker. I just couldn't sleep. I had to talk to you."

She closed the door behind him and smiled. "No, how could you sleep? You're dressed for a walk in the park." He was fully dressed, and even carried his new jaunty cane in his hand.

"Couldn't creep down the hall in the altogether, could I?" he growled. "Be enough to give the maids fits."

They both snickered.

"Sit down," she said, gesturing to a chair by the window. "I'm happy to see you any time. What troubles you?"

"I talked to Miss Lovelace," he said as he sat, and motioned her to sit nearby.

She pulled up the footstool that was by her dressing table, and sat beside him.

"And she told me she'd lectured you, which is all good and proper," he said, frowning. "But she didn't tell all, because she couldn't. There are things that for all her experience, she don't know." He looked at Lisabeth and sighed. "It's my own fault. I brought you up with stories of the good old times, filled your head with nonsense about pirates and highwaymen. Very romantic, they were, or at least so I described them, I see it now. But you took me too much to heart. And I forgot I was speaking to a girl who had never seen a real pirate or a real highwayman, never lived in the age when they was feared by all citizens, good and bad alike. And then there were those damned portraits to fire your imagination.

"Lisabeth," he said soberly, "pirates were lice-ridden, selfish pigs, they was. Outcasts of the land, and dogs of the sea. They killed, raped, murdered for nothing but money, and half the time, just for fun, for few of them could find enjoyment in much else but drinking. They couldn't read nor write, nor reason right neither. They had no respect for anything, nor fear of death, because I reckon they decided nothing could be worse than the lives they led. Sewage, they were, the filth of the land run off into the sea. Bad cess to them all. I'm glad their numbers are dwindling, for I make my living from importing and exporting, and I'd be ruined if they still ruled the seas.

"Oh, there be a few left, but they mostly plunder now in the New World, since we've gotten so fierce with them. They went with the old century, most of the greatest, or worst, of them. I met Captain Cunning the once, when I was just a lad. He had manners and charm, aye, that he did. But I daresay he was no better than any of them, only smarter, and meaner, which is the only way a pirate could take command of a ship."

Lisabeth listened, eyes wide. She'd never heard her grandfather talk so cruelly about any man.

"And highwaymen?" he asked. "Your lord's father was a bad one, by which I don't mean that he was cruel or wicked. I only mean to say he wasn't cruel nor wicked enough. He was no true highwayman. A true highwayman would shoot before he thought, and kill without blinking. Poor fellow was killed on his first venture out, wasn't he? He was trying to get money to set up a home for his wife and child. It was the wrong thing for him to do, on all counts. I knew him and I liked him, and he didn't have an ounce of slyness in him. Nor good sense. I offered him money, but he, and my fool of a son, decided to go out and get their own, God rest their foolish souls."

He fixed Lisabeth with a sad look. "I don't blame you for falling for Lord Wylde, darlin', I don't. He's smart and handsome enough, and he knows his way around a woman, but I don't think that's what turned the trick for you. I think it was because you thought he was like his great-grandfather and his father. It's a good thing he's not. He's not a fool or a monster, not he."

"He still isn't," she said.

"Maybe," her grandfather said on a shrug, "but he isn't who you thought he was, is he? He was different when he was with us at Sea Mews, wasn't he?"

She nodded.

"Want to know why?"

"I do, Grandy," she said with feeling. "I really do. Do you know?"

He shook his head. "I think so. He was shocked when I told him about his father, and then he was fascinated by tales about his wicked great-grandfather when he came to us. That made him act different, I think, like he was trying on their lives to see if they fit. But believe me, I can see that now he's back in his own waters, he's himself again."

She hung her head. "Yes," she whispered. "That's the problem. He seems to be."

"Aye," her grandfather said, sighing. "Now you have to think. He *is* an honorable man, and he'll marry you if he thinks he has to. But that don't mean he's the right one for you. Can you fit into his tight little world? And does he really want you to?"

"I don't know," she said. "But I mean to find out. And if I must, can we leave for home as soon as may be? Because I'd rather be without him than sitting at a table with him, and still be without him—or at least, without the man I came to London to find. Can you understand that?"

He rose to his feet slowly, like a very old man. "Aye, my love, I can," he said. "We'll leave the minute you say you want to."

"I'll tell you tomorrow," she said. "I can't take this much longer. But you and Lovey have to leave us alone for a few minutes. I promise I won't fall into his clutches, or he, into mine," she added with a crooked smile. "If we kiss, it will either be: 'hello, there you are at last,' or 'good-bye.' But we really have to talk, alone."

"Consider it done," he said, "watch for the moment."

They were going for a drive around the city the next day, with a stop to see Elgin's marbles, Constantine had said. Lisabeth dressed in a new russet walking dress, topped by a fine bonnet to shade her face and eyes if the sun was too strong. She had a shawl to wear if the weather changed, which it often did at the turning of the season. She also carried a parasol covered by an oilskin, in case they took an open carriage and it rained suddenly. She was prepared for whatever happened. But she didn't know how she could find a way to get Constantine alone so she could talk with him.

Still, after she'd dressed she found she had an hour to think and plan before she was to meet him in the hotel lobby. She was sitting by the window, plotting, when her maid went to answer a tap at the door.

"A Miss Winchester to see you, miss," her maid said.

Lisabeth shot to her feet. "Show her in," she said. She remembered the name, and wished she could say no. But she had to see the lady and hear why she had come here, and what she had to say. For the life of her, she couldn't understand why a woman who didn't want a man because of his ancestors' pasts would care about the man's future.

A tall, slender woman in an elegant blue walking dress came in through her doorway, followed by a servant, dressed in black.

"Miss Bigod?" the slender woman said, nodding her head in the slightest bow Lisabeth had ever seen, one step from insult.

"Yes?" Lisabeth said, feeling invaded, but holding her head high, as she studied her visitor's face.

Miss Winchester wasn't a pretty woman, or even

309

a fetching one. She was, however, regal, cool, and unapproachable, with icy blue eyes. Her blade of a nose was pinched as though at a bad odor, and her thin lips were tightly compressed as she studied Lisabeth from her nose to her toes. She might look better if she'd been happier, but Lisabeth thought she was the sort of female that people called "handsome" because she wasn't precisely ugly, or attractive. And she certainly looked hostile.

Lord! Lisabeth thought. Were I a man, I'd sooner snuggle with a snake. What had Constantine been thinking of when he proposed to this woman? Then Miss Winchester spoke, and Lisabeth knew.

Miss Winchester's accents were upper class, and her modulated, cool voice was the sort used to command. "Miss Bigod," she said, "it has come to my attention that my former fiancé has been seen about town with you of late."

Lisabeth straightened her back. She'd never followed the command of anyone she didn't either love or respect. "But if he is your former fiancé, as you say," she said, "then what business is that of yours?"

"Ah!" her visitor said with a cold smile. "I see that you are defensive. With reason, I suppose. My business, Miss Bigod, is that I've known Lord Wylde for many years. I know his family. Or knew of it as well as he did before he met your grandfather. His behavior since he returned from his visit to your home has changed drastically. I've spoken with his uncle, and those friends of his who truly care about him, not those care-for-nothings Kendall and Blaise. We believe that you somehow have trapped Lord Wylde into a situation he cannot, as a gentleman, extricate himself from. And so I am here to tell you that those of us who care for him will not let him give his life and his future away.

"Lord Wylde had visions of a seat in Parliament," Miss Winchester went on, her hands neatly folded in front of her as she spoke. "He had a future bright with promise as a force behind the very throne. And yet, since you came to London, he has been seen embracing you, in public, like a commoner. That, I am convinced, is not the man I know."

Lisabeth stared. This cool creature didn't recognize Constantine's behavior. But neither did she. Which was the man they knew?

"If you care for him, as you say," Miss Winchester went on, "will you let him throw his brilliant future away?"

"Who says he'll throw it away?" Lisabeth demanded, her hands on her hips, until she realized,

from Miss Winchester's slightly amused superior
stare, that the gesture made her look like a wash-
erwoman. So she hurriedly took her hands off her
hips and hugged herself instead. That made her
look as though she were trying to protect herself.
But she was.

Miss Winchester's smile was not warm. "You
want to be his wife? Do you know how to enter-
tain the cream of London Society? Are you known
to any of the statesmen, politicians, or poets of the
land? Related to any living peers, or to anyone of
note in town? No, I didn't think so."

"Constantine never said that was one of the
qualifications for being his wife," Lisabeth said.

" 'Constantine' is it?"

"It is," Lisabeth said. "And I can't see how a
woman who claims to care for him, and wanted to
share his life, would toss him away because of who
his ancestors were." She bit her lip the moment she'd
finished speaking. That was not what she'd meant
to say. She didn't want to make the horrid woman
change her mind about how desirable Constantine
would be as a husband. What would Constantine
do if Miss Winchester did decide to take him back?
Could she legally do that? Would he care even if she
couldn't?

"I did not come here to argue with you," Miss Winchester said. "Actually, I wanted to see the sort of female you were. Now, I have done. And I begin to understand much that had escaped me before. You are pert, and attractive, in a countrified way. And you are without scruples, obviously. So I leave you with this: I have not inconsiderable influence. I will have you, and your grandfather, and all your family investigated. And I will see that you are made to pay if coercion was used on Lord Wylde during his visit to you. His past, you see, is never so important to me as his future. Nor is it to him either, I believe. I suggest you think on that.

"One thing I know even now. You will never be admitted to the best places in London or in all of England, for that matter. Poor Lord Wylde may think he has no choice in the matter of whom he eventually weds. I shall try to show him that he does. And, I promise you, whether he marries you or not, I will make sure you never forget it."

"You only say that because you're mad as fire that he's not languishing for you!" Lisabeth blurted. "And I can't blame him!"

"I doubt you know what he is feeling, Miss Bigod," her visitor said, as she turned to leave.

"Lord Wylde has excellent address, superior manners, and is not a man to wear his heart on his sleeve. Have you not noticed?"

And without waiting for an answer, she left the room, leaving Lisabeth furious, frightened, and challenged.

Chapter 19

No one looked at Lisabeth as she walked through the museum. No one so much as peeked at her at the restaurant where Constantine brought her and Miss Lovelace afterward, for ices. And no one glanced at them as they rode back in their open carriage, through the park. But Lisabeth knew she was being watched out of the corner of every eye by the way heads hastily turned away when she felt someone's gaze on her. And she felt it often.

"I must speak with you," she told Constantine as he steered his team round the lake in the park on the way to the gate. "Just you and me. It has to be somewhere private. Miss Lovelace and my grandfather agreed that we may."

"Only not for too long, and never where anyone can observe you," Miss Lovelace said casually from the back seat, looking to the side, as though she were paying no attention to them.

Constantine smiled. "I can't take Lisabeth to the end of the world," he said. "We can't be observed going to my town house. We can't be seen going upstairs together at her hotel. What do you suggest?"

"There are two chairs to the side of the hotel lobby," Miss Lovelace said. "They are far from everything else."

"But near enough so that two people alone, in close conversation, will be noticed," Constantine said. "Being private is no problem. London has many places where one, or particularly two, can be alone together. Being seen going or coming from somewhere private is the difficulty."

"True," Miss Lovelace observed, with a frown.

Lisabeth felt as though she might explode. "Be damned to gossip and convention," she said angrily.

"Do you mean that?" Constantine asked, eyebrows raised, as Miss Lovelace swelled with indignation.

But before her old governess could chide her, Lisabeth spoke up again. "Maybe I did. But excuse me, I'm sorry I said it." She looked around in despair. "Wait! Look there! It's mild, it's late in the season but it's still summer," she said quickly. "Why don't we rent a small boat, and go rowing, there, on the lake, like some others are doing? The only way anyone can eavesdrop is if they hang on to the back of the boat. And you, Lovey, can't fit in without us capsizing, so no one will stare if we don't have a chaperone. And if you can get up to anything in a boat made for two, my lord, well then, more power to you!"

Constantine's mouth twitched. "Excellent idea. Can you row, Lisabeth?"

"I'll swim if I have to," she said through clenched teeth.

Constantine rowed the little rented boat out into the lake. The lake was wide, and if not blue as the open sea that Lisabeth was used to, then at least the water seemed clean, though green, because of the growth of pond weeds. In the distance, on the shore, they could see people walking,

children and dogs playing, milkmaids and ped-
dlers, and Miss Lovelace dwindling to a little figure as she sat patiently on her bench, still watching
them.

Constantine had taken off his jacket, because it
fit so well. As he said, he'd burst the seams if he
exerted himself in it. He was in a white shirt and
a blue waistcoat, and Lisabeth admired his broad
shoulders as he rowed. It was odd, she thought
sadly, that she'd been intimate with this man and
yet had never seen him without his clothes on.
Still, she understood that many couples married
for years had never undressed for each other. Was
that also done in Society? She hoped not. Then
she remembered that mightn't matter anymore.

She held her parasol over her shoulder and
turned it to prevent the sun on her face, because
she knew a white complexion was so highly prized
here in London. And also so that she could peek at
him without him knowing,

"Yes, I do cut a manly figure," he said.

She wanted to bat him with her parasol, but
forced a grin instead. "I never knew your name
was Narcissus, my lord," she said. "So we've come
to the perfect place. All you need do is look down
in the water to be happy. But not for too long, if
you remember what happened to the original

Narcissus. By the way, I ought to have asked before we went sailing, but then I knew the lads could save you. Can you swim?"

"Like a fish," he said. "And you?"

She laughed. "I grew up by the sea. I'd be a fool if I couldn't."

What was it, she wondered, about Constantine and the outdoors? It brought out the humanity in the man. Though they sat opposite each other, she felt closer to him than she had since she'd come to London. He was warm and natural with her again.

"So," he said suddenly, "out with it. I enjoy rowing; the view from here is lovely, of you especially. That parasol isn't doing you much good. I spy freckles. They're charming. But I'm curious." He rested the oars on either side of the boat and let it drift. "What do you have to say that's so secret?"

"Lots of things," she said, trailing an ungloved hand in the warm water. She looked up at him again. "But before I do, I suppose I ought to tell you: Miss Winchester came to see me this morning."

That startled him. His dark eyes opened wide. "Did she, though?" he asked. "About what?"

"About me. And you," she said, casting her gaze down to the water her fingers were in. "She said I— Well, she as much as accused me— No, she

319

didn't 'as much as,' she accused me of 'coercion,' of somehow blackmailing you into a . . . Constantine," Lisabeth said, sitting up and confronting him, "she said if I continued to see you, she'd make certain I'd be punished for it. She said I'd ruin your political ambitions. She intimated that she cared for you, as I did not. She said I had no scruples. Oh, and that she'll see my family is investigated."

"Much good that will do," he said. "They had me investigated without coming up with a sniff of Captain Cunning or the truth about my father."

"Is that all you can say?" she yelped in indignation. "She must have had us watched."

"Everyone who is anyone in London is always watched," he said. "And by the way, I never mentioned that I'd any interest in politics, except in a trifling way, about making speeches now and again in the House of Lords. Parliament is Miss Winchester's ambition talking, I think."

"Not yours?"

He shrugged. "Not that I know of, but one day, who knows? The future is a closed book."

"She was very angry with me," she said. "And she acted superior, as though I were a servant, and she the fine lady. Well, I suppose she is a fine lady. But I don't consider myself an inferior. I didn't want to talk to her for very long because I was getting angrier, and if I spoke without thinking, as I often do when I'm in a fury, she'd have won her point. So I never asked. But I'd like to know: did you tell her?"

"Tell her?

"About me."

He picked up an oar and stroked it in the water, sending their boat slowly revolving in place. "No," he said. "I've told no one. Certainly not Miss Winchester. Blaise and Kendall, for once, have been discreet. We, I fear, were not. We must have been seen at the theater, or in the restaurants, or driving, or walking, or all of those things. And we kissed in public, you know."

"I know," she said softly.

"We were very foolish," he murmured. "Rather, I was. I sent for you too fast. Of course she'd take note of rumors about me being seen about town with a new lady, so soon after I'd broken off with her, or rather, forced her hand so that she had to do it."

"I suppose," Lisabeth murmured. "But if she really cared for you she wouldn't have minded what your ancestors were. There's something else, my lord."

" 'My lord?' " he mused.

"Yes," she shot back. "Why should I use your given name? That implies intimacy. We may have kissed and even more, but we don't have any kind of intimacy anymore. In fact, you've never even invited me to call you 'Con' as your friends do. We were never friends, only intimates. And we aren't really engaged.

"That's the other thing," she said sadly. "I don't recognize you these days. I can't say I know you anymore, if I ever did. Back at home, at Sea Mews, you were a different man, and different toward me. You were freer, easier, more filled with humor, closer to me. You're a gentleman of means and title here, all manners and morals, and aloof. You laughed out loud at Sea Mews. You smile here. You're Lord Wylde here and Constantine in the countryside. Which man are you?"

"Which one has insulted you?" he asked, his eye on the oar in the water as they turned in a circle. "Which one traduced you? Or ignored you, perhaps?"

"No, neither one of you, and none of those things," she admitted. "But you're different. It's as if you have another face here in London: faintly amused instead of really happy, disapproving instead of curious, and the rest of the time I can't tell what you're thinking. Truth to tell, my lord, you were like that when you first came to Sea Mews, and I didn't like you then. Further truth," she said, watching his eyes as he avoided hers. "I loved what you warmed up to become. Which you aren't anymore. And now I don't know if that was you. Or ever really you."

He looked at her then, his expression unreadable. "You think, perhaps," he said, "that I was more like my father and my great-grandfather then?"

"I suppose I did," she said, looking away from his penetrating stare.

"Ah," he said quietly. "Then it could be argued that you never found me attractive, but only the shadow of the men you wanted to love. I liked them too. But, yes, I'm not either of them."

"I know that, now," she said, leaning toward him. "So what I came to say is that I don't know you anymore, and that perhaps you don't really know me, and so maybe we're rushing things. I'm not with child. You're free. And so am I. I'm saying that it may be best if I leave London now, for a while, or forever. We'll see."

"You can't. You're ruined," he said flatly. "I ruined you."

"For what?" she cried, so agitated she began to stand up. She sank back when the boat rocked.

"Listen, my lord," she said, gripping the sides of the little boat so hard her knuckles hurt. "I'm not ruined. Maybe if I were a London girl, I would be. We're not so . . . provincial in the provinces. We're more tolerant of human error, especially if one's grandfather is influential and has money. I expect much the same is true in your Society."

"It's not," Constantine said. "A fellow who ruins a lady is expected to marry her. If he doesn't, she's married off to a man who needs the money or influence. That's not a happy life for her."

"Or for her husband," Lisabeth retorted. "I suppose the same might be said back home, but maybe not. We're a smaller society, and a more closed one. I'd be gossiped about, but the blame would be put on you. You'd be considered a devious rake, and me, your victim. But what would you care? Sea Mews and its village are a long way from here. As for me? I'm not a virgin, but I'm still me. Ruined? How? I look the same, and think differently only in that now I know what to expect in the marriage bed. I can still read and write, cook and sew, dance and sing, be a good wife to some man one day, and with luck, maybe even be a mother too. There are lads at home who've known me forever and would still have me as a wife. How am I 'ruined,' then?"

"Here," he said flatly, "you would be."

"But I won't be here much longer," she argued. "And I don't aspire to Society. You clearly do, and there's the problem." She put her head to the side, and studied him. "You're such strange creatures, you London toffs. I heard once a lady's married and has a child or two, she can be joyously ruined again and again, and her husband will look the other way, and so will Society."

"Sometimes," he admitted.

"And here too," she persisted, "I hear a man can be married and have as many mistresses as he likes. He can have his own bedchamber, his own bed, and his own life too. Well, I tell you, sir, that he could not, not where I live, not without his wife reshaping his head for him if she has any spirit. And I do."

She took a long breath, and looked at him directly. "You said you didn't expect me to live in your pocket. I wouldn't. But I wouldn't let any husband of mine range free either. So what I came to say is that I don't think we'd suit. Isn't that what a lady is supposed to say when she rejects a gentleman? Oh, right, there's more. I'm grateful and honored by your proposal, which you never really made the right way, I remind you. 'I want to marry you' is to the point, but not very romantic. But it wasn't romance that impelled you."

"How can you say that?" he asked.

She stared at him, and he looked away.

"But rest easy," she said. "I'm not asking you to ask me again." She lowered her gaze. "I'd only ask that you never tell Miss Winchester, or any other female, about me. I'll never know, of course. But I'd rather keep thinking that you didn't. We had a stroke of midsummer madness, I think," she said. "I'm not holding you to it, nor will I set my whole future by a course I drifted into one fine summer's day."

He looked pained, but didn't speak.

"The point is," Lisabeth said, "she wants you back. And I think you might be better off with her."

"And you?" he asked, looking at her directly. "Will you be better off?"

"Me? I've seen how you swim in your home waters, my lord. And they're not mine. I think that if I try to net you and keep you for my own, you'd die, slowly, but surely like any sea creature a child takes home and keeps in a bucket of seawater. And if I tried to live in your life, I know I'd as surely suffocate, like any fish out of water."

He said nothing. He only put the other oar in the

water, and began rowing again. Lisabeth looked back to see the tiny figure of Miss Lovelace fading away. Then the boat went round a little bend, and Constantine steered toward the shore. Wordlessly, he brought the nose of the boat to touch the edge of a long lawn, where giant willows with long weeping branches touched the water. Constantine bent, uncoiled a long rope on the bottom of the boat, then lightly leaped out. He splashed through the water, disregarding the certain ruin to the high shine of his boots, and tied the rope to a nearby tree, mooring the boat. Then he returned, and held out a hand for Lisabeth.

She took his hand, and he lifted her in his arms, took a few steps, and let her down on the edge of the shore. They were blocked from sight of the lake and the shore as they stood under a huge willow, its streaming canopy of leaves forming a green tenting around them.

Then, finally, he spoke. "You're certain?" he said.

And though she'd hoped against hope that he'd taken her here to woo her back, now, at last, she knew she'd done the right thing, for him, at least.

She nodded.

He stayed still, his hands on her shoulders, looking deep into her eyes. "Because of Miss

Winchester? Because you're afraid you'll be shunned? I would not allow that, you know."

"You can't control that," she said softly. "And you know it full well."

"We wouldn't have to live in London, or visit often, or at all," he persisted.

"And you'd like that?" she said.

He stayed still, watching her closely. "I don't want you to be unhappy," he finally said.

"Life makes people unhappy sometimes," she said. "And I know that in time I'd make you so. I don't want that, and not because I'm a saint. An unhappy husband would be the very devil."

"I'd never make you suffer for my actions," he promised, his expression stark.

"Nor would I make you do so," she said. "Don't you see?"

His eyes searched hers. "You are sure?"

She nodded, not trusting herself to speak. She'd hoped against hope that he'd laugh at her, reassure her; tell her she was being foolish. But they both knew she wasn't.

"I'll never forget how we made love," he said in a husky voice, reaching out to touch a loosened strand of her hair. "I'll never forget you. I was a different man with you, for you, and I liked that man. But you're right, try as I may, I can't find him again. And I've tried. I won't go back to Miss Winchester, never think that. I don't know that I'll ever be able to forget you. But I can't be the man you fell in love with, and believe me, I know you'd never have made love to me if you hadn't. I'm sorry, Lisabeth. Sorrier than you can know."

She nodded again, and her smile quivered. "I'll never go berrying again," she whispered, "without the memory of you. I'm sorry too. But I know I'm doing the right thing now."

He kissed her then. She knew he would. This time, their kiss was shocking in its intensity. She clung to him, molded herself against him, tasted the dark rich sweetness of his mouth, shivering as his hands traced her body. She could feel his arousal against her and it made her want to sink to the grass with him again.

But she was the one who ended it. Because she realized that if she didn't, they'd be making love again.

"This," she said, her face buried in his chest, "still works. This may be the only thing we have that still does, Constantine."

He stroked her hair. "I know," he said. "Lisabeth, maybe we can still try . . ."

She stepped back. "Love doesn't try," she said. "It is. What we have is attraction. Magnets have that. And how long would even that last if either of us bent to the other's way of life? I'd hate your world here in London. I'd feel so constricted and mutinous I'd rebel and shame you. You'd perish of boredom at Sea Mews, or anywhere like it, and begin to feel cheated of the life you led before. Let's remember what we had, what we might have done, and consider ourselves lucky."

"Lucky?" he asked bitterly.

"Yes," she said. "I think that love turned sour is worse than love remembered as one wild, memorable incident, even if it was a foolish one. Now please take me back. I don't want to see Miss Lovelace swimming out to find us. She would, you know."

He laughed, and so did she. But there was no merriment in it for either of them.

Chapter 20

"I still say it's running away," Miss Lovelace grumped.

"And I say it's just a tactical retreat," the captain argued.

"As if you ever retreated!" Miss Lovelace retorted.

"Aye, and I did, as any sane man would if he knew he was cornered. Hide a while and then spring out again. It's a good maneuver."

"But she's not going to spring out again," Miss Lovelace said. "She's going to hide, all right, but never will she take up arms against him or those who want her gone. I know her!"

"And I am her," Lisabeth said, sighing. "Have you two forgotten I'm here, sitting right next to you? Though I vow, if I had a horse, I'd get out and ride home by myself. In fact, I'm tempted to rent one at our first rest stop if you two don't stop talking about me as if I couldn't hear every word. I left him because I'd already lost him, if I ever had him. Because the truth is he himself doesn't know who he is. I don't want a husband who isn't sure of wanting me. I certainly don't want one who isn't sure of himself. I'm a fighter, but that sort of man isn't worth fighting for."

The other two fell still. They sat in the carriage, Miss Lovelace at Lisabeth's side, the captain opposite, and those two had been arguing for the last ten miles. Since they'd only gone ten miles out of London, Lisabeth had felt it was finally time for her to speak up.

"Aye, there's that." The captain sighed. "Poor lad was brought up stiff and proper, and no wonder his eyes lit up when he found out there was wild blood in his veins. Must have been everything he'd secretly dreamed about."

"After he got over the first shock of it," Lisabeth murmured.

"And secret dreams fulfilled don't always bring happiness above the moment, that I can tell you," Miss Lovelace said sadly.

"Aye," the captain said.

"Did you want me to marry someone who regretted me, hid me away, or even if he didn't, passed the rest of his life ruing the day he met me?" Lisabeth asked. "Not I. I'm to blame too, you know. I should never have believed the change in him, or trusted him so soon and so completely. There, I've said too much. Can we speak of something, anything, else?" She bent her head and sorted through her pockets.

The captain handed her his handkerchief. "No," he said, "you were what we brought you up to be: honest with yourself and your feelings."

"And I'm as much to blame," Miss Lovelace said. "I forgot that there aren't many honest maidens in England anymore, and for good reason, because there are fewer honest men."

"That's not true," Lisabeth murmured.

"Maybe not," Miss Lovelace agreed. "But there's fewer honest gentlemen, that's for certain."

"He didn't know which he was," Lisabeth said. She raised her head. "Let's be done with this, please. I acted rashly. I'm glad I have you two, because you

333

didn't insist I act even more rashly in order to save my reputation. Thank you."

"Your reputation is still good with us, and still good at home," the captain declared. "There's many a lad who still pines for you, and no one I know who would blame a lass for falling for a handsome stranger with smooth and studied wiles."

"Especially if he's the image of old Captain Cunning," Miss Lovelace said.

"He didn't use smooth and studied wiles," Lisabeth said, remembering who had started her seduction. She'd been honest with them about everything, but that still embarrassed her too much to speak of. Perhaps one day she could. That led her to another melancholy thought. "That's over and done," she said softly. "But surely, another man, a different man, any man that marries me, will always think I could have been more moral and will always hold it over me. Because I will not lie about my past."

"Nor should you!" the captain shouted.

"Just let him say one word!" Miss Lovelace cried.

"The men at home aren't that stupid. And I don't care if you never wed," the captain blurted. "Though I'd love to see great-grandchildren, I admit I'd miss you something terrible. You light up my house and my days. So if you do marry, I'd be better pleased if you married a good honest lad from home. I'm just as relieved that you left London for good. Tell the truth, I don't think a lass can trust a man from there."

"A *gentleman* from there," Miss Lovelace said on a sniff.

"Truth is," Lisabeth said, "I don't think he knows what he is."

They were quiet after that, and so Lisabeth could think about the man she was leaving. She didn't know if he'd ever leave her heart, and she didn't want him gone from her memory. She'd felt a connection to him as she'd felt for no other being. It might have been brought about by his resemblance to the dream men of her childhood, but certainly there was more to it than that. She wasn't a fool. Surely she hadn't just succumbed to her overwhelming desire for the face and the body of the man in the portrait? The real man had been beyond her imaginings. She'd fallen in love with a kindred soul, or so she'd thought. Someone wise and learned, with manners and morals and charm, yet with spirit enough to act foolishly sometimes, to play and to laugh, and yet be a man who knew right from wrong, and would never stray.

She ought to have known how impossible that was. She still didn't blame him. She wished him joy with his Miss Winchester, or another female like her, the sort he'd surely eventually marry. But she knew, in her heart, that he, in his heart, would never be satisfied with a wife and a life like that. She knew she wasn't the one, but she didn't think he'd ever know what was right for him.

In that, she felt blessed. Because she was only one sad woman, and she'd wager he was and would always be two confused men from now on.

Lisabeth stared out the carriage window but closed her eyes and mind to everything but her new resolve. She was going home, sore at heart. But she wouldn't sit and pine and wither to a disappointed old age. She'd wait her sorrow out, and then go find herself a man she could trust and desire, and then maybe, one day, love—if she could only forget Constantine. The feel of him, the taste of him, the ecstasy in his embrace, the laughter and the moments of pure foolishness she'd shared with him were too delicious to abandon for all time. So she decided she wouldn't.

She resolved to keep a proper mourning period for the dream that had died, and then keep the memory of it someplace in her heart. But she'd never let it rule either her head or her heart again.

Then one day she'd be able to make a future for herself in reality, knowing it would never be as thrilling or bright as her dream. But, at least, at last, it would be something real and right.

"Miss Winchester," Constantine said, bowing over the lady's hand.

She greeted him in her salon. The slight smile on her lips was one of triumph. She shot a knowing glance to her mother, who sat in the room while morning callers visited, as was proper. But the only guest in the salon this morning was Lord Wylde. Miss Winchester's mother had managed to hastily shuffle her daughter's few lady friends out the moment she'd heard Lord Wylde had called and was waiting in the hall.

Miss Winchester had suffered since she'd last seen him. Her mother had shrieked when she'd heard of her daughter's decision to let him go. Her father had been beyond fury. But the notice of the canceled engagement had been put into the paper when Lord Wylde hadn't come back to plead for a reprieve.

"Are you mad?" her father had thundered when he'd heard the news. "Your good blood will wash out his bad. And this is the nineteenth century. Who the devil cares about yesterday? He's one of the most eligible men in London town, and would be if his father had been a . . . cannibal!"

"Go see the slut who turned his head while he was gone," her mother had advised her. "She's no one, a country nobody, I've asked. Go see her, and let her know what damage she's done—and what will be done to her if she stays with him. The *ton* will not accept her, and that will destroy him."

"How can I forgive him?" Miss Winchester had moaned, her hand to her forehead, because she doubted she'd be asked to.

"Forget it. Every man has a moment of madness," her father had commented, earning himself a sharp look from his wife.

Miss Winchester had definitely suffered. But now, here was Lord Wylde again, bowing over her hand. And gossip had it that the strange woman from the countryside had left town. "I'm pleased to see you again, my lord," she said, with heartfelt sincerity.

"Are you?" he murmured. "I wonder. You see, my dear Miss Winchester, I've come here to scold you, and I don't know a female alive who'd welcome that."

Her smile grew broader. "Scold" was such a playful word for a gentleman to use with a lady, and he didn't look at all angry or annoyed. "Whatever have I done?" she asked in a teasing way.

"You've interfered in business that was none of yours," he said coolly. "You've hurt an innocent female's feelings, and I believe that while you were at it, you've also traduced my name."

"I beg your pardon?" she said, as her mother's head shot up.

"Well, you should," he told her. "We ended our alliance because you couldn't endure my family's past reputation. I understood. We parted friends, I thought. And that, my dear Miss Winchester, ought to have been that. What motivated you to try to end all my future alliances?"

"She was clearly not worthy of you," Miss Winchester said, growing red-faced.

"She was worthier than I am. Her family's reputation is spotless. And even if it were not, what business was it of yours? We no longer have a connection, Miss Winchester. What sort of nonsense was it for you to go to Miss Bigod and tell her that I aimed for a future in politics? And what sort of spite to infer that if her name were linked with mine, my plans would fall to dust? All untrue, all surmise, you didn't even know what my plans were for myself, or for her."

"Yes I did!" she shot back. "You were seen kissing her!"

"I see," he said. "And this offended whom? Public morality? In this day and age? I doubt it. You? Why should it?"

"I'd hoped . . ." she said, and paused. "When I considered matters at length, after we'd agreed to part," she went on, "I thought I had been too hasty."

"You weren't," he said.

His face became expressionless, but there was a dangerous glitter in his dark eyes that she'd never seen before. He towered over her, and cast a shadow. She suddenly remembered that she had let this man go because of his pirate forebears.

"There's no question of a reconciliation between us," he told her. "But I guarantee, Miss Winchester, there is definitely a question of a libel suit, or perhaps one of harassment, or maybe neither, but at least a good deal of gossip about your actions in the highest circles of the *ton*. I may not aim for a political life at the moment, but I have many friends who are so occupied. And even more flighty fellows who live for rumor. So I warn you, my lady: no more of this. Forget me, my diversions, my life and my plans, or be prepared to have your own life and motivations examined by everyone in London town.

"And ma'am," he said to her mother, who was

standing now, her mouth slightly open, "I beg you to counsel your daughter wisely in this. I don't care to be the subject of vile rumor, and your daughter, I know, cares for it even less. Good day, ladies. And good luck."

He turned, and left them standing there. As he reached the front door, and a footman handed him his high beaver hat, he could hear them begin to berate each other. He clapped on his hat, and then, at last, he smiled.

But not for long.

"You're terrible company," Blaise said.

"No fun at all," Kendall agreed.

Constantine waved a hand. "Then go. No one invited you, no one's holding you here, and I assure you, no one cares."

His two visitors exchanged glances.

"Stupid insult," Kendall said. "Not creative or funny. Might be if you were jug bitten, but you're not. Unless you've drunk yourself into the blue sullens, that is. That happens. Get very happy, and then so miserable you could die, and the more you drink, the worse it gets."

"That, we could understand," Blaise said. "If you were, we'd leave you in a happy, or unhappy, stupor. But I believe you're stone sober, and have been for days; in fact, your face even begins to look like a stone. Unshaven stone, that is. Obviously, you haven't let your valet near you in days. You look ghastly."

"Thank you," Constantine said, staring into the fire crackling in his hearth. "Then go away so you don't have to look at me."

"Can't leave a friend in distress," Kendall said sorrowfully. "Not done."

"Do I look as though I'm in distress?" Constantine asked, from where he lounged in a deep chair, as he had every evening this week.

His friends gazed at him.

"Actually, no," Blaise said. "You look beaten, defeated, drowned, and dead. A man in distress has some energy, he at least struggles to live."

Constantine chuckled. It was such a strange rusty sound coming from a man who had been brooding for days that his friends cocked their heads.

"That's what I've been doing," he said, sitting up straighter. He ran a hand over his stubbly chin and then through his hair. "Lord! I didn't realize how long it's been. Even I'm tired of myself. Gads. I don't know why you put up with me. Why do you, by the way?" he asked curiously. "And don't say it's what friends do. I want to know why you are my friends. Honestly."

"Honestly?" Blaise said. "That's difficult for me. But in truth, I suppose because you have a sense of humor. You've always been fair, and always been honest with me. I don't know, Con. I met you years ago, and liked you, and have had no reason to dislike you since."

"Even though I'm straitlaced, and hard-shelled?"

"Wouldn't say that!" Kendall put in. "I agree with Blaise. Everyone knows you're a bit of a stick. But you know? Truth is, not really. I mean, think on. You never ratted on us and our nonsense at school. Never lectured us then, or since. Thing is, you try to live like a parson, but you aren't one. Not at heart, I don't think. Couldn't stand one of those."

"Kendall has it exactly," Blaise said. "You're a good friend, Con, and we hate to see you like this."

"So do I," Constantine said. "But how would you feel if you were raised a tortoise, only to discover you want to leap like a hare? Bad analogy," he said. "The point is that I got to this great age and only just discovered what I am. I wasn't really happy before."

"You're overjoyed now?" Blaise asked.

Constantine chuckled again. He stretched. "I will be. But, I think, at this point, I need your help."

"Always ready," Kendall said.

"Be pleased," Blaise said. "How?"

"I have to do something foolish. Daring. Dangerous. Even stupid. But I have to do it to make a point. Care to join me? But wait! There really may be danger involved, and if I see it coming, I'll ask you to leave me so you aren't involved."

"Going to kidnap Lisabeth!" Kendall crowed. "Capital idea!"

"No, no," Constantine said. "Nothing that stupid. Anyway," he said with a slight smile, "she'd kill me if I tried."

"Are you going to do anything about her?" Blaise asked. "I thought all this had to do with her."

"Perspicacious of you," Constantine said with a tilted smile.

"Told you he wasn't drunk," Kendall said. "Couldn't say 'persip-whatever,' if he was."

"I'm not drunk," Constantine said. "I've just been thinking, and now I know what I have to do. I was never happier than when I was with Lisabeth. Only I was too stupid to realize it. I was raised to be prudent and cautious and proper, while all the time my inner self has wanted to be the opposite. My uncle was half right. Morality is next to godliness, and wildness should be shunned. But he was half wrong too. No good can come of being either thing completely. Wildness is not necessarily evil. Morality may only be cowardice, a fear of facing life."

He rose from his chair and faced his friends. "A man needs balance: wildness and caution, excitement, and time to think. I'm not cut out to be a pirate or a highwayman; I know that. I wouldn't want to take what wasn't mine, nor would I prey on the helpless. Though I know now that if I *had* to, I could. That was hard to accept. I'm not running from it though. Acceptance of a thing doesn't mean you have to practice it.

"But now I also know that I'm not the sort of man who'd be happy spending my evenings talking nonsense at Society dos or sitting in a window seat all morning reading the *Times* until it's time to go to church. What I need is a chance to be myself at last. What I need most of all is another opportunity, and a woman who will give me one. Damn it all, but I need Lisabeth."

Kendall clapped his hands. Blaise grinned.

"But I have to make it up to her," Constantine said. "By God, I let her go! That must have been devastating for her. I know it was for me. She trusted me, and I let her down. I let myself down too, but that doesn't matter now. The worse of it is that I let her go thinking it was because I doubted her worthiness, when all the while it was because I didn't know myself, and so of course, what I doubted was myself. Kidnapping her is a lovely thought, my ancestors' blood races in my veins at the very thought." He laughed. "But I don't want to steal her away. I want her to want me. *Me*, not my ancestors, good or bad. And I want to let her know she matters more to me than any gossip, rumor, uncle, person in Society, or any other female in the land."

"Huzzah!" Kendall cried. But then he frowned. "Good idea. But not easy."

"Hellishly difficult at this point, I'd imagine," Blaise said.

"Yes," Constantine agreed. "But the thing is, my vanity is such, or my instinct, or my faith in her, that I believe I can convince her. I just need to do something so different from what she'd ever think I'd do that she knows I'm finally accepting my true self, asking her to forgive me, and risking myself in order to show her I want her to join me as my wife, for life," he said, grinning. "What I want to capture is her attention, her interest, and make her laugh. And then I have to plead with her to forgive me."

"Excellent," Blaise said happily. "What do you want us to do?"

"Be accomplices," Constantine said.

Chapter 21

The only clouds were shredded ones, scurrying across a waning sickle moon. The night was dark and filled with fading stars, the sea was calm, the hour was as close to midnight as it was to dawn. Three ragged, desperate-looking men, dressed in black and breathing hard, stood near some brush where the rocky beach began to tilt down to the sea.

"Perfect," Constantine said, drawing a deep breath. He looked around the deserted beach. There were no shadows, no ships, not even a rowboat on the shore.

"You sure this is the place?" Kendall whispered.

"He's right," Blaise said, low. "How can we be sure? We must have walked through miles of forest. This place is all bracken and stone, puddles, beach and hidden inlets. Gad! I'm glad you talked me into wearing these rags and oversized boots. Nothing fits, but when I think of the sand and earth and damp! It would have ruined my good clothes."

"It would have ruined you if you'd come waltzing through looking like a gent on the strut on Bond Street," Constantine said. "Even the foxes around here would have known you didn't belong. Now you look like every other fisherman in the village. Better still, you're all in black, and so the hope is you don't look like them, or anyone. The idea is not to be noticed." He pulled a crumpled piece of paper from an inner pocket and studied it in the scant light. "No doubt, this is where we're supposed to be."

"Where are those others who are supposed to be here too? And the boat?" Blaise said, shivering.

"*That* is a problem," Constantine said, frowning.

"Didn't trust that Frenchie above half," Kendall said darkly. "That oily Henri. He didn't like you above half neither, Con. Just like him to send you to the wrong place and make a fool of you."

"It was William who drew the map, and he's honest as the day is long. And, I might add, he was delighted to see me," Constantine said.

"Yes, he and Francis. They like you, and thought it was a jolly good idea," Kendall said. "But that Henri was giving you a cold and fishy eye."

"They're the only ones he has," Constantine said. "Still, if they don't arrive by sunrise, we'll leave."

"Another tramp through the underbrush," Blaise groaned in hollow tones. "At least a fishing smack, however odiferous, would have been preferable."

"If they let me down I'll think of something else," Constantine said, as he settled himself, crouched on his haunches, looking out to sea. "Arriving unexpectedly on Lisabeth's doorstep, tossing pebbles at her window to wake her, taking her for a sunrise ride on the sea, was a good idea. Still, if it can't be, there'll be something else. But we'll have to act quickly, before word of my arrival spoils the surprise."

"William was right though," Blaise said, hunkering down beside him, careful that the damp sand didn't touch anything but his high boots. "She might be so angry she'll refuse to go with you."

"I don't think so. She's a reasonable person. But if she is, I'll carry her back with me anyhow. Not quite a kidnapping. Not quite an invitation either. I'll let her go when the sun rises, and I'll tell her that too. That's what you're here for. You, Kendall, steer the craft. You, Blaise, assure her of my worthiness. I'll do the rest."

"And if she denies you?" Blaise asked.

"I don't know what I'll do," Constantine said, all laughter gone from his voice.

There was a sound, not of the sea, at the edge of the beach. All three men stilled, and tensed. They heard an eldritch cry, not human, or any animal they knew. And then they heard it again. They waited.

"Blast!" a harried voice whispered. "Don't you London gents know an owl?"

"You shoulda have done a sparrow, Will," another voice said. "That, they'd understand."

Constantine rose to his feet. "Welcome," he said, as he strode down the beach to the two men he could now faintly see. "We've been waiting." He shook hands with the men. "I see you've the same fishing smack. Excellent. Shall I pay you now, or later?" The tallest man shook his head, but before he could speak, Constantine went on. "I know I'm

351

taking away a day of your fishing, and I know it's your livelihood, so please don't protest."

"Well, then, later," William said in an embarrassed voice. "Now, Henri's still aboard. When your friends have got the smack in hand, he'll leave. Just set him down after you board Lisabeth. It's you who'll be the pilot, isn't it, Sir Kendall?" he asked as Constantine's friends joined them. "You know about sailing?"

"I do," Kendall said. "Just give me the bearings."

"Done," William said, handing him a crumpled map. "Now sail close to the shore, hug it without hitting the rocks. I've drawn them on the map. Go due north by northeast, five miles, exactly. The wind's rising, and it's with you. Two rocks that look like fangs mark the inlet you want. Remember them, Lord Wylde?"

"I do," Constantine said.

"Good. When you reach them, anchor near the shore. There you can be put down, you know the way to Miss Bigod's house from there."

"Yes," Constantine said.

"And, oh," William said casually. "We may be there as well, so don't be surprised. The thing is, we owe the Bigods and I want to be sure Miss Lisabeth takes this in the right spirit. If she don't, we'll be there to take her home. Agreed?"

"Agreed," Constantine said, taking his proffered hand.

"And don't mind Henri," William added, before he and Francis disappeared into the stunted trees at the edge of the beach. "He's always fancied her, much good it did him."

Henri scowled at them when they boarded the fishing smack. Blaise gasped, and covered his nose with a handkerchief.

"It's the memory of fish," Constantine said. "I didn't think they did night fishing. But maybe they do. What's under there?" he asked Henri when a cloud tore off the face of the moon to show a heap of tarpaulins at the end of the smack.

"We don't feesh by night, m'lor," Henri said with a mocking bow. "But we have got to have that with which to keep feesh in."

"Right," Constantine said, as Kendall strode to the wheel.

Kendall instructed Henri to raise the anchor and the sail. Constantine stood at the prow as the sail caught the wind and the smack began to move with the winds that now smelled of incoming rain.

Constantine hoped she'd be amused. He prayed she'd be amazed. He thought of his long-rehearsed speech, and ran through it one more time, just to be sure he'd touched on all the points he had to make.

He was sorry, he'd been a fool; he needed her to forgive him. He couldn't think what he'd do if she laughed at him, not with him, and stalked away. He refused to consider it. He was no pirate bold, nor any kind of highwayman. But he was desperate, and hoped this foolish escapade would remind her of the men she'd hoped to find an echo of in him.

The fishing smack sailed on up the coast, running silent and smooth even in waters that began to rock, the ship as steady as Kendall's hand at the helm. Even Blaise was enjoying himself.

"You get used to the stench," Blaise told Constantine. "Or else, the sea wind brushes it away. No worse, and actually somewhat better, than that of a gentleman's gaming hell at dawn. At least it's fresh. And the fish have bathed recently."

"Shh!" Henri suddenly whispered. "Not another word. I hear something."

They fell still, listening.

They heard nothing. But Henri was scowling. He peered into the shadows. Constantine saw nothing. But Henri did.

"We go!" Henri shouted. "Spread the sail, we run for it!"

And then he jumped overboard.

Constantine stared at Kendall, while Blaise looked down into the water, dumbfounded. Henri went under, and came up in front of the fishing smack he'd just abandoned. And then, his arms stroking hard, he disappeared into the vanishing night.

"Heave to!" a booming voice shouted. "We'll fire if you don't."

"Might as well," Kendall told Constantine. "I'm sailing into ink, I don't know these waters. But whoever is at the helm of that cutter does."

Constantine looked round to see a long low cutter approaching them faster than the wind, on their leeward side. "What the devil!" he said. "That's an official-looking craft. By God! I think it's that revenue officer . . . Nichols. Yes, that was his name. He had a *tendre* for Lisabeth. Do you think he found out what I'm up to and is out to stop me from speaking to her?"

The sound of a pistol shot rent the night.

"I know he's out to stop us," Kendall said, then shouted, "Hold your fire, man. We're stopping!"

"Well, he won't stop me," Constantine said grimly. "I mean, he can stop the ship, but not me. I have a pistol too."

"But he has the law, and four men, with him," Blaise commented as the cutter threw a line to them, and the man in the bow of the boat pointed to the shore.

The fishing boat was dragged to a rocky beach by the cutter.

"What is the meaning of this?" was all Constantine could say as he stepped ashore.

"Well, if it isn't the fine London gent?" Nichols said. "I recognize the voice, if not the clothes."

Constantine's eyes narrowed. The customs agent seemed to be gloating.

"You don't look so fine now, my lord," Nichols said, circling around him. "In fact, you look exactly like a moonraker."

Moonraker? Constantine thought the fellow would say he looked like a fisherman.

"And these must be some gents from the House of Lords, no doubt?" Nichols asked with barely controlled elation. "Times must be hard if you fellows come down here to make the money to pay off your gambling debts. Poor Miss Bigod. I believe she really thought you were interested in her, and not in the riches to be gained by plying your trade right at her doorstep."

"What," Constantine asked, his hands on his hips, "are you talking about?"

"I'm talking about your cargo, my lord," Nichols said.

"Fish," Blaise said. "Actually, the last remains of stinking fish."

"Oh, yes?" Nichols asked gleefully. He strode to the fishing smack, lightly leaped aboard, and beckoned for his men and Constantine and his friends to follow.

As they all stood in the fishing smack, Nichols bent, and then with a theatrical gesture, swept back the tumble of tarpaulins at the back of the boat.

Constantine stared. Blaise, for once, was speechless. Kendall groaned.

"Fine kettle of fish, indeed, gentlemen," Nichols said happily, reaching down into the boxes of bottles. "The finest port wine, brandy, and liquors, direct from France, and . . . yes, without so much as one tax stamp on them. A good haul, indeed, for me. Hands behind your backs, my lords, if you really are such. You'll need to be tied together for the journey back to my offices. I'm pleased to be showing you the accommodations we have for smugglers. Not so comfortable as those at Sea Mews, but I doubt you'd be welcome there. No one likes to be used. And for you, gentlemen, my lodgings certainly will do. Until, that is, you go to London again, in chains."

The room was dank and dark, but never so dank or dark as Constantine's mood.

"How could they do this to us?" he said again as

he tried to pace the little space with crablike steps, the best he could do with his ankles in chains. "They must be laughing their heads off. I *trusted* them." He sank to the narrow bench on the side of the room. "I suppose I deserve it. She trusted me, didn't she?"

"Well, I don't deserve it, at least not this time," Blaise said. "Blast, but I itch," he added, as he wriggled on the bench. "Do you think I've picked up lice or fleas in this ghastly place?"

"Ain't bugs, I don't think," Kendall said gloomily. "Dried salt water, and the damned itchy wool these clothes are made of would make a statue itch."

"If she finds out she'll be amused, all right, but in all the wrong ways," Constantine said, standing again. "I tried to emulate my daring ancestors, and didn't even do as well as my poor father. At least he was killed in his first endeavor. I just look like a dupe and a fool."

"Better than dead, I'd say," Blaise murmured, scratching his chest. "Or in prison. Do you think they've grounds for tossing us in Newgate, or sending us to the Antipodes? I suppose I could try to make a fortune there, as the Earl of Egremont and his wild crew did. But that took a generation to accomplish, and I don't care to leave my home. I'd lose it long before I got back—if I ever did. Even if we use influence and get off with fines and warnings, there go my chances of ever making a marriage that could save the estate. The one thing a fortune hunter doesn't need is a criminal past. That insures everyone will think he's up to even more than no good."

"I thought you were investing as I advised you," Constantine said.

"I am, I was, but it takes time for my ships to come in."

"Don't care about making a fine marriage," Kendall said sadly. "But I'll be tossed out of the four-in-hand club for this. Not to mention my other clubs. I'll miss fencing and riding, and—"

"There's no saying what will happen," Constantine said, sinking to the bench again. "Except my dreams have been shattered. I doubt we'll go to Newgate, but I know I've been made to look foolish. A woman, especially one like Lisabeth, can pardon a man many things, but not being a dolt. And I don't blame her."

He put his head in his hands.

"Gentlemen," Nichols said.

They looked up. The customs officer stood at the door to their cell, and he looked about as happy as they were.

"You're to come with me," he said.

"Where?" Constantine asked warily, visions of midnight hangings making him step back.

"To see your attorney at law, and to make another inspection of the craft we caught you in," Nichols said.

Constantine frowned, as did his friends, but no one said a word. What attorney? Constantine's law firm was an old one, firmly lodged in London. And no one had sent word to anyone since they'd been arrested.

"No need to get back in the cart," Nichols said. "We confiscated, then towed your vessel to the harbor at the foot of this street. It's under guard. Your attorney only wants us all present when he sees the goods so he can see what you're charged with. Come along, step smartly."

"Difficult to do," Constantine said, as he shuffled forward, his chains clanking.

"Do it," Nichols snarled. "I'm not risking anyone diving into the water and trying to get away. With chains on, do you jump in, I doubt you'll be able to come up again, much less swim off."

Nichols, his guards, and their prisoners clanked and shuffled out of the customs office, and out the door.

Constantine squinted up to see the sun rising

over the sea. The fresh winds of the night had blown
the clouds away; it bid to be a fair day, the night
mists already drifting off. They made their slow
passage to the little harbor at the end of the village
street. The tide was out; all the boats anchored there
lay crooked in the mud. Only the smart little cus-
tom's cutter sat in the sea, looking as though it were
ready to chase anything anywhere to the end of the
world.

A plump little man, dressed soberly and well,
stood pacing on the dock. Constantine had never
seen him before.

"Welcome, my lord, it's been a long time," the
man said to Constantine, offering his hand. "Tsk!"
he said when he saw how Constantine's wrists were
bound. "Chains for a gentleman? Come, Mr. Nichols. Surely this isn't necessary, I give you my word.
As I'm sure the gentlemen do."

Nichols hesitated.

"Come, my good fellow," the man added angrily. "Have I ever lied to you?"

"Often," Nichols said gloomily.

"But always legally," the man said, shaking a
finger in the customs officer's face. "Now, off with
the chains, if you please. It will make it easier for
us all to inspect the evidence. And easier still,

when I show you that my clients are innocent, and you have to let them go."

"Innocent?" Nichols yelped. "I caught them with the goods. I don't know who called you, Mr. Makepeace, or who's paying you for your work, because I doubt Lord Wylde ever clapped eyes on you before, neither him, nor his men. But I tell you the goods are there. Brandy, champagne, port wine, the best. Unstamped, untaxed, and unreported . . . until now."

"Very good," Mr. Makepeace said. "Now, if you will be so kind as to unchain my clients, we shall all go see for ourselves."

Nichols had his prisoners unbound, and did it with bad grace. But he was smiling when he let them follow him aboard the fishing smack. The attorney, Nichols, Constantine and his friends, and three somber guards, all walked carefully on to the ship. It was mired in mud, and tilted, so they had to walk uphill to the back of it. The tarpaulins were still in place.

Nichols went straight to them and, bending, whisked them off again.

Mr. Makepeace held his nose. Constantine blinked. Kendall grinned. Blaise let out a deep sigh. And Nichols raged.

They saw a mound of half-rotted fish: fins and tails and heads.

"Who did this?" Nichols shouted. He kicked at the fish and then, in a fury, bent to dig under the stinking pile of guts and pieces, using both hands to do it. He only uncovered more of the same.

His men looked at each other.

"Weren't there guards here all night?" Nichols demanded, straightening, his hands dripping slime and coated with scales.

"Two," one of his men said. "I were one of them. I didn't hear nothing, nor see a thing. Why, look for yourself, Mr. Nichols. There ain't even a foot-print in the mud, sir."

"I see," Mr. Makepeace said comfortably. "These fish, you claim, Mr. Nichols, are filled with fine port wine, brandy, and champagne? Do tell me, my lord Wylde, I should like to catch some of those. Pray, what was the bait you used?"

"My secret, Mr. Makepeace," Constantine said, because he was as numbed and shocked as Nichols.

"I fear you'll have to let my clients go, with an apology," Mr. Makepeace told the customs officer.

"I know what I saw. I don't know how this was done," Nichols said through tight lips. "They can go. But I'll be listening and watching close to find out what happened."

"Everyone needs a hobby," the attorney said sweetly. "Come now, gentlemen, I can provide transportation back to where your fishing trip was so rudely interrupted."

Blaise grinned. Kendall raised his head. Constantine looked to the end of the dock where two coaches waited. There was also an open carriage there. Constantine winced. The open carriage was driven by a lovely young lady, dressed in sunrise pink and gold to match the growing day. And she was laughing at him.

Chapter 22

Constantine sat silently, as Lisabeth raised the whip and set her horse trotting back up the hill, following the other two coaches. Kendall and Blaise were in one, Mr. Makepeace in the other.

"Your friends are going straight to Sea Mews," she said, as they drove on through the little village. "They need baths, and rest, and good food."

"And me?" he asked dully.

"Oh, you and I have to talk."

"There's nothing to say," Constantine said. "I tried a stupid trick. It was to win your admiration. No, it was supposed to be amusing, so you'd forgive me. No, why lie? It was supposed to remind you of my great-grandfather and my uncle. They were the ones you found dashing. I'm not. Try as I might, I'm still a stick. I met with your fishermen friends, borrowed their craft, and was going to persuade you to come with me for a daring night of sailing, while I tried to convince you of what a fool I'd been and how much I regretted it. What I did was to show you what a fool I still am."

"Why go to all that effort?" she asked calmly, as the carriage moved up the street, out of the village, and into the open countryside again.

"I didn't know if you could forgive me my hesitation to marry you immediately, out of hand," he said. "I didn't know because I couldn't forgive myself. How could I have let you go? Because, I suppose," he said sadly, "the truth is that I'm not daring, or dashing. I may feel stirrings, but I can't defeat my upbringing. Can you imagine a portrait of Captain Cunning sitting in a prison cell? He was bold. I'm cautious to a fault." He laughed. "But as it turns out, not cautious enough. Why, by the way, did your friends switch their cargo from fish to alcohol when they lent me their craft?"

"They thought Nichols wouldn't stop you, and

that if he did, you could get out of the snare. You did."

"I didn't," he said. "Who did?"

"Oh, changing the wine into fish? It wasn't a minor miracle," she said, still smiling. "We have many friends. Poor Mr. Nichols. He has none."

"And Mr. Makepeace?"

"Grandfather's man-at-law. A very good man."

"Yes, I will, at least, recompense him for his efforts," Constantine said stiffly.

"No, Grandy wouldn't hear of it." She turned her head. "You are a little ripe, my lord."

"The wind changed," he said. "Even I can smell it."

They drove out into the countryside, following one of the coaches they had left the village with.

"So," she finally said, carefully, "the plan was to take me out for a moonlight sail, and convince me that . . . ?"

"That I loved you," Constantine said, looking down at his hands. "That I didn't want to contemplate life without you. That I wasn't the man you wanted to fall in love with, but that I'd try to be, for you. And I confess, for me as well. Because the time I spent with you was the happiest of my life, and I didn't want to go on without you."

"And you needed to look like a pirate for that?" she asked.

He shrugged. "I honestly don't like stealing. So I couldn't hold up a coach for you. Though I confess, I thought about it. But I knew it would have to be your coach; how else would you know about it? And if I did, you'd shoot me dead before I got a chance to explain. So a night's sailing seemed right. I look more like my ancestor in the dark."

She looked at him steadily.

He noticed how the rising sun turned her brown eyes gold. He looked at her face, and felt his heart ache. He'd never seen a lovelier face.

"Nonsense," she said, and he realized he'd said that aloud. "You're a London gentleman, you've seen the greatest beauties in England. Only I must admit," she said, grinning, "Miss Winchester certainly wasn't one of them."

"I wanted to apologize for that too," he said.

"For not picking a prettier fiancée?" she asked with a show of innocence.

"For her, entirely," he said. "For how she upset you."

"Why, did you send her?"

"No, but she wouldn't have come to see you if I hadn't gone back on my own word, and kissed you when and where I shouldn't have."

She turned the carriage off the high road, and they drove on in silence for a while longer.

"Why did you do that?" she finally asked. "Kiss me where and when you shouldn't have?"

"Because I couldn't help myself. I may not be bold, but you make me forget that."

"I see," she said. She wrinkled her nose. "You know, my lord, you really do smell bad. Not as bad as poor Mr. Nichols must, but very bad indeed."

She slowed the carriage, and stopped it under a willow tree.

"I understand," he said, as he rose, and stepped down from the carriage. "You want me to get out and walk. I don't blame you. I'll go straight to the inn near Sea Mews, if you'll point me in the right direction."

"Oh, they wouldn't let you in!" she said, wide-eyed. "Not as you're dressed, and certainly not as you smell."

"Then what?" he asked, looking up at her.

"There's a pool here, and a fresh running stream. I suggest you rip off those clothes, and beat them on the rocks, and then wash until every last fish scale and bit of prison stench is off you."

He nodded.

She smiled. "Don't you remember?"

He looked around. And then whipped his head around to look at her.

"Yes," she said. "We were here that day. Go," she said, waving her hand. "I want to talk, but only when I can't smell you."

Wonderful, he thought, as he trudged up a little hill and went upstream. This was the icing on his cake. He'd made a fool of himself, and now she treated him like a child. There was no coming back from this. But he'd try, he vowed, even if he had to do something drastic again. Drastic, he reminded himself, and much better planned. He mightn't be as inventive as his ancestors, but he was at least doggedly determined. He amused her now. He'd build on that.

He stripped off his wretched clothes and stepped into the stream, shivering as he did. The summer was over; the chill in the water confirmed it. He washed, using handfuls of sand to scrape his skin. He went downstream and ducked into the pool, submerging himself again and again. When he lifted his head at last, there was no sign of Lisabeth anywhere in the vicinity. He went back upstream again, leaving his clothing on the rocks. A season of winter storms wouldn't cleanse them, but he had to wait for them to dry.

He lay down on the grass, on a bank surrounded by ferns, and closed his eyes, letting the morning sunshine dry him.

He felt a shadow over him, but kept his eyes closed.

"You really look better this way," Lisabeth said. Her voice was a little shaken.

"Don't let looks deceive you again," he said, not moving. "I am what I am. I can try to be the man you want. And I will. But I'm not the men you loved in your imagination."

"No," she said. "But you tried to be, for me. I didn't really want that. What I want is you, and now, you're my own private pirate, entirely."

The shadow moved away, and he sighed. Then he felt her settle on the grass next to him, and her arms went around his neck.

"I'm naked," he said.

"I can see that," she said.

Instinctively, his hand moved to cover his groin, because chilled as he was, still the sound of her voice stirred him, and it showed.

"So can I," she whispered, from very close. She giggled. "You have a big hand, my lord. But not quite big enough."

He opened his eyes and turned his head. She lay

beside him, and she wore nothing but a quavering smile. He sat straight up. He stared at her body, and started to stand up as well.

She put a hand on his shoulder to keep him from rising. "How else can I show you that it's you, and not the man in the portrait, that I love?" she whispered.

When she'd come upon him, where he lay on the grass, she'd caught her breath. He was as good to look at as he'd been the day they'd made love. Only today, because she'd caught him unaware, she could look her fill. He was well made, muscular, perfect in her sight. She'd taken off her gown, and joined him.

She'd never expected him to be so withdrawn from her.

He shook his head. "We started our problems by making love that day," he said. "What it did was to take away the element of choice. As a gentleman I had no recourse but to offer for you. As a clever woman, you heard the doubt in my voice, and left me. This time," he said, taking her into his arms, covering their nudity with his body, "I want you to know that I offer for you because I must. Not in the eyes of Society. But in my own heart. Good God, Lisabeth, if you don't marry me I'll have to keep making a fool of myself, and I don't like that. Lord! You can't like that." He bent his head, and whispered, "And your grandfather would hate it."

He felt her laughter against his heart. He also felt how her soft breasts moved against his chest, and the warmth of her heated him to the point where he felt as though he had a fever.

"I didn't really want a pirate," she said. "They plunder and loot and kill. And highwaymen can be killed. Once I grew up I realized I wanted a man who could amuse me and challenge me, and support me. I suppose I'm still enough of a romantic to also want one who could risk all for me. You did that. And you didn't seem a fool to me," she said, her hand tracing the soft fuzz on his broad chest. "What you did was brave. For a man who always observes the proprieties, it was very bold indeed. And you did it for me. What more can I ask?"

"What I do for you now," he said, with difficulty, "is let you go, so that you always know I chose you for yourself and for no reasons of propriety."

"I know that," she said, curling closer to him.

"Well," he said, his eyes closed, as he kissed her neck, and breathed deeply of her scent. "We can maybe do something. Not, perhaps, everything. But enough to please you, and me, and bind us to nothing in the eyes of Society."

"Which society?" she asked dreamily. "The birds? The fish? The trees?"

"All," he said, turning so that she lay on the grass, and he looked down at her. "Miss Bigod, will you marry me? As soon as possible? Or will you condemn me to the life of an ass, and a lifetime of regret? I have an estate; my uncle lives there now. I have no taste for it, but I do have funds. We can build a home here, not far from Sea Mews. I like it here."

"And we can live in London in the autumn," she whispered. "I'd like to live there, at least for part of the year." Her eyes searched his. "But no separate quarters. No separate beds. I don't care to live a pocket, but I will not be set apart from your life. And if I ever find you've taken a mistress, I'll kill her, and you."

"Agreed," he said, as he sank to her side again. "And as for you: no lovers, no midnight sailing with your male friends. And a promise to tell me whatever distresses you, now, and then, and later."

"Good," she said. "To start with, I wish you'd make love to me again, Constantine. And oh! May I call you 'Con'?"

"Repeatedly, please," he said, and kissed her until she couldn't call him anything but "darling," and "my heart," and "oh, my love, yes."

Avon Romantic Treasures

Unforgettable, enthralling love stories, sparkling with passion and adventure from Romance's bestselling authors

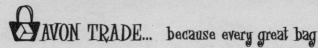